# HELL'S HALF ACRE: THE BUTCHER OF BAXTER PASS

# HELL'S HALF ACRE: THE BUTCHER OF BAXTER PASS

William W. Johnstone
*with J. A. Johnstone*

PINNACLE BOOKS
Kensington Publishing Corp.
www.kensingtonbooks.com

PINNACLE BOOKS are published by

Kensington Publishing Corp.
119 West 40th Street
New York, NY 10018

PUBLISHER'S NOTE
Following the death of William W. Johnstone, the Johnstone family is working with a carefully selected writer to organize and complete Mr. Johnstone's outlines and many unfinished manuscripts to create additional novels in all of his series like The Last Gunfighter, Mountain Man, and Eagles, among others. This novel was inspired by Mr. Johnstone's superb storytelling.

All Kensington titles, imprints, and distributed lines are available at special quantity discounts for bulk purchases for sales promotions, premiums, fund-raising, educational, or institutional use. Special book excerpts or customized printings can also be created to fit specific needs. For details, write or phone the office of the Kensington sales manager: Kensington Publishing Corp., 119 West 40th Street, New York, NY 10018, attn: Sales Department; phone 1-800-221-2647.

PINNACLE BOOKS, the Pinnacle logo, and the WWJ steer head logo are Reg. U.S. Pat. & TM Off.

ISBN-13: 978-0-7860-3948-7
ISBN-10: 0-7860-3948-5

First printing: September 2015

10  9  8  7  6  5  4  3  2

Printed in the United States of America

First electronic edition: October 2017

ISBN-13: 978-0-7860-3598-4
ISBN-10: 0-7860-3598-6

# CHAPTER ONE

*Dallas Mercury,* June 14, 1865:

## MASSACRED

## NOTHING SHORT OF MURDER !!!!

### *200 Brave Boys from Texas Butchered at Baxter Pass*

#### PRISON CAMP COMMANDER REFUSED TO SEND 1ST TEXAS SOLDIERS HOME

### SHOCKING DETAILS!

#### Is This What We Can Anticipatse Now That Our Valiant Cause Is Lost?

### By M.O.V./Special Correspondent

BAXTER PASS, OHIO (MAY 31) — Much savagery has been witnessed during the past four years of just but forlorn rebellion, but none—not even the butchery at Gettysburg, nor the shocking sights of brave young men full of ideals and courage struck down in the prime of youth at the slaughters of

Sharpsburg, Shiloh, the Wilderness, and Franklin—has been seen as horrific as what happened late last night on the Ohio River.

With word of the surrenders of Confederate armies (General Robert E. Lee's Army of Northern Virginia at Appomattox; General Joseph E. Johnston's army at Durham Station, North Carolina; General Richard Taylor's army north of Mobile, Alabama; and, most recently, Lieutenant General Kirby Smith's command of the Trans-Mississippi Department in New Orleans) reaching the prisoner-of-war camp southeast of Cincinnati and just across from Kentucky, the 4,230 prisoners at Baxter Pass were sent home after taking the Oath of Allegiance to the victorious but damnable Union.

More than 4,000 soldiers of the South, many of whom had spent three years in the wretched conditions of Baxter Pass, including some 200 of what had originally been 450 boys of the famed division led by that gallant Texas leader, John Bell Hood. Hood's 1st Texas Infantry, glory be their name, Hood's Texas Brigade! Yes, 450 1st Texas boys had been sent to Baxter Pass after their unfortunate capture at Sharpsburg in September of 1862, a bloody, savage encounter in Maryland that the Yankees have called Antietam.

Four hundred and fifty . . . reduced to 200 from disease and privation and butchery . . . now all gone to Glory.

Slaughtered. Murdered. Incarcerated in a field fit not even for trash, these men had become mere skeletons, having had to fight for coarse cornmeal and rancid bacon for three years. Living off rats and mice with little more than greatcoats turned into tents during the worst of winters.

If ever there was a Hell on Earth, it was at Baxter Pass.

Our brave soldiers had survived buck and ball at Eltham's Landing, the horrific grapeshot that cut down soldiers by the scores at Gaines's Mill during the Seven Days Battle, they had helped turned the tide and send the Yankees running at Second Manassas, only to run into rotten luck at Sharpsburg, where so many gallant Texans fell to Yankee shot and turned a cornfield into a death field. Our 450 survived, only to be captured and sent to Ohio as prisoners of war since Mr. Lincoln and his black Republicans had refused to allow any more prisoner exchanges.

So they rotted. They died.

And all the while, Lincoln Everett Dalton, the commandant of the prison camp, the Butcher of Baxter Pass, watched, and laughed.

But with the unfortunate end of the war, the Butcher had to let his prisoners go. Oaths were pledged, the paroles issued, and the gates to the filthy camp were opened. Four thousand soldiers, once men, now practically ghosts, walked past the "dead line"—where many prisoners had been shot by Yankee guards taking target practice, where others had stepped across to die by musket ball rather than cough or rot to death—and past the cemetery where hogs rooted out the dead, where markers were unheard of, where mounds and mounds—thousands of them—were reminders of what once had been soldiers. They left weakly, but with dignity, for they are the future of our glorious South.

Some returned to South Carolina. Some decided to cross the mighty Ohio by ferry and walk—take the "ankle express," as they called it—back home to whatever home awaits them in Tennessee and Alabama and Georgia.

And 200 brothers of Texas were given passage on the stern-wheeler *Fancy Belpre* that was bound to the mouth of the Ohio at Cairo, Illinois, and then to steam south down the mighty Mississippi River to New Orleans, Louisiana, where they might find transportation back home to Marion County . . . to Livingston County . . . to Harrison County . . . Tyler County . . . Anderson County . . . Houston County . . . San Augustine County . . . Galveston County . . . to mothers and fathers and sons and daughters and brothers and sisters and neighbors and friends . . . and wives—and ladies who had pledged to wait for their brave men's return before they were to wed.

Some soldiers wrote letters to their loved ones to let them know they would be home soon.

Instead of home, however, this morning their mangled bodies are washing up by the scores on the banks of the Ohio. Slaughtered by the Butcher of Baxter Pass.

At 10 P. M. last night, those paroled soldiers of South Texas boarded the *Fancy Belpre*, an old packet, tried and true, that has been carrying passengers and cargo down the Ohio and Mississippi since 1857. With no berths available on the passenger deck, our Texas boys bound for home sat on crates that lined the main deck. General Dalton, the Devil Incarnate, watched from the balcony of the Union Hotel, where he has made his headquarters since taking command of the prison camp two miles south of here in August of 1863. The Union Hotel is known for its catfish and fried chicken, smells that are much more pleasant than those foul scents that attack one's nostrils at Baxter Pass.

Shortly past 11 P. M., the packet pulled away from the landing, to begin its journey south. But she never made it to Cairo—our brave Texans never made it home. Indeed, the *Fancy Belpre* never made it more than three hundred yards from the landing at Baxter Pass.

For gunfire, practically unheard of in this quaint city of 750—except the occasional muffled sounds of musketry from the prison camp—erupted at 11:10 P. M.

A Gatling gun—that Yankee-created monster of a weapon  opened fire on the *Fancy Belpre.* General Dalton himself cranked the handle, turning the multiple rotating barrels, and sending lead projectiles ripping into the hull of the old packet—and into the bodies of soldiers of Texas who had survived so much.

General Dalton murdered 200 Texas soldiers, but he also killed the crew of the packet and 58 civilian passengers. He triumphantly told a reporter that the Texas boys had escaped, but the war is over—which, naturally, he knew, unless his evil brain has been rotted to insanity; therefore he changed his story and told authorities and the press that the Texans had found weapons and had pirated the ship and opened fire on town. He said the Texas boys had already killed the crew. He, of course, lied.

As leaden projectiles from the Gatling gun ripped into men and women and wood and Negroes, the boiler on the steamboat exploded. Fire swept through the *Fancy Belpre* like a tinderbox. The wonderful old stern-wheeler sank quickly to the Ohio's murky depths. Bodies began washing ashore, some drowned, some horribly burned, and others ripped apart by those awful heavy slugs from that unholy creation of Mr. Richard Gatling.

Crews this morning are still recovering bodies. General Dalton has ordered that any body identified as a former prisoner be returned to the camp at Baxter Pass and be interred there.

Already there are calls from Yankee newspapers that the commander at Andersonville, Georgia, should be tried and hanged. He is considered a monster—but in Ohio, the Cincinnati newspapers have already labeled the Butcher of Baxter Pass as a savior of Ohio, a hero. Some have suggested that he run for senator of Ohio . . . or *President of the United States*.

Lincoln is dead. The war is barely over. The horrors that face the South, and Texas, have just begun.

# CHAPTER TWO

*Monday, 7 a.m.*

Winter had settled over Tarrant County, Texas, which made Sheriff Jess Casey quite happy.

January meant a lot of things in Fort Worth. It meant that the stockyards were practically empty of cattle, which meant that Hell's Half Acre's saloons and gambling halls and cribs and gutters were mostly empty of cowboys. The bulk of the notorious district's gamblers had departed for warmer climes and hotter decks of cards. Luke Short had gone to San Antonio. Others had opted for Arizona Territory or New Orleans. Railroad workers had blown off most of their steam during the summer and fall, and now they were settling down for the winter. The trains still arrived, but not many people got off in this cow town, and those that did were welcomed here to peddle their merchandise or pay their respects. Legitimate businessmen. Women visiting families.

Families relocating, for Fort Worth kept right on booming.

Kurt Koenig, Fort Worth's city marshal, and Jess's and the marshal's deputies had taken a train that eventually would deposit the lawmen and a handful of prisoners at the state penitentiary in Huntsville, which meant that the jail cells in the sheriff's office were also empty. Oh, sure, Koenig had asked Jess to look after the town while he was gone. Like Jess wasn't always doing town work in addition to county work, but this time, Jess didn't mind. Winter. January. Cold, clear, but pleasant.

This time of year, what would he be doing other than patrolling the streets for dead dogs and picking up trash? Maybe there might be a drunk to arrest, or some vagrant to send along his way, but . . . Jess had other things in mind.

Winter. In the old days, back when Jess had been cowboying, winter would usually mean riding the grub line, drifting from ranch to ranch for a meal and maybe a bunk for the night in exchange for some trivial work: Chopping wood. Mending some tack. Feeding the stock or mucking a few stalls. Maybe digging a hole for a new privy if picks and shovels could cut through frozen ground. But now that Jess had become well established as the law in Fort Worth, having survived a slew of gunfights and fist-fights and drunken brawls and sober fights, having been rewarded with a nice rocking chair and a fancy gold badge—but mostly with his life—Jess figured that winter meant catching up on some much-needed, much-appreciated sleep.

He had dragged that old oak rocking chair—the one

Mayor Harry Stout had awarded him (by salvaging it from the City Hall garbage)—from outside his office (actually the jail), where he liked to sit and rock and watch people ride down Belknap Street, inside, where the hard-coal Duke Canyon stove kept the front office toasty and the coffee warm enough.

The Regulator clock let him know that it was seven in the morning, maybe a half hour before sunrise, though gray light already crept in through the slits in the window shades. He could sleep now; sleep as long as he wanted, to noon or midnight or February. The hard coal would keep the stove pleasant for hours, and Jess had finally gotten everything perfect. The pillow behind his head, the one he had procured from one of the, ahem, "sporting houses" in Hell's Half Acre, felt comfortable, and smelled really sweet, like one of Ma Shirley's girls. He had the rocker positioned perfectly, his hat had been pulled down just at the right spot, and his boots, crossed at the ankles, had found a comfortable place on the edge of his desk.

Now all he had to do was think about what he would like to dream about. A cold beer maybe. A good horse. A fifteen-pound catfish hooked. A morning without interruption. A winter with nothing to do but. . . .

The door opened, letting in a cold wind, and feet stamped on the floor. The door slammed. Jess Casey did not budge. He had found the perfect position and was not about to change anything.

"Marshal!"

Jess did not answer. One of these days Clint Stowe

might remember at least that Jess was the county sheriff and Kurt Koenig was the city marshal.

"You awake?"

Jess's eyes remained closed. He could hear Clint Stowe shaking a piece of paper.

"No," Jess said. He wet his lips and wondered if he could just imagine an office without a Clint Stowe.

"He's a-comin'!" Clint Stowe said urgently.

*Maybe,* Jess thought, *if I just tried counting sheep.* He had never done that before. After all, Jess had started out cowboying back when he was fourteen years old, some twenty years earlier. Cowboys did not count *sheep.* Unless, of course, they were killing them.

"Sheriff Casey?" Clint Stowe pleaded.

Well, since old Clint had gotten Jess's title right, he had to react to that. Slowly, Jess's eyes opened, and he removed his brown hat.

Clint stood in front of the door, still shaking that flimsy piece of yellow paper in his right hand as if it were burning hot and he was trying to shake out the flames. If Jess guessed right, the temperature outside was hovering around thirty degrees, but Clint had left the telegrapher's office without his bowler, woolen scarf, or his overcoat. He stood there in his cotton shirt and sleeve garters. Not only that, beads of sweat, which had somehow not formed into bits of ice, rolled down his forehead.

The telegrapher had to be in his fifties, with a head as bald as a cue ball except for that thin band of gray that ended right above his ears but, surprisingly, produced enough dandruff for ten or fifteen teenagers. He had a potbelly, long fingers meant for tapping out Morse code on a telegraph, plaid woolen trousers, and scuffed-up black gaiters, which, Jess noticed, had been pulled onto the wrong feet. Clint usually sat in the office by the depot barefooted. Probably because he hailed from Alabama and still was not used to wearing shoes.

"He's a-comin'," Clint repeated.

Jess nodded. "Well . . . ," Jess picked the hat off his lap and began to return it to his head. "Let him come."

"But it's . . . him."

With a heavy sigh, Jess tossed the hat on his desk, uncrossed his ankles, brought his feet down to the floor, and leaned forward in the old oak rocker. He snapped his fingers and waited for Clint Stowe to deliver the telegram.

"It's from Paul Parkin," Clint told him.

Parkin was the city constable in Dallas, roughly thirty miles east across rolling Texas prairie.

*What does a Dallas constable want with me?* Jess asked himself as Clint gave him the telegraph slip. Dallas and Fort Worth mixed like oil and water, like cowboys and farmers, like . . .

In a matter of seconds, Jess Casey was wide awake.

GEN DALTON ARRIVED DALLAS
YESTERDAY STOP YOU MIGHT BE
TOO YOUNG TO REMEMBER HIM STOP
JUST ASK ABOUT THE BUTCHER OF
BAXTER PASS STOP I SENT HIM YOUR
WAY STOP ENJOY HIS VISIT STOP
PARKIN DALLAS

Yeah, Dallas and Fort Worth did not mix. The two cities were rivals in everything, so Paul Parkin had run Lincoln Dalton out of Dallas and sent him to Fort Worth. Not that Jess Casey could blame Parkin. Had the Butcher of Baxter Pass arrived in Fort Worth first, Jess would have run that damn Yankee east to Dallas.

"You just get this?" Jess asked.

"Uh-huh. Came in a little past six."

After a quick glance at the Regulator, Jess scowled at Clint Stowe.

"Well," the telegrapher began, and stuttered, and stopped, and wet his lips, and finally found a handkerchief in his trousers pocket and wiped the sweat off his face. "Well, sir, I figured the mayor should know . . . and . . . um . . . well . . ."

"The telegram was sent to me," Jess said.

"Yeah. And I brung it to you . . . just as fast as . . . well . . . you know . . ."

"Don't you telegraphers have to take some kind of oath about . . . confidentiality?"

"Confound what?"

Jess moved toward the wall where his shell belt hung, along with the holstered .44-40-caliber Colt.

"What time does the train get in from Dallas?" Jess asked.

"Which one?"

"The next one!"

"Seven thirty-seven, if it's on time."

The gun belt was buckled on now, and Jess had pulled out the Colt, opened the loading gate, and was spinning the cylinder. Five fresh shells. He wondered if he should fill it with six. Most men—most *smart* men—kept the chamber under the hammer empty to prevent that accidental discharge, which might blow off a toe or a foot or a leg. Jess didn't consider himself much of a gunman, certainly no fast-draw specialist. As a cowboy, he had used a Colt primarily as a hammer when he drew the unfortunate duty of riding a fence line. As the law of Tarrant County, Texas, however . . .

"You can go now, Clint," Jess said, and plucked a brass cartridge from the belt.

"Where?"

*Back to Tuscaloosa, please,* Jess thought, but held his tongue. Instead, he just glared some more, and as the telegrapher turned to the door, he added, "Clint . . . if you get another telegram from Dallas, bring it to me . . . first."

"Yes, sir." The door let in a numbing blast of wind. The door slammed shut as Jess snapped the gate shut on the revolver and dropped it back into the holster.

He moved toward the coatrack and fetched his Mackinaw. That old red-and-black-plaid coat had been with him forever. Smelled like it, too. "'You might be too young to remember him,'" Jess said as he slipped on the woolen coat. No, Jess wasn't that young, or green. He had been, what, six years old or right around there when the Civil War—no, the War for Southern Independence—had erupted. Too young to fight, of course, but he had certainly killed a lot of invading Yankees back when he was playing war while his older neighbors were fighting that horde of blue-coated tyrants. Anyone who had grown up in Texas or the South remembered the war, and no one would ever forget Brigadier General Lincoln Everett Dalton and what he had done to two hundred paroled soldiers at Baxter Pass, Ohio.

Shot them down like dogs.

The Butcher of Baxter Pass.

"Thank you, Paul Parkin," Jess said, and added a few phrases that insulted the Dallas constable's mother as much as Parkin himself. Next, Jess stood in front of the gun case and thought about grabbing his Henry rifle. Instead, he withdrew a Parker twelve-gauge with the sawed-off barrels. Opening the breech, he found two shells already chambered. He snapped the barrels tight and grabbed a handful of fresh loads, which he dropped into the pocket of his Mackinaw.

Another glance at the clock on the wall. Then at the stove. He could use some coffee but not to keep him awake. No, Paul Parkin and Clint Stowe had remedied that. Later, he thought.

*If I'm still alive.*

He opened the door, stepped into the cold, predawn air, and almost got trampled to death by a herd of angry citizens.

"Casey!" Big-bellied Harry Stout pointed a fat finger at Jess. "Where are your deputies?"

Stout wasn't alone. Through the white vapor of breath and flaring nostrils, Jess could make out bowler hats and even some bell crown hats, and woolen caps, and coats and ties, and a few diamond stickpins. Even a dressmaker and the Methodist preacher's wife.

Jess wondered if Clint Stowe had told all of these people about the impending arrival of General Dalton.

"You and Kurt and the county commissioner and the district judge sent them to Huntsville," Jess reminded the appropriately named Mayor Stout. "Remember?"

"He ain't stayin' here!" someone drawled.

"He ain't welcome here," another man said.

"Maybe the Butcher wants to murder some more of us Texans!"

Jess sighed. Tucking the Parker's stock underneath his shoulder, he reached for his pocket watch. Only . . . he must have left it. . . . Now, he remembered. He had stuck the old Illinois in his desk's top drawer, thinking that he wouldn't care what time it was until spring.

The mayor, however, had brought out his watch, opened the hunter case, and was saying, "It's—"

"Thanks, Mayor Stout," Jess said. He glanced at the time, shut the case, and slipped the heavy, gold watch into the pocket of his jacket. "I'm just borrowing this. I'm going to the depot, and when General—"

"General!" someone spit. "You mean *murderer*."

"When Dalton arrives, I'll tell him to stay on and head west. Let the town marshal in Abilene worry about the Butcher."

Back in the early 1870s, when the railway had been chartered, the idea was to send trains all the way to San Diego, California, but the Texas and Pacific had only reached Abilene. Jess hoped Abilene's town law wouldn't send General Dalton back East.

"Now . . . if you gents will excuse me, I'll—"

Gunfire erupted from—where else at this time in the morning?—Hell's Half Acre.

The Butcher of Baxter Pass and Stout's citizens' committee would have to wait.

Frigid air left his lungs burning by the time Jess reached the White Elephant Saloon in the cow town's notorious anything-goes district. Two saloon girls stood in the muddy street, shivering like crazy in their skimpy attire. The bartender, his face pale, had pasted himself against the outdoor wall. One drunk was urinating in the horse trough, and another squatted beneath an empty hitching rail with both fingers in his ears and his eyes squeezed shut.

Jess saw the splintered wood from three bullets in the batwing doors.

A horse farted, and Jess stepped away from the stink.

"Bennie," he called out.

The bartender craned his head but refused to leave the front of the saloon, as if he were holding up the wooden façade.

Bennie managed to free one finger.

One man. But how many shots had he fired? Better yet, how many guns did he pack?

A muzzle flash lit up the dark interior of the saloon, and glass shattered, which forced Bennie the barkeep to squeeze his eyes back shut and return that extended pointer finger into a tightly balled fist.

"Yeeee-hiiiiiiii!" Spurs chimed, drawing closer

to the doorway, so Jess Casey leveled the Parker and thumbed back the double hammers. The girls took their shaking bodies a bit farther down the street.

Jess saw the figure first, mostly a big Texas hat, and then the doors swung open, sending pieces of the shot-up door falling back inside. A tall man in shotgun chaps and tall boots with Lone Stars inlaid in the uppers staggered onto the boardwalk. A smoking Remington .44 was in the man's right hand, although the barrel—for the time being—was pointed at the ground.

He was leathery and hard and drunk. The spurs were big, and so was the man's head, and his face bore the reminders of too many chuckleheaded horses and even more saloon brawls. Bunkhouse brawls, too. Hoot Newton had a reputation for fighting anyone, anywhere, though he had never tangled with Jess Casey. Which was a good thing, Jess figured, because Jess had never seen Hoot lose a fight.

"Hoot." Jess took a chance and lowered the hammers on the shotgun. "What are you doing?"

For a few seasons, they had worked together on Nathan Swift's ranch. Swift, of course, had wound up firing Hoot Newton. Said Hoot made it hard to hire good cowboys who had better sense than getting their ribs broken and noses busted, and, hell's fire, Swift had grown tired of paying doctor bills. That had been three years back. Of course, Swift had also fired Jess Casey, which is one reason Jess found himself wearing a fancy star on his new blue bib-front shirt instead of riding the grub line this January.

Hoot Newton turned and narrowed his eyes, which refused to focus. His mouth drooled, and he staggered a bit, but he managed to keep his feet and his hold on the Remington. The pistol wasn't one of those late-model Remingtons, either, but an old cap-and-ball relic from the days of the Rebellion. Most men would've had that antique converted to take brass cartridges, but not Hoot Newton. He still used copper percussion caps, black powder, round balls, and grease.

Finally, Hoot smiled. "Long Jack Muldoon!" he said, chuckling. "As I live and breathe."

Yeah, Hoot was really in his cups. Long Tom—not Jack—Muldoon had cowboyed with them, too, and Jess Casey didn't look one thing—thank the Lord—like that old cowboy, though Jess certainly was getting more and more stove up.

"It's Jess," Jess said. "Jess Casey."

"Who?"

Jess sighed. "What are you doing, Hoot?" he repeated.

"Celebratin'." He raised his pistol, thumbed back the hammer, and squeezed the trigger. The drunk underneath the hitching rail grimaced. The one who had been urinating turned and staggered deeper into Hell's Half Acre. The pistol, however, only puffed, though Jess couldn't tell if the old percussion cap had misfired or if the Remington was indeed empty.

"It's . . . Robert E. Lee's birth"—a burp, then "day!"

Hoot stepped off the boardwalk, grinning, slurring, slobbering, and said, "Let's have a drink, Jeff."

"Pard," Jess said. "I've got just the place to drink," he added, thinking on his feet, despite the fact that the sun was just rising over toward Dallas way. "I have a bottle of Old Overholt," he said. "Good rye whiskey." Hoot wrapped his arm around Jess's shoulder and almost pulled the both of them to the muddy, cold street.

Jess tried to hold his breath. *And a new bar of Pears soap,* he thought. Which he would hate to use on Hoot Newton.

Bennie the Bartender moved from his spot against the wall, nodded a pale thanks at Jess, and went through the batwing doors. The saloon girls followed. The batwing doors sang out, and the drunk underneath the hitching rail keeled over.

Jess tried to remind himself to come fetch that walking whiskey keg later and have him sleep it off in a cell.

With Hoot hanging on Jess's shoulder, they wandered back toward Main Street, Hoot singing— if one could call it singing:

> *Oh, I'm a good ol' Rebel*
> *Now that's just what I am*
> *And fer this Yankee nation*
> *I do not gives a damn*
> *I'm glad I fit ag'in her*

> *I only wisht we'd won*
> *I ain't askin' any pardon*
> *Fer anything I done*

They were just about to the office when the train whistle blew.

# CHAPTER THREE

*Monday, 7:30 a.m.*

Jess stopped and stepped from underneath Hoot Newton's heavy arms. He expected the drunken old cowboy to fall facedown in the street, but Hoot kept his feet, though he swayed every which way but loose.

Seven thirty-seven, the telegrapher had told him. Jeff was opening the mayor's watch. The train from Dallas had not come in late. The damned thing was early, which rarely happened.

"Hoot," Jess said. "I gotta meet somebody. Important." He stopped, tried to think.

He was just a cowpuncher with dreams of making enough money to buy his own ranch. Run his own cattle. Ride for his own brand. He really had no clue how this law job was supposed to work. Especially with no deputies, and no Marshal Kurt Koenig.

"What . . . about . . . *burp* . . . our drink?" Hoot Newton slurred.

"I'll fetch an extra bottle," Jess said, which made Hoot grin and drool some more.

"Hell," Jess added. "I'll need an extra bottle. Wait here. I'll be back in a jiffy."

He started running. The sun was rising. Hoot Newton kept swaying, and Fort Worth was slowly waking up.


Thick, pulsating black smoke pretty much ruined whatever sunrise was shaping up to be. Not that sunrises ever meant much to Jess Casey, especially in Tarrant County. He stopped to catch his breath as he stepped onto the platform and got out of the way of a black porter who almost trampled him. Jess wet his chapped lips and looked at the train.

The 4-4-0 locomotive was one of those relatively new Class J's from Baldwin, and not many people were disembarking from the coaches it pulled. Jess stopped himself and tried to refocus. He had been looking for some monster in a Union shell jacket, maybe a fancy kepi with a French braid. Cloven hoofs and a pointy tail and horns sprouting from the top of his head. The war had been over nigh twenty-five years now, and whatever the Butcher of Baxter Pass had been in 1865, he'd have to be practically an old man by this day and age. Jess spotted a drummer in a tan plaid sack suit and another man helping an elderly woman off the train. She certainly wasn't General Dalton, and the man was one of the station hands Jess had seen in town though he couldn't pin a name on the gent.

THE BUTCHER OF BAXTER PASS      23

He shifted the shotgun, and a new thought crept into his mind.

What if Paul Parkin, Dallas city constable, had been playing Jess Casey, thirty-a-month-cowhand turned reluctant lawman, for a fool? Get the greenhorn's goat. Tell him that the most despised man south of the Mason-Dixon Line was coming to torment his fair city. See if Casey would arrest a drummer or a spinster by mistake. Or if Casey would soil his britches.

He wouldn't put it past anyone from Dallas. People there thumbed their noses at the Panther City.

That's when one of the wooden doors to a freight car slid open, and Jess watched a ramp fall into place. Briefly, still the cowboy with a deep appreciation for good horses, he forgot about Lincoln Everett Dalton and looked with envy at the fine sorrel stallion coming down the ramp, followed by a black Morgan and maybe the best-looking Tennessee walker that Jess had ever laid his eyes on. Good horses with fine saddles—clean saddles, too, and Jess knew you could tell a lot about a man by how he kept his saddle.

Or his guns.

Which reminded Jess about that star he packed.

He scratched a thumb on one of the hammers of the Parker and walked toward the car.

The three men looked younger than Jess but only by a few years. Their hair was close-cropped, and each kept his mustache well-groomed. Even from the distance, Jess could guess that all three were brothers. They had pulled on linen dusters but swept the tails behind their gun belts.

Black hats. Gray-striped trousers. Good boots and Crockett spurs. New clothes, store-bought duds. They wore two-gun rigs, which a body didn't see much, even in Fort Worth. The leather looked a lot older than the duds but recently cleaned, just like the revolvers in the holsters. Right-hip Colts with the butts to the rear and the revolvers on the left hips facing butt forward. So all three had to be right-handed.

One of the riders had been about to swing into the saddle when he noticed Jeff making a beeline toward them. He said something, and the other two men stepped around. The tallest of the three hooked his thumbs in the gun belt. The other one simply put his right hand on the butt of the Colt on his right hip. The last one, the one with the savagely pockmarked face, gripped the stock of a Winchester sheathed in the scabbard.

The Parker felt cold in Jess's hands, but then he realized that it was only thirty-something degrees this morning. It was the weather, he tried telling himself, not some premonition.

He stopped when he figured he was close enough to take down two of those boys by triggering both barrels of the scattergun.

If it came to that. Jess sure hoped it wouldn't.

"Morning," he said, but did not smile.

The oldest one, the tallest one, nodded. None of the brothers spoke.

"Good-looking horses," Jess said. "Riding out?"

The one with his hand on one of his revolvers nodded.

"Good." Jess nodded at their guns. "You see, we have a town ordinance. We don't allow firearms worn in the city limits. That keeps a lid on things."

*Sometimes,* he thought, but did not say. *Actually, rarely. But we mean well by that law. After all, it had worked in some towns.*

"Figured," the oldest said in a deep Texas drawl, "that we'd just grab us some breakfast, then lope on home."

The young one sneered. "If that's all right with you, law dog."

"Burt," the oldest said. "Be sociable."

"Yeah," the middle one said. "Man's just doin' what he thinks is right."

"Breakfast is all right," Jess said. "Take your pick of where you want to eat." He stared at the young one, the ugly one, the one Jess decided he really did not like. "Then you see to it that you do ride home."

"Or what?"

Jess waited. Even as ugly as that boy was, he couldn't be that stupid. At last, his eyes landed on the shotgun Jess had casually brought up. When the boy saw that, Jess thumbed back both barrels. Then, Jess smiled.

"You ain't Marshal Koenig," the middle brother said.

"Nope."

"Where's Kurt?" the oldest one asked.

"Taking some prisoners to Huntsville."

With mention of Huntsville, the middle and older brothers glanced at one another, and the older one even grinned. "We must've just missed him," he said, and chuckled to himself.

"I'm the sheriff," Jess said.

"You ain't Hank Henley, neither," the older one said, no longer amused at his private joke.

The youngest one said nothing. He just stared at the shotgun and kept his hand on the Winchester's stock.

"Hank's dead. I'm Jess Casey. New sheriff."

"I've heard of you. . . ." The youngest one had finally regained his voice. Jess studied him a bit, though never taking his eyes completely off the two other gunmen. The ugly one shot a look at his two older brothers. "Chink Dublin said the Tarrant County law was greased lightnin' with them pistols."

Jess didn't think of himself that way, though he had been lucky in a few ruckuses. And some folks had said he had this instinct, this natural ability when it came to pistol-fighting. Jess, however, would rather swing a loop with a lariat or slap some branding iron on a calf than start shooting at men shooting back at him.

Chink Dublin, Jess knew, had been convicted of assault with intent to kill in Dallas and sent to Huntsville. So now Jess, although he had suspicioned as much when he first approached the trio, knew for certain that these three brothers were likely fresh out of the state pen. And remembering that telegraph he had received from the Texas Rangers on Friday, he knew who he faced.

"Like I was saying, Tom . . ." He nodded politely

at the older brother. "And Neils." Another greeting at the middle brother. "And even you, Burt." The pock-marked one glared. "Have your breakfast. Then keep riding. Down Stephenville way, isn't it? But if you stay for any length of time after breakfast, check your Colts with me or the bartender at whatever watering hole you frequent. All six of them." His head tilted at the Winchester Burt McNamara still touched. "And keep the rifle in that scabbard."

"You that fast, law dog?" Burt asked with a scowl.

"Don't have to be too fast to pull two triggers on a scattergun," Jess said. But, just to show these ex-convicts, these McNamara brothers, that Fort Worth was really a friendly city, he decided to lower the hammers on the shotgun.

Jess had learned to read people, and these brothers—even the ugly one—looked like they weren't worried, that they did not want to start a fight that would leave some of them, if not all three, dead.

He started to back away from the gunmen when the breath whooshed from his lungs. Something had slammed into his back, a mean, vicious, hard punch in the kidneys. Blurred as his vision turned, he saw the shotgun scattering across the warped planks of the station platform and felt himself dropping to his knees. Next, his head rang out in pain and orange and red lightning bolts flashed across his vision.

Which explained why the three brothers had no longer looked worried.

Too late he remembered something else that the Texas Ranger had mentioned in the telegram.

MCNAMARA BROS RELEASED FROM
HUNTSVILLE STOP PROBABLY WILL
ARRIVE IN FT WORTH STOP THEN
RETURN TO ERATH COUNTY STOP
BROTHER DAN MIGHT MEET THEM
AT STATION STOP NONE OF THEM
WORTH SPIT

Jess's ears rang, but he figured he could hear the
brothers—Burt, at least—cackling. Anticipating another blow, he made himself fall to his right and roll.
That was a lucky, and good, anticipation, because if
he had not dropped when he had, Dan McNamara
likely would have taken his head off with a single-
tree he must have found on the platform being unloaded for Farwell's Livery. The momentum from the
force of the swing carried Dan, who looked nothing
like his other brothers but did resemble those illus-
trations Jess Casey had seen of gorillas and cave
men, past him.

Jess stuck out one of his boots and watched the
big brute—seven inches over six feet tall, and Dan
wore moccasins—cry out in a high-pitched yelp as
he fell onto his face. He came up spouting curses and
spitting blood, looking for this slippery little cuss
who had just made him look foolish in front of his
brothers.

First, Jess shot a glance at the three ex-cons, but
they had moved away from their horses and stood
grinning, watching the fight. By then, Dan
McNamara was up, lunging toward Jess. For a man
that size, he moved like a prairie rattlesnake. And
punched like a mule.

Jess moved with the blow, stepped to his right and under the big cuss's left. He jabbed a right into Dan McNamara's side, but that was like hitting that Baldwin locomotive that was hissing and moaning. Or was that sound coming from Jess? He sent a hard right into the big man's kidneys as McNamara went past him, and that didn't even hurt anything . . . but Jess's right hand.

"Stomp him till he ain't nothin' but a puddle of grease!" Burt McNamara called out.

He could reach for his Colt, Jess told himself. No, that wasn't fair. Besides, as soon as his hand touched that walnut grip, Tom, Neils, and Burt would fill him full of holes. So he swung and missed and fell when Dan McNamara punched but did not miss.

Jess spit out blood as he sat on his buttocks. He blinked, shook his head, and watched the six-foot-seven monster grin.

"I'm a-gonna stomp you till you ain't nothin' but a puddle of grease," Dan McNamara said.

Apparently, McNamara wasn't much when it came to original thinking.

He let the big man come toward him, and then Jess showed that he could move like a rattler, too. His hands found the singletree and he swung it like a scythe, catching Dan McNamara right on the knees, and down Goliath toppled.

The hell with fighting fair! Jeff had decided, and he palmed his Colt, lightning fast, slammed the barrel against the big man's head, and heard him fall like a cottonwood tree crashing to the ground.

Next he turned, thumbing back the hammer, waiting to start the ball with the other brothers.

Jess blinked away blood and pain and wondered why in blazes Burt, Neils, and Tom McNamara had done nothing. Folks called them clannish. Fight one, you had to fight them all. With guns, knives, fists, blacksnake whips. . . . One McNamara, Jess figured, was aplenty in a go at fisticuffs.

He had expected bullets to be singing, but all he heard was the ringing in his ears and the mechanical groans of the Baldwin at the depot.

Aiming the .44-40 in the general direction of the freight car and the three other McNamara brothers, Jess waited for his vision to clear and breath to return to his lungs.

Tom, Neils, and Burt McNamara stood in front of their horses, hands raised above their heads. Standing in front of them, covering all three with the Parker shotgun Jess had dropped, stood Hoot Newton, who looked relatively sober.

# CHAPTER FOUR

*Monday, 8:45 a.m.*

He dropped the McNamara boys' gun rigs and the Winchester carbine on the bench by the office door, before he staggered to the washbasin, to work on his face. Hadn't lost any teeth. That was a good sign.

"Where's that . . . *burp* . . . whiskey, Jess?"

Jess reached for a towel and gestured. "Big drawer," he said, "Desk." He never realized how three words could bring so much pain. Jess tested his jaw while Hoot Newton staggered over toward the desk and pulled on a drawer. Jess returned to his face, testing his nose, which was bleeding but not busted, his ears—he still had both of those—and running his fingers gently through his hair. Just a few knots and none larger than a Texas pecan.

Hoot Newton sat in the chair and took a long pull on the bottle of rye. Jess dabbed a few cuts and moved to the stove for some coffee, then decided he had better sweeten it with the rye before Hoot Newton emptied the bottle. With coffee in his hand, he collapsed in his rocker and took a sip of pleasurable brew.

"Thanks for your help, Newt," he said.

"Hoot."

It took a moment before Jess realized his mistake. He took another sip, wondered if Dan McNamara might have damaged his brain.

"Hoot. Right. Thanks."

Hoot Newton burped a nasty, smelly burp.

Jess could have arrested Dan McNamara, but figured he might as well leave well enough alone, especially since he had confiscated the brothers' weapons and recommended that they grab breakfast at Tio Julio's Café and pick up their hardware on their way out of town. Let the law in Stephenville worry about the McNamara brothers. As soon as they were out of Fort Worth, Jess might be able to catch up on his sleep.

They had roused McNamara and had been soaking his head in a water trough while Jess and Hoot Newton had gone to the telegraph office, briefly, and then moseyed back to the jail on Belknap.

Hoot Newton set the bottle, now empty, on the edge of the table. "Thought you said you was gettin' another bottle."

Jess closed his eyes. "Later. Don't you think you've had enough?"

"Robert E. Lee's birthday," Hoot said.

Robert E. Lee, the South's greatest hero, the general who had almost won independence for the Confederacy. How long had Lee been dead? Jess couldn't remember, but he seemed to recall that the old gray fox had died within five or six years of the surrender.

Twenty years. Was he born on January 20? No, Hoot started his drinking on the nineteenth? Did Jess really care?

Jess opened his eyes. "Did you fight in the Rebellion, Hoot?"

The big old ox stared at Jess dumbly.

"Huh?"

"Did you fight? In the Civil . . . in the War Between the States?" Hoot was a good deal older than Jess, old enough to likely have served. Maybe not smart enough, but then again Hoot Newton might have had a few moments of coherence thirty years back, before he had started beating the tarnation out of cowboys and railroaders and drummers and muleskinners and freighters and lawmen and soldiers and blacksmiths and wheelwrights and coopers and miners and even a few professional boxers.

Hoot sniffed, looked at the empty bottle, wiped some drool from his chin, and nodded.

"Second . . . no . . . Ford's . . . uh . . . Mounted . . . um . . . Cav'ry."

Jess's eyes widened, and he lowered the cup of rye-flavored coffee without taking another sip. "Rip Ford?"

The old cowboy had to think, before recognition and pride came to his dull eyes, and he nodded. "Uh-huh."

Jess knew about Rip Ford. Anyone who had spent any time in Texas knew about Colonel John S. "Rip" Ford, who ranked right alongside Sam Houston and those heroes at the Alamo when it came to legendary Texans. Ford hailed from South Carolina, came to Texas as a young man just months after San Jacinto, but these days was living down in South Texas, which is where he had spent most of his life. He had fought in the Mexican War, ridden with the early Texas Rangers—back when they were fighting Comanches and Mexican bandits and not tracking down felons—served in the Texas Senate, had even been a newspaperman. And during the War Between the States, he had fought any Yankee who dared try to invade the Lone Star State. The Second Texas Mounted Rifles was his command, later to become the Second Texas Cavalry. Those old boys had whipped the Yankees at the Battle of Palmito Ranch down around Brownsville. In May of 1865. The last battle of the Civil War, a month after Bobby Lee had surrendered to Ulysses S. Grant at Appomattox.

If Hoot Newton had ridden with Rip Ford, then he must've been some type of man thirty years ago. By thunder, Jess thought, Hoot was still a man to ride the river with. If Hoot hadn't wandered after Jess hoping to get some more whiskey, Jess would undoubtedly be lying in a pine box at the undertaker's while Mayor Stout argued with him about who'd have to foot the bill.

The door opened—the blast of wind felt a bit warmer now that the sun was up—and Clint Stowe walked inside, holding another flimsy piece of cheap yellow paper but not shaking it as if it were burning this time.

"Here's your answer, Marshal." The bald man—with gaiters on the right feet this go-round—came inside. He still wore his hat and his coat, so this message wasn't so important, at least, to Clint or the mayor or anyone else the blabbermouth might want to tell.

Jess took the slip and tipped the old Southerner, thinking that Clint had followed instructions and had not told half the population of Fort Worth what the telegram said.

As soon as the McNamara brothers had wandered off, Jess had sent another wire back east to Dallas. He had instructed Clint Stowe not to dillydally when Constable Paul Parkin answered . . . if Parkin answered.

Well, the Dallas lawman had. Jess read the wire.

NEVER SAID I PUT THE BUTCHER ON A TRAIN STOP

With a curse, Jess figured he could hear Paul Parkin laughing all the way across the Trinity River in ugly, miserable, mean Dallas.

"You got any whiskey?"

Crumpling the yellow paper, Jess shot a glance at Hoot Newton, who sat staring like a pathetic hound dog at the telegraph operator.

"Huh? Uh . . . no. . . ." Clint pocketed his nickel and hurried out the door. The telegram went toward the wastebasket but missed. Jess didn't bother picking it up.

Instead, he sipped more coffee.

Hoot Newton yawned, and Jess hooked a thumb at the door behind him.

"There's a few empty bunks back yonder," he said. "Some shut-eye would make you feel better."

The big lunk's eyes hardened. "You arrestin' me?"

Jess smiled. "I sleep back there myself." When

there happened to be an empty bunk, which wasn't often, especially during the cattle season.

"And you'll have some rye waitin' for me when I wakes up?"

Jess nodded. He could use a bracer himself.

The big man started to rise and stopped. Jess tried to guess how much Hoot had had to drink, which reminded him of something else.

"You got any money on you, Hoot?"

"You need a grubstake, Jess?"

Jess grinned. If only . . . Enough money to buy that ranch somewhere. Hire a smithy to make his brand, the J-C. Slap it on some longhorns. Register it with the state. Yep, that was a dream.

What Jess figured he might need, however, at least from Hoot Newton, was enough to pay Bennie the barkeep at the White Elephant and maybe settle everything without having to face a judge. He could have arrested Hoot for disturbing the peace—and Jess did collect a percentage of any fines issued. In fact, that was his plan once he had gotten the drunken old cuss in the jail. But after Hoot had stopped the McNamara brothers from taking a hand in his little set-to with big Dan McNamara, he wasn't about to lock up Hoot Newton. Hell, they'd ridden together.

Hoot was fishing in his vest pockets. There was a rabbit's foot. What looked like a token to one of the bawdy houses. Tobacco. An arrowhead. He deposited a few more items, including some coins, on the desk, and this time pushed himself to his feet.

"Old . . . Overholt . . ." The big man staggered toward the door that led to the cells. "Remember."

"As soon as you're awake," he said. Considering the amount of booze that cowhand had consumed, Jess figured he might have until Wednesday to fetch a fresh bottle.

The door shut, and moments later came the squeaking of a cell door being opened or maybe closed. Followed by the roaring snores that the door and the distance did not muffle.

Jess fingered the items Hoot had deposited on the desk. Eight cents. Plus one tarnished peso. Well, maybe Jess could cover the damages himself.

Suddenly Jess decided Hoot Newton had the right idea. After placing the empty mug on the desk, he positioned himself perfectly in the rocking chair, propped his feet up, ankles crossed, stuck that pillow behind his head, and pulled his hat down over his eyes, which he closed, and tried to think pleasant thoughts.

Which were immediately interrupted by the muffled sound of gunshots from—where else?—Hell's Half Acre.

# CHAPTER FIVE

*Monday, 8:50 a.m.*

It sure beat the slop they served behind the red-brick walls of the Texas State Pen down in hot, humid, miserable Huntsville. Or even the peanuts, crackers, and coffee they'd managed to live on during the train rides from Huntsville to Fort Worth.

Greasy enchiladas smothered in chili, refried beans, honest-to-goodness rice, fresh tortillas, and real coffee, not the watered-down crud the railroads and the prison cooks had served. Best of all, there was beer. Maybe not cold—after all, a grimy ramshackle shack like this café probably didn't have an icebox—but this was winter, so who needed an ice-cold lager?

Three of the McNamara brothers wolfed down the Mexican chow and the beer. Big Dan McNamara merely held his throbbing head. At least, Tom McNamara figured, Big Dan didn't throw up all over the warped table and ruin the first decent chow they'd eaten in five years.

"Hey, señorita!" Burt snapped his finger, then banged the empty mug on the table, which caused Dan to groan and move his elbows off the table, as he leaned back in the chair and squeezed his eyelids tight. "How 'bout some more beer, sweetie pie!"

It was not a request but more of a demand.

Neils McNamara set his fork and knife on the empty plate and looked across the table at his kid brother. "Best go easy on that, Burt," he said. "That's six already."

"And it ain't . . ." Tom glanced at the wall on the clock hanging between two calendars, one for this year, one six years old. ". . . even nine this morn."

The plump waitress swept Neils's mug off the table without a by-your-leave or kind smile, and for a fat petticoat, she was mighty quick. Neils couldn't even pinch her rear as she raced back to the kitchen.

"I got five years a-drinkin' to catch up on, *Mommie*!" He winked at both brothers, shot a look at Big Dan, and shook his head at his third sibling.

Tom and Neils glanced at one another. Big Dan slowly shook his head, cursed, sniffed, and mumbled something about that low-down law dog who had come mighty close to crippling him with that single-tree and then maybe cracked his skull with his six-shooter.

The waitress returned with Burt's beer, slamming the mug down in front of him, sending most of the suds and some of the brew sloshing over the rim and puddling on the well-worn checkered tablecloth. She did not apologize and vanished once again.

Tom sighed as Burt picked up the mug and drained about half of the beer. Tom and Neils had each had one beer; Dan hadn't had a thing. Their kid brother was well in his cups now.

Not that Tom blamed the youngster. If Tom hadn't been saddled with the job of being pa and brother to his younger brothers, he likely would have joined Burt in some drinking contests. Burt was the youngest, but twenty-seven now, not a kid but a man. A man old enough, five years back, to know better than to rob a bank, but that hadn't stopped Burt, who had always been wild. Neils, now thirty years old, had joined him. "Because he's my brother," he had told the judge, "and he needed me."

Tom hadn't even known what those two had been up to until they rode home with a posse barely behind the dust the two brothers' well-lathered horses had raised up. All Tom had seen was a bunch of strangers sending bullets after his two kid brothers, so he had opened fire. Hadn't killed anyone, as luck would have it, but he had knocked two out of the saddle and dropped two other horses.

Of course, neither the judge nor the jury—and probably not even that pettifogging lawyer who had represented the three brothers in that trial back home in Stephenville—had believed Tom's story. Even after Burt and Neils had testified that they had planned the robbery on their own, that Tom was just defending his sorry brothers.

At least, no one thought ol' Dan had taken part.

And at least, Tom figured, the judge had taken mercy on the McNamaras. He had given them only seven years, but the warden had recommended that two years be knocked off that sentence, for good behavior.

"I knew your father, Tom," the warden had said when he told the three brothers they would be getting out early.

Same thing the judge had said in Stephenville before passing sentence.

*I knew your father.*

Which is something Burt couldn't say. By thunder, Neils couldn't even remember Walter Bass McNamara. Even Tom, at thirty-five years old now, and Big Dan, thirty-three, had only vague recollections of their father, but, oh, those stories Ma would tell before consumption called her to glory.

Bass McNamara was tougher than Pecos Bill, Paul Bunyan, Hercules, and Samson all rolled into one. He'd been born in Kentucky, or somewhere along the Cumberland Gap, and came to Texas shortly before Sam Houston had won Texas's independence at San Jacinto back in 1836. He fought Indians—four Comanche and three Kiowa scalps still hung over the fireplace mantel in their home— rode with the Rangers, and cleared about two hundred acres by himself. He had once lifted a piano over his head, had killed an alligator down along the Gulf of Mexico with nothing but a knife, and had befriended the likes of Deaf Smith, Jack Hays, and even Sam Houston himself.

Then came the war, and Bass had been among the first to join up, riding down south to enlist in what became Hood's Texas Brigade. Some muckety-muck had offered him a commission, but Bass had said he'd be danged if he'd be giving any orders and cowering with some yellow-livered general. By thunder, Walter Bass McNamara was a fighting man, and that's why he had joined up. To fight. To kill Yankees. He even hated it when they made him don sergeant's stripes, and he refused to carry the colors. He would use his Enfield rifled musket. He wanted to fight, to kill blue bellies, not wave some damned flag.

So he had fought, practically winning the fight at Gaines's Mill by himself—if you believed those tales—until that September day in Maryland when the Yanks had taken Bass McNamara and hundreds more prisoners after that bloody, savage day at Sharpsburg. The Yanks had carted them all off to some hellhole on the Ohio River, to starve, to rot, to die. But you couldn't kill a man like Bass McNamara.

You couldn't. . . .

Unless you lined him up after the damned war had ended, turned the crank on a Gatling gun, and ripped him apart. Murdered him. And many more.

Tom thought about ordering a whiskey, just to kill the memory, to wash that gall out of his mouth. He looked at his coffee but did not drink. Burt was laughing at something, but Tom didn't hear what was so funny. Right now, nothing was funny. He felt the blood rush to his head, and he dropped his hands beneath the table, put them on his thighs, and clenched his fists until his hands shook and his arms ached.

The Butcher of Baxter Pass.

That yellow-dog Yankee had killed his pa. Murdered him.

Tom himself had been only eleven years old when

his father had been shot down like a rabid dog. Assassinated. Before then, everybody down around Stephenville had bragged on what a good boy Tom McNamara was, how he would likely go to college, maybe become a lawyer, a doctor, maybe governor of the great state of Texas. Perhaps even president of the Confederate States of America—after Texas had whipped those blue-bellied tyrants.

After the murder of Bass, however, things changed. Carpetbaggers came flooding to the South. Yankees wanted everything, and they could take much of it. Take anything they wanted with Yankees running the Texas government, the county government, and the crooked State Police. And even after those long, bitter years of Reconstruction, things had not really improved. Oh, many of the Yankees had headed back north, to steal from their own people, but things remained hard in Texas. And every time Tom would read about that butcher, that killer of some two hundred paroled Rebel soldiers, Tom would seethe with anger.

Brigadier General Lincoln Everett Dalton was free to roam across the North, and even the West, giving speeches, showing off Gatling guns or other weapons—for which gun companies paid him a healthy stipend—or kissing babies and the like. While he, Tom McNamara, had to tend to his younger brothers, manage the farm, pay the share-croppers who had once been slaves owned by Bass McNamara, and watch his mother cough herself to death.

She had never really, truly, recovered after word reached Stephenville of her husband's death. Most times, she'd just sit in her rocking chair on the porch and talk to Bass. Talk to herself. To her memories. By the time Tom was sixteen his mother could barely get out of bed, and even when she could manage that, she'd just sit, too weak to rock herself by then.

When she died, back when Tom was two weeks shy of eighteen, everyone said it was a blessing.

Tom McNamara never thought of anything as a blessing. Blessings came from the Lord. To Tom's way of seeing things, everything since May 30, 1865, had been damned.

"Tom?"

He blinked, made his hands relax, and wondered if his face was as scarlet as it felt. He forgot those bad memories, tried to put aside that hate, and lifted his left hand for the mug of coffee.

"Yeah." He saw Neils hook a thumb at the portly waitress who stood behind him.

Tom looked up at the Mexican woman.

"You pay?" Her accent thickened the words.

With a sigh, Tom drained the coffee.

Any money they'd managed to earn in prison had already been spent. On new duds. On ammunition for the guns that had been returned. And on food and on some horses and tack they had bought at a livery in Dallas before the law had sent them back onto the train. Mostly on the horses. The McNamaras had always admired good horses. Good horses. Good guns. Take care of both, and they'd take care of you.

"Dan?" Tom asked.

The simpleton brother lowered his hands. His eyes looked rheumy, his face pale.

"How much money do you have?"

Dan blinked. "Mo-ney?"

Neils cursed. Burt laughed. The waitress frowned.

Tom wondered what the home place would look like after five years. Maybe the sheriff down there had already claimed it from back taxes.

Tom dropped his hand to his belt, thinking maybe he could trade the gun belt for the meal, but then found himself, as the saying around here went, "undressed." The sheriff had taken not only their guns, but also their shell belts. There was that one Winchester carbine Burt had insisted on buying in Huntsville. . . .

Tom cursed again. No, the sheriff had taken the Winchester, too.

"How much?" he asked.

*"Dos dólares y diez centavos."*

He dipped his fingers inside his vest pocket, glaring at his two brothers—but not addlebrained Dan—to do the same. When it was all said and done, they had thirty-one cents among them.

The waitress put her hands on her thick waist and barked something to her boss in rapid-fire Spanish.

Tom was standing, turning toward the Mexican owner, starting to say that he would bring them the money as soon as he saw the sheriff, but when he turned, he saw that the big man with the apron was bringing up a single-shot bird gun from behind the bar.

"Are you crazy?" he yelled. "It's two bucks and a dime!"

The man was slow, and Tom was already moving. You had to be fast, even in prison, especially in Huntsville, if you wanted to stay alive in that place, where life was worth even less than two dollars and ten cents. He figured he could get to the middle-aged man before he could even thumb back the hammer on that big shotgun, jerk the weapon out of the man's big hands, and make everyone understand.

He had practically reached the hombre, was extending his hands to grab the barrel, when something boomed behind him and heat flashed past his left ear, and the right ear of the big Mexican disappeared in an explosion of red.

# CHAPTER SIX

*Monday, 9 a.m.*

The shotgun's barrel went upward, away from Tom, as the Mexican fell. The single-shot weapon boomed, punching holes into the tin ceiling and filling the little eatery with clouds of pungent white smoke. Whirling, reflexively bringing up his hand to his burning, now ringing, ear, Tom McNamara saw Burt grinning wildly, moving. Yet even before he had seen the café owner/cook's ear shot off, Tom knew what had happened.

He had not forgotten the little .32 Burt had pocketed at the hardware store where they had bought the Winchester and bullets for their revolvers.

"Don't!" Tom yelled, but Burt did not listen. He'd never listened, not even when he had been a little kid.

The stout waitress was screaming, and Burt slammed the pocket pistol against her head, dropping her onto the sawdust-covered floor.

Neils also moved, jerking the groggy Dan out of his chair, which fell backward.

A couple of cooks pushed through the door to the kitchen, saw Burt aiming the little popgun in their direction, and the door slammed as they retreated. Another door opened, and Tom saw the other customers fleeing into the streets.

"Best ride!" Neils yelled, and he was dragging Big Dan over the unconscious waitress's body, following the café's patrons.

Behind and beneath the bar, the wounded Mexican groaned.

"Don't leave without me, Neils!" Burt yelled, and he leaped over the bar, moving toward the cashbox. A place like this, it dawned upon Tom, was too cheap to have a cash register.

Tom looked around, found the beer mug that Burt had been cherishing since they'd arrived at the restaurant, and fetched it, spun, and sent it sailing after his brother. The glass smashed the wall at the end of the counter, just as Burt reached the cashbox. The kid had to raise his arms to protect himself from the shards of glass that sailed toward his face, and then he spun, pointing the little .32 at Tom.

"Get out!" Tom yelled. "You ain't robbin' these people."

His brother lowered the gun, glared at Tom, and cursed, but this time he actually obeyed.

Tom followed him through the door, checking both directions on the street.

The town had filled up, and so had the boardwalks, but nobody wanted to stick his nose in somebody else's business. Businessmen and passersby kept a respectful distance. At least the streets were clear. For now.

Neils had managed to get Big Dan onto that big mule he had ridden all the way from Stephenville, and the big cuss leaned low in the saddle. The mule did not budge. Neils's horse, on the other hand, was rearing, eyes wide and full of fear, the hoofs slashing down as Neils fought to keep his grip on the reins.

"Easy. Easy! Easy!" Neils tried to coax his horse.

Burt had untethered his horse and was leading it down the street, away from Neils and that little rodeo dance his horse was doing. Tom's horse was pulling at its reins, threatening to break the hitching rail in half, and Tom knew he needed to get to his mount or he would be afoot in this cow town with a wounded café owner and an unconscious waitress—not to mention a two dollar and ten cent bill, less thirty-one cents, to account for.

So he moved, grabbing the bridle straps on the horse's head. Prison hadn't softened any of Tom McNamara's muscles. He jerked the horse's head, saying in a firm voice. "No." That was with his right hand. His left was unloosening the reins around the rail, and then Tom's right hand was moving toward the saddle horn, and he felt himself leaping into the saddle from a standstill.

He spurred the horse down the street to prevent Neils's mount from escaping. With relief, he saw the panicking horse calm down, just enough for Neils to get control and get himself mounted.

Clucking his tongue, Tom guided his horse between Neils and Burt, moved over toward that worthless mule carrying Big Dan, and slapped his hat on the mule's rump.

"Hi-ya!" Tom shouted. "Get a-movin'! Get a-movin'!"

The mule started to move. The streets remained empty, and for a brief moment, Tom McNamara thought that they just might get out of Fort Worth unscathed, get back home to Stephenville, and put the past five years, and especially this morning, behind them.

That's when he heard that voice that somehow, deep inside him, Tom knew he would hear.

*"Hold it!"*


Sheriff Jess Casey took everything in. The McNamara brothers. The open door to Miguel Sanchez's little café. Nobody on the boardwalk on this side of the street, but across the street, dozens of people kneeling, staring, pointing. He also saw the little pistol in the youngest brother's—the pock-marked kid, Burt, yeah, that's the name—right hand.

The kid's horse reared, came down, and Burt McNamara was smiling. Tom, the oldest, yelled. Sounded like "Don't!" The mule with the big brother, Big Dan, who had come mighty close to stomping Jess Casey until he was just a puddle of grease earlier this morning, had stopped again. The other one—Nelson, no, Neils—he had his hands full managing his own mount. The only one with a weapon, it appeared, was Burt McNamara.

And the kid was leveling that gun at Jess Casey.

Jess blamed everything on the morning. It had been too busy, and he was too tired to think straight. Otherwise, he wouldn't have left his office without a double-barreled shotgun. He only had the Colt hanging on his hip, but in a situation like this, that .44-40 was all he really needed.

He moved to his side as the little pistol popped. The column near him splintered as the .32 bullet tore at its side. By that time, the people across the street were ducking behind water troughs, or columns, or some bales of cotton, or moving back into their businesses or residences. Jess had swept the Colt into his right hand, thumbed back the hammer, and pulled the trigger.

The horse screamed and blood spurted from its neck. That sickened Jess Casey. He never liked to hurt a horse. In fact, he hadn't meant to kill this fine animal, but he had rushed his shot, and the horse had come down from another jump in an area Jess had not anticipated. Otherwise, the bullet would have, should have, caught Burt McNamara in his right kneecap. And that would have ended all of this unpleasantness.

Instead, the horse fell to its side, and Burt McNamara kicked free of the stirrups and dived to his right. He landed with a thud, stirring up clouds of dust. As far as Jess could tell, however, the ex-con had not lost his hold on that little popgun.

Jess moved, sizing up the scene, as he leaped over the empty hitching rail, cocking the Colt again, as he raced toward Burt McNamara.

Big Dan had fallen off the mule and lay in the street, curled up like a baby, wrapping his big head with both of his massive arms. Neils was turning his wild horse around in a circle, a move that an ex-cowhand like Jess Casey had to appreciate. Good horsemen were good people. Usually. Unless they were also bank robbers.

Tom McNamara had swung down from his horse and started moving toward Burt, who was coming up. Burt was on his knees now, trying to stand, or maybe just trying to bring his gun hand up. The dust was too thick for Jess to tell for sure. The .44-40 was cocked in Jess's hand, though, and all he had to do was squeeze the trigger.

Which he did.

But only a warning shot that sent mounds of dirt clods up in front of Burt McNamara. He heard Burt's curses, and then he was moving to his right, thumbing back the hammer again. He would not give the boy another chance. He couldn't afford to.

That's when Tom McNamara kicked his brother in the back. Jess heard the *oomph* and saw Burt slam face-forward in the dust. Tom was moving around, as his kid brother tried to bring up his gun hand, but Tom's boot planted on the boy's right hand, burying his hand and the pocket pistol in the dirt.

By then, Jess stood only a couple of feet from those two McNamara brothers, and his Colt .44-40 covered both of them.

"Why'd you do that fer, Tom?" Burt managed to say, through coughs and sniffles and spitting out dirt.

Jess took a quick look behind him. Big Dan still lay in the dirt. Neils had his horse under control but sat still in the saddle, frowning, and keeping his hands away from his horse and his person, showing that he was making no play for any weapon he might have on his person.

Tom McNamara took his foot off his kid brother's hand and picked up the little gun in his right hand. He blew the dirt off it, broke open the action, and withdrew a .32 bullet from the barrel, which he dropped into his vest pocket.

The gun was a Marston. It held only three shots. Apparently, Burt had fired only two, and one of those had been at Jess Casey. He looked at the door to Miguel's place. Then he looked hard at Tom McNamara.

"I had hoped," Jess said, not lowering his Colt, "to be taking my nap right about now. And my mood grows mighty sour when I don't get my nap."

# CHAPTER SEVEN

*Monday, 9:10 a.m.*

He slipped the Marston that Tom McNamara handed him into the back pocket of his britches. Keeping the Colt leveled at the oldest brother, Jess Casey knelt and slapped one iron bracelet on Burt McNamara's left hand. He wasn't worried about the kid's right hand, for Tom's boot had taken care of that one. From a glance, Jess figured the boy's thumb and two or three fingers were busted, but Jess did not care.

He dragged the screaming, cursing kid toward the hitching rail, where he secured the other end of the handcuffs to the sturdy post. Then he said, "Nobody leaves."

That was likely a wasted breath. If everything he had heard about those brothers was true, they wouldn't leave one of their own.

Then Jess went inside Miguel Sanchez's little café.

* * *

Fifteen minutes later, Jess sat on the edge of the water trough in front of the restaurant, surrounded by the county solicitor, Mayor Stout, and the McNamara brothers. Tom, Neils, and Big Dan stood in the streets; young Burt remained chained to the hitching post, his mangled hand resting on his dusty thigh. Doc Amanda Wilson, who had arrived in Fort Worth and hung up her shingle just a few weeks back, was inside the café, working on Miguel's ear and his sister's head.

"Attempted murder on Miguel," said Solicitor Mort Thompson. "Assault and battery on Ramona. Attempted robbery." Thompson grinned. "We can add vagrancy, resisting arrest, and petty larceny for the meal they wanted to eat for free."

Everything about Mort Thompson was wrong, from the custom silk shirt from Bloomingdale's to that fancy overcoat of black mohair, and the blue corkscrew suit that had been tailor-made in St. Louis—which clashed with the high-crowned Texas hat, a spotless white, and its leather chin strap and his polished black boots and handsome spurs. Trying to fit in with Fort Worth, Jess figured, with the hat and boots, but especially the spurs. Mort Thompson likely had never been on a horse. Probably was scared of them, and Jess had never met an honest-to-goodness Texas cowboy or cattleman who needed a chin strap to hold his hat on his head.

Jess Casey did not care much for Mort Thompson. Besides, he knew Miguel Sanchez.

"That Mex," Tom McNamara said tightly, "was pulling a shotgun on us. That was self-defense."

"You're free to act as your brother's counsel, McNamara." Thompson grinned.

Jess hoped that miserable politician would get creamed in the next election.

"We would have paid the Mex," Tom said.

"Yeah. With thirty cents."

"Thirty-one," Jess corrected.

"We would have hocked one of our guns. Spurs. Hat. Something." McNamara shook his head. "For God's sake, man, it was over two dollars."

"And ten cents." Mort Thompson was a low-down Yankee weasel. Jess wondered how he had managed to get elected in this day and age. Reconstruction had ended years ago. Fort Worth did not need some slick-talking, baby-kissing skunk from South Bend, Indiana, to handle prosecutions in Tarrant County.

Mayor Stout mumbled something. Probably worried if the café would be able to open for dinner. The mayor ate there a lot, probably because he was a bigger miser than Miguel Sanchez.

"You haul Burt off to jail, they'll send him back to Huntsville in a blink of an eye." Tom's face flushed. "Make him finish those two years."

"And add a few more years to that sentence." Thompson pointed a fat finger in the oldest McNamara brother's face. "Ask me, all of y'all belong behind those brick walls."

Jess cleared his throat and stepped off the board-walk between Tom McNamara and Mort Thompson. He even turned his back on the McNamara boys, hoping to defuse the situation.

"Miguel's a skinflint," he said. "Pulling a shotgun

over a two-dollar bill is extreme, even for that old boy."

"I'd call shooting a man's ear off extreme, too, Sheriff Casey," Thompson said icily.

"A man has a right to defend himself," Casey said.

"This is a town matter, Casey," Thompson said. "Not the county."

"But Kurt left me in charge while he's out of town."

"And I say who goes to trial and who doesn't."

"No," Casey corrected. "That's actually up to a grand jury. And I'm thinking, once they've heard what happened, the good citizens on that grand jury would no-bill these boys."

"He just wants those ex-cons out of town before . . ." Mayor Stout stopped himself, cleared his throat, and looked uneasily at the Fort Worth men and women who had gathered around.

"I can pay Doc Wilson for her troubles. I can pay the two dollars and ten cents for these boys' breakfast. Turn them loose. Let them ride home."

"Let Stephenville's law worry about them," Mayor Stout said.

"No." Jess wondered if he would be no-billed by a grand jury if he up and shot Mort Thompson right now. The solicitor waved that fat finger in Jess's face. "Take him to jail. You have the charges. We'll see what the good citizens of Fort Worth say when he goes before the grand jury."

"When would that grand jury be?" Tom McNamara asked.

"A week," Thompson answered.

"You boys could ride home and come back," Mayor Stout suggested. He had started to sweat.

"We might wait around here," Tom said.

"There's a law against vagrancy," Thompson said.

"We'll sell one of our horses. Maybe two."

A cold silence filled the morning air, and Jess Casey wondered if he could find a job punching cattle up around Jacksboro. Maybe just ride the grub line for the winter. Drift on to Kansas. Dodge City. Maybe on up into Montana. He had heard a lot of good stories about cowboying in Montana. There weren't as many fences in that part of the country, and there sure weren't many Mort Thompsons and Mayor Stouts up north.

"Take him to jail, Sheriff." Mort Thompson turned on his heel and shoved his way through the crowd as he sought out his office. Good, Jess thought. The solicitor had knocked off one man's bowler hat. That'll likely cost him a vote in the next election.

Shaking his head, Jess knelt by the hitching post and fetched the key to the handcuffs from his vest pocket. He gave Tom McNamara an understanding look.

"My hand's all busted up," Burt wailed.

Jess rose, tugging on the manacles as Burt McNamara struggled to his feet, then pulled the kid's left arm behind his back, took the swollen right hand, and gently locked that bracelet in place.

"Send Doc Wilson to the jail when she's done here," he told Mayor Stout.

The mayor nodded, then asked, "Have you heard anything about . . . you know who?"

Jess's head shook, and he pulled the watch from his vest pocket. "Stage is due at eleven. I'll be there."

"That's my watch," Mayor Stout said.

Jess returned it to him and walked the sniffling Burt McNamara through the crowd.


"You want me to do what?" Hoot Newton asked. "Be a law dog?"

The old cowboy slurped coffee, sweetened with Old Overholt, in the cell across from the one where Jess Casey had deposited Burt McNamara.

"It pays a dollar a day," Jess said. "And it's only till my regular deputies get back from Huntsville."

"I don't know, Jess . . ."

So Jess topped off Hoot Newton's coffee with more rye whiskey. Actually, regular sheriff's deputies earned seventy-five dollars a month, but if Jess was going to have to keep Hoot Newton supplied with whiskey, he figured thirty a month would be more in line with what he could afford. He wasn't sure the county commissioner and Tarrant County's cheap treasurer would approve of hiring an extra deputy, so this money would likely come out of Jess Casey's own meager bank account.

"Newt . . ."

"Hoot . . ."

"Right. Hoot. Thing is, ol' hand . . ." Jess figured it the right time to thicken that Texas drawl. "Here's what's going on in Fort Worth." He jerked his thumb behind him toward Burt McNamara. "This boy is here in jail on some charges that could send him

back to Huntsville. Which makes no never mind to
me. But his brothers—those boys who raised such a
ruckus down at the depot earlier this morning . . . you
remember that, Hoot? How you saved my bacon?"

Hoot Newton focused on his coffee, which he
quickly drained, and then looked back up at Jess.
Hoot's face revealed nothing but blankness.

"Doesn't matter," Jess said. "McNamara here has
three brothers. In town. Right now, they are unarmed,
but you know how easy it is to get a pistol in the
Panther City, right?"

Nothing.

"So that's one problem I have. The other is this."
He leaned forward. Inside the office, he heard the
chimes on the clock. Then the door opened and a
voice called out, "Sheriff Casey?"

"Wait a moment," Jess said and moved down the
hall. He opened the door and leaned inside his office.

"Hi, Doc. Thanks for coming."

Amanda Wilson closed the front door. She held
her black satchel and smiled. Her smile was the best
sight Jess had seen all morning. She was probably in
her thirties now, but she didn't look it. Red hair.
Smartly dressed. Green eyes and a face full of freckles.
He had heard that her husband had died back in
Jefferson, an old cotton town in northeast Texas, and
had moved to Fort Worth to start over. But she didn't
wear black, so maybe she had stopped mourning.
She sure was pretty.

Jess got the keys and motioned Doc Wilson to
follow. Back in the jailhouse, he unlocked the door

to Burt's cell and held the heavy door open as Amanda Wilson eased inside.

"Let me see your hand," Amanda told Burt.

"It's busted." Burt's voice had lost its whine, and he sat on his bunk like a bantam rooster. "But I can sure . . ."

"And I can bust your other hand," Amanda said, and for proof, she pulled one of Burt's fingers.

The boy yelped like a kicked dog.

Doc Wilson was all right, Jess decided, so he turned his attention to Hoot Newton. He kept the door to the cell open, though, just in case he needed to get in there quickly.

"All you'd have to do, Newt . . ."

"Hoot."

"Right. Hoot. I need some coffee." Actually, he could use a couple of morning bracers of rye whiskey, but that was out of the question. On this day in particular, Jess Casey knew he needed to keep his mind clear.

"You'd just be the jailer. Wouldn't have to leave the office. Just keep an eye on Burt yonder." He hooked his thumb again, just as Burt yelled as Amanda Wilson set another one of the fingers his big brother had busted.

"I just sit here."

"Just for a while. Week. Probably no more. Maybe a little less." Maybe, Jess thought, the judge could convene a grand jury early enough, or even better, someone could talk Mort Thompson and Miguel Sanchez out of pressing charges. But that wouldn't happen. Although if Tom McNamara filed a civil suit against Miguel Sanchez, or even pressed charges against that miserly Mexican then . . .

That was a wild dream. Jess stopped himself. He didn't know Tom McNamara at all, but he knew enough about the man. Tom McNamara would not go to a lawyer, or a judge, or a hired gun. Tom McNamara would do his own fighting, his own killing, and his kid brother might not be worth a hoot in hell, but he was blood kin, a McNamara, and those boys fought together.

Jess sighed. "Hoot. There's a fellow coming to town. Anyway, he's supposed to be coming to town. And I think when he arrives, things might get hot in Fort Worth. I can't babysit this McNamara kid all day and all night. Not if this fellow comes."

"Who's this fella?" Newton asked.

"His name is Lincoln Dalton and—"

Behind him came a roar of pure rage that drowned out Doc Wilson's girlish yelp. Dropping the bottle of Old Overholt, Jess whirled to see Burt McNamara racing toward him, hatred filling his eyes.

# CHAPTER EIGHT

*Monday, 10:25 a.m.*

Jess reacted more out of instinct than anything else. Amanda Wilson was lying on her buttocks on the filthy jail floor, and Burt dashed out of the cell. Instead of drawing his Colt—fearing a wild shot might injure or even kill Amanda—Jess reached out with his left hand, grabbed the edge of the iron-barred door, and swung it with such force he grunted and fell to his knees.

He heard the crunch of iron meeting bone and flesh, followed by a feminine shriek and an unlady-like curse, and came up. This time, he did draw the .44-40, but as soon as he was standing, he holstered the Colt.

Burt McNamara, his nose gushing blood, lay atop Amanda Wilson, who pushed him off her body, pulled herself up, and while brushing the filth off her dress, she spit in the kid's bleeding face, cursing him like a sailor before her eyes fell upon Jess Casey.

"I'm . . ." She blushed. "Sorry."

Jess grinned. "I've heard worse."

Behind him, Hoot Newton said, "Bottle didn't break."

Jess looked at the cowhand, who had picked up the bottle of Old Overholt and took a long pull. Wiping his mouth, Hoot gestured with the bottle at Burt McNamara. "You don't need nobody to mind your pris'ners. You does a good job your ownself."

With a chuckle, Jess pulled open the door and stepped inside Burt's cell. He unloosened his bandana and handed it to the dazed prisoner, who seemed to know enough to wad up the piece of calico and press it against his nose, which, Jess could tell, was busted. Next, he leaned down and lifted the punk onto the bunk and stepped back.

Recovering and remembering her upbringing, Amanda knelt to pick up her satchel, then righted the stool and sat back down. She started to bring a cotton ball toward Burt McNamara, then she stopped and looked up at Jess, who was leaning against the iron bars of the cell.

"You said . . . Lincoln . . . Dalton . . . ?"

Jess nodded. He stared into Amanda's pretty green eyes, but Burt McNamara said something in a nasal voice, and Jess found himself looking at the kid's bloody face.

"He . . . killed . . . my pa."

Jess frowned.

Burt McNamara continued. "The . . . Butcher . . . of Bax-ter . . . Pass. Ouch!" He flinched from Amanda's touch, and this time she turned back to Jess.

"The Butcher of Baxter Pass . . . is coming . . . to Fort Worth?"

"He's a murdererin' son-of-a . . ."

In the hallway, Hoot Newton burped.

"How old are you?" Jess asked.

Amanda glared at him.

"No. Not you, ma'am. How old are you, Burt?"

The punk answered with a curse.

"How could Dalton have killed your father . . . ?"

"I'm . . . twenty-seven." He pulled away as Doc Wilson set his busted nose.

The math there worked out. At least, it was mathematically possible, though he doubted if Burt McNamara would ever have met his father.

"They . . . was . . . marchin' out of that . . . hellhole. And . . . Dalton just . . . gunned 'em . . . all down."

"Like dogs."

Now Jess found himself looking into those green eyes of freckle-faced Amanda Wilson, who no longer looked so beautiful, but angry, and her eyes did not register anything resembling Hippocrates or Florence Nightingale.

"My cousin," she said. "Corporal Vincent Groves."

She went back to doctoring the patient, and Jess Casey backed out of the cell.


In his office, Jess stirred honey into the coffee he had just poured and passed it across his desk to Doctor Amanda Wilson. A quick glance at the clock told him he had enough time for a chat.

"Your cousin?" he said.

She sipped the coffee, calmer now, not as angry, and she had wiped the blood and remnants off her face and hands. She relaxed, leaned her head back, and let out a little sigh. "Vincent Groves. Mama always told us how he'd been wounded at Sharpsburg. Everyone thought he was dead. He was Mama's brother's oldest son. I barely knew him. When the war started, I was only . . . well, that doesn't matter. Anyway, three months later, Mama got word from Uncle Vin—that was Vincent's pa, Mama's brother—that Vincent had died in that pesthole at Baxter Pass. They even put up a headstone in the family plot in Galveston County. That's where I grew up."

Jess nodded and stirred his own coffee, even though his was black.

"And just when the war had ended, Mama got a letter from Uncle Vin. Turned out, Vincent had not died after all. You know how rumors get started and all. Vincent was alive. And he was coming home. And then . . ." She shuddered and looked down at her lap, at the coffee cup that trembled in her hand. When she looked up, Jess had to search every pocket and drawer before he found a decent handkerchief, which he handed her.

Amanda wiped her eyes. She set the coffee cup on the edge of Jess's desk.

"You don't know what it's like," she said.

"No, ma'am."

"That was in '65. I was . . . well, that doesn't matter . . . but I was old enough to understand. My cousin was coming home. Alive. He had survived all those awful things, Sharpsburg, Baxter Pass. He was coming home. Mama and Papa even made jokes about taking Vincent to the cemetery, show him his grave, his tombstone. They'd have a good laugh over it. And then . . ."

Tears poured, and she sobbed without control, but without shame. Jess knew that those tears needed to run their course, and he waited. Finally, she wiped her face again and shivered.

"Maybe the worst part of it was reading about it in the newspaper a neighbor, Mister Clavin, brought us. That's how we'd learned that . . . that . . . that . . . Vincent wasn't coming home." She picked up the soaked handkerchief and dabbed her eyes again.

Despite all that crying, her swollen eyes, Jess thought that she still looked lovely.

"General Dalton . . . the damned Butcher . . . he had lined them up against the prison wall. He had made them recite the Oath of Allegiance to the Union. And while they were doing that, he gave the order, and the Gatling guns barked . . . and . . . and . . ." She shuddered, tossed the handkerchief away, and found the cup of coffee.

"He shot them down like dogs."

Jess leaned back in his chair. "I read . . ." he began, but she silenced him with a stare.

"Did you fight in the war?"

His head shook. "Too young." He frowned. *How old does she think I am?*

"I'm from Texas." He felt that she needed to know this. "And not from one of those Union-loving counties."

"I'm sorry." She gave him a weak smile.

"You said that the prisoners . . ."

"Two hundred of them."

"Yes. You said they were in the prison camp at Baxter Pass. That's when Dalton . . . the Butcher . . . gunned them down with the Gatling gun."

"Guns. I think they had a dozen at that wretched, wretched place."

Jess nodded.

Her eyes still held a spark that reminded Jess of a percussion cap. Ready to pop and ignite a chamber, or maybe a barrel, of gunpowder. He had stared into friendlier looking eyes belonging to a rattlesnake coiled up and whirring its tail. This was a subject, Jess knew, that would need careful phrasing.

He hooked his thumb at the closed door that led to the jail cells. "Burt . . . he said something else. He said they were marching out of the prison camp when Dalton began firing."

She shrugged. "He was just a baby when that happened. What—two, three, maybe four years old?"

His head nodded, but he kept talking. "I guess I've heard that story before. The general opens the gates to the prison, tells all those Johnny Rebs they were free to go home, and as soon as they were out the door, through the gates, the Gatlings opened up and brought them down like a McCormick's Reaper."

Amanda shook her head. "Yes. There are all sorts of stories."

Jess went on. "Yet I remember reading in a magazine . . . no, it was a newspaper. The *Dallas Mercury*. That's the paper." It had been used to paper a wall in a line shack when he was cowboying. Faded and hard to read all those years later, but he had read that article, had been drawn to it like a moth to a flame.

"That paper, if I remember right, said the prisoners had been loaded onto a ship. The *Fancy Belpre*!" That amazed Jess, even excited him that he could remember that little detail from a newspaper he had read one winter night alone in a line shack down around Waxahachie way. "The steamboat was to carry the prisoners home, and as soon as it got into the middle of the Ohio, General Dalton began . . ." He stopped.

Amanda's head had dropped.

"I guess there are many stories about what happened," she said.

Jess could only nod. This was, after all, Texas. The Lone Star State. Bigger than anything and full of braggarts and liars. How many men had he met who had been with Sam Houston at San Jacinto? How many had ridden with Sam Bass? Had lived in a cabin where Davy Crockett had slept on his way to the Alamo? Had seen John Wesley Hardin gun down somebody in some saloon or in some street? Had fought with Ben McCullough during the war against the Union? Had taken part in one or even both fights up in the Panhandle at Adobe Walls?

"What I remember," Amanda says, "is what I remember. They were in the prison. Dalton opened fire."

Jess nodded. "I guess that's one thing that's

consistent to the story. Dalton . . . he was always the one cranking the Gatling gun."

Her eyes hardened. She was the rattler, and now she struck. "No, Sheriff Casey, there's one more consistent, undisputable fact to the stories out there."

He knew what she would say.

"Two hundred paroled soldiers were murdered . . . by that damned butcher."

She stood, and he pushed himself out of the chair. The clock on the wall chimed, and he moved toward the office door as Doctor Wilson gathered her belongings. She opened the satchel, pulled out a tincture, and dropped it on the desk. "The prisoner can have one of those to help with the pain," she said, and headed to the door, which Jess pulled open.

The air remained cool.

"How much do I owe you?" Jess asked.

"Three dollars."

He paid her, thought about asking for a receipt, so he might ask the treasurer to reimburse him, but decided that would be in poor taste.

She dropped the three greenbacks into the satchel, snapped it shut, and stared back at Jess.

"Do I look . . . presentable?"

Her eyes were redder than scarlet, puffy and swollen, and her face was streaked with tears and dust. Her nose even was swollen and red from blowing it and sobbing so much. Somebody might even think she'd been drinking a few snootfuls.

"You're lovely," Jess said, and he meant it.

That got him a grin.

"Flattery, Sheriff Casey . . ."

"I am sorry," he said, seriously now, and her grin faded, but her eyes lacked that deadly intent. "I didn't mean to bring up unpleasant memories."

"It's all right, Jess." Good. She was back to calling him by his first name. "I hadn't thought of Vincent in a long time. Years." She drew a deep breath. "Do you really think he's coming . . . here . . . to Fort Worth? The Butcher of Baxter Pass?"

Jess answered: "I hope to hell not."

# CHAPTER NINE

*Monday, 11:17 a.m.*

The stage from Dallas was late.

Casey leaned against the wooden façade, sipping the thick tar Hank Joseph called coffee. It probably had been coffee when the old stationmaster first brewed it, maybe two or three weeks ago. It tasted awful, but no one could ever complain that it was weak or watered down.

Hank wandered out of the station and settled onto the bench in front of the stagecoach stop, pulled out a sack of Bull Durham from his coat pocket, and began rolling a cigarette. He was grizzled and old, with a face like shoe leather and teeth stained brown from tobacco and coffee. He shaved once every two weeks, maybe three, bathed every other month, and spoke only when spoken to. His cavalry-style boots were brown and scuffed, holes in the bottoms, and patches covered his denim britches. An ancient kepi topped his balding pate. It was the kepi that Jess Casey noticed. He had always found Hank Joseph inside the station and had never actually seen him with a hat on his noggin.

"Hank," Jess called out.

The rail-thin old man turned, licking his cigarette, and staring with dark brown eyes. He said nothing.

Jess gestured with his coffee mug. "You fought in the war?"

"Which war?" The cigarette went into his mouth, and he found a lucifer in his pocket, struck it against his thumb, and fired up the smoke.

Which war? Answering that question incorrectly had caused a few fights during Jess Casey's time in bunkhouses, saloons, and even church socials. For the most part, people called it the War Between the States or the War for Southern Independence in Texas. Ladies often referred to it, politely, as "the recent unpleasantness," and Yanks called it the War of the Rebellion. A lot of folks would use the Civil War, but from the stories Jess had heard about the fighting, there had not been one damned thing civil about those four bitter, bloody years.

Those brown eyes, set deep in that bronzed face, were hard to read, but that kepi told Jess how to answer.

"The Rebellion."

Old Hank snorted, might even have grinned, and pulled hard on the cigarette, tilted his head back, and blew a smoke ring toward the awning.

"Risky," the old-timer said. "Callin' it by that handle." Hank's accent sounded pure Texan, not Yankee.

"Union kepi," Jess said, nodding at the cap.

"Coulda taken it off a dead blue belly."

Jess grinned but said nothing.

For a minute, Hank Joseph smoked, watched a buggy clip down the street, moved his outstretched legs to let a woman pass, then took the smoke out of his mouth and looked back at Jess.

"Hailed from Cooke County," he said.

Jess nodded.

"Union country," he said.

"Like Jack County," Jess said. He had cowboyed up in that part of Texas, and had known quite a few men who had refused to vote for secession.

"Yeah, but the difference between Jack County and Cooke County was that the boys up in Jack thought they was Texans first. Over 'round Gainesville, their blood was blue. Union blue."

That was more than Jess had heard Hank Joseph say in six months.

"Hung a bunch of folks there, you know, in '62."

Jess lowered his cup, surprised. "I didn't know that."

"Yep. Said they wasn't loyal to the Confederacy. Hung a ton of 'em. From a tree in Gainesville's town square. Hung two of my uncles, a cousin, and my pappy."

Jess cursed softly.

"So you're damned right I fit for the Union. And that's why I ain't ashamed to keep this here hat on my head."

The coffee tasted worse than ever, so Jess poured out the remnants onto the street and stepped inside the office, dropping the cup by the table near the stove. When he returned, the old stationmaster was crushing out the butt of his smoke on the boardwalk.

"He ain't gonna be on the stage," Hank said, "if the damned thing ever comes in."

"Who?"

Hank Joseph snorted. "Who? Who else, ya knucklehead? Lincoln Everett Dalton. Brigadier General. Hero of the North. Savior of Ohio. The Butcher of Baxter Pass."

The old Yank had been staring out in the street, which saw little traffic now, but turned and let his dark eyes bore into Jess Casey.

"Stout." Jess spit over the hitching rail.

That got a chuckle out of Hank Joseph. "Mayor couldn't keep a secret to save his hide. I tol' him the same thing. Dalton won't be on the stage."

Since the old man seemed to be windy this morning, Jess decided to wait. Push a man like this, and Hank might press his lips together and not speak for another week.

"Seen him oncet," Hank said after a moment, "ten years, nah, a dozen years, back."

"You knew him?" Jess asked. "Did you serve . . . ?"

"I fit with the 7th Wisconsin Volunteer Infantry— the Iron Brigade—from Brawner's Farm to Petersburg. I didn't hide in no stinkin' prison camp."

He fetched a plug of tobacco from another pocket, bit off a mouthful, and tried to soften the rock-hard quid.

"He give a lecture in Council Bluffs once," Hank said. "Gen'ral Dalton. Come ridin' into town on some fancy wagon, gal playin' one of 'em steam pianies a body could hear ten miles outta town. Pretty gal. Real pretty but just a kid. Bet she's a right handsome woman now, though. But that steam piany given me a blasted headache. Ain't never heard such a racket."

This time, Hank Joseph removed his kepi, ran bony fingers over his bald head, returned the cap, and sent a stream of tobacco juice through the cracks in the boardwalk. His aim, Jess marveled, was perfect.

After wiping his lip, Hank Joseph continued. "Buntin' on the sides of that wagon, flags flappin' in the wind, and Gen'ral Dalton standin' atop. A Gatlin' gun was secured atop that wagon, too, and the gen'ral, him in his blue uniform, brass buttons a-gleamin' in the sun, purple ostrich plume tucked up in his Hardee hat."

"Did you attend his lecture?"

"Hell, no." Hank shifted the quid to the opposite cheek. "I couldn't stand to hear that steam piany. Crossed the ferry and went to Omaha. But I seed him. Gen'ral Dalton. He was somethin'."

He stood then, and moved to the column, putting a weathered hand on the rough wood and looked east. Old Hank had a set of ears on him, for a half-minute later the red and gold stagecoach wheeled around the corner, the driver's blacksnake whip popping over the ears of the six mules churning up mud and dirt as the Concord stage plowed its way toward the station. The messenger, holding a sawed-off shotgun, looked mighty pale when the stage slid to a halt in front of Jess and Hank.

The driver set the brake, leaned over, spit his own river of tobacco juice into the dirt, and bellowed, "Fort Worth. Get off now or you'll be walkin' back from Belknap."

Mayor Stout and a few of his associates hurried

down the boardwalk. Apparently, the mayor didn't take Hank Joseph's word that the Butcher of Baxter Pass would not be aboard the stage. Hank was jerking open the door, and Jess Casey watched as a potbellied man in a sack suit leap onto the boardwalk, turn quickly, and catch a gaudy carpetbag that the messenger was tossing off the top.

Next stepped a tall man in black broadcloth shirt and a gold brocade vest with thistle designs. Tinhorn, Jess decided, and when the man took his grip, Jess moved toward him.

"Gamblers are welcome in Hell's Half Acre," Jess said. The man's face was deeply pockmarked, and his eyes were hidden by his shaded wire-rimmed spectacles. His hair was black, greased down, and his mustache had been trimmed pencil-thin. "As long as they don't deal from the bottom."

The man said nothing.

"But I'll take that derringer."

Jess held up his left hand, palm up, and waited. His right hand rested on the butt of the .44-40.

The man fished a Remington over-and-under .41 from the vest pocket, and laid it gently in Jess's hand.

"What name should I put it under?"

"Luke Flint," the man said.

"Very well, Luke Flint. Pick it up on your way out of town. Sheriff's office. Up yonder way."

The man's grin held no humor. "Aren't you going to wish me luck, Sheriff?"

"You don't need luck," Jess told him, and stepped out of the man's path, watching him amble through Mayor Stout and his followers, moving away from Fort Worth proper and toward Hell's Half Acre. Jess slid the derringer into his rear pocket and turned back to the stage.

The crew was already at work, changing the team of worn-out mules for a fresh batch. They were a marvel, those three young black men and the Mexican, replacing the team like they'd been doing it for twenty years. Professionals. But honest men, doing honest work, not like Luke Flint. Just another headache that would probably trouble Jess Casey until Kurt Koenig returned to his marshaling duties. But at least Jess had evened the odds by relieving the cardsharp of that derringer.

"Sheriff," the drummer in the sack suit called out, "where's a decent place to eat some decent chow? That won't blow my expense account."

Jess started to gesture down the street. "Well . . ." No, Miguel Sanchez likely would not reopen today. Maybe not tomorrow. What was left of his ear had to hurt like blazes, and all the blood on the floor and counter might turn a body's stomach.

"Get the blue plate at the Trinity River Hotel," he suggested, and watched the drummer waddle in the general direction.

That was it. No more passengers getting off for Fort Worth and nobody climbing aboard for the journey north and west. The stable hands were leading the mules across the street toward the corral, and Hank Joseph was slamming the door to the coach as the messenger settled back onto his seat in the driver's box.

With a blast of profanity and the pop of the whip, the westbound stage pulled out of Fort Worth.

"He wasn't on the stage," Mayor Stout said, his voice resigned in defeat.

Snorting in contempt, Hank Joseph went back inside the office.

Harry Stout's eyes lifted toward Jess Casey's. "Maybe he won't come."

"Maybe," Jess said, and thinking, but not saying, *And maybe you won't tell everybody this side of Dallas that he is coming.*

"Well." Stout turned. "Time for dinner, boys." He walked down the boardwalk, followed by his minions.

Jess didn't care and only half-heard the mayor's comment. He kept watching Luke Flint. Even before he pinned on that nice gold badge, he had learned a few things on his own as a cowboy: Gamblers would never give a cowhand an even break. No honest gent sported a pencil-thin mustache. And any gambler who wore a brocade vest was a dirty, rotten cheat and one dangerous hombre. Jess would stop at the telegraph office and send a query about one Luke Flint to the Dallas constable. Not that that smart-aleck son of a cur dog would give him an honest answer.

He turned and walked down the street, away from Mayor Stout, away from Luke Flint.

"Sheriff."

Jess looked back at Hank Joseph, who had stepped out of the office. He wasn't wearing that Union kepi. Probably had hung it on the rack behind the desk.

"You ain't gonna tell nobody nothin' I tol' you. 'Bout me bein' in the war with the 7th Wisconsin."

"I don't bring up a man's past," Jess said.

Hank's thin head nodded.

"Like I done tol' you, I don't know Gen'ral Dalton. Just laid eyes on him that one time up in Iowa. But the man you oughta talk to, iffen you's interested, is the perfesser."

"The professor?" Jess asked.

"Uh-huh. Perfesser Mitchell Vogt. Teaches 'em petticoats and them boys who ougtha be wearin' petticoats at that thar seminary place down by Thorp Spring."

Jess waited, and for a long while thought maybe that was all the information he would get from Hank Joseph. After all, the man had been an open book for the past half hour.

"Vogt served with Hood's boys. And he was at Baxter Pass."

# CHAPTER TEN

*Monday, 11:45 a.m.*

Professor Mitchell Vogt. Jess moved down the boardwalk, taking in the aroma of the myriad restaurants in Fort Worth as dinnertime approached. Chicken-fried steaks, fried potatoes, coffee that smelled more pleasing than the tar he had sipped at Hank Joseph's stagecoach station, beef brisket, cornbread, enchiladas, beans. . . .

Professor Mitchell Vogt. Jess didn't know the man, and he knew little about that Christian college that had been founded, originally here in Fort Worth, but now about forty miles south at Thorp Spring near Granbury.

The way Jess had heard the story, brothers Addison and Randolph Scott from somewhere over in East Texas had established the Male & Female Seminary of Fort Worth here in town back in '69. The brothers had been part of that Second Great Awakening and the Restoration Movement and really wanted to educate the day's youth. So they bought five blocks in Fort Worth and started to teach the students. The problem was . . . where they'd set up their college.

That's where Luke Flint would be by this time. The original site of the Male & Female Seminary of Fort Worth would soon be crowded with dance halls, bawdy houses, saloons, cribs, brothels, and plenty of drunken cowboys in Hell's Half Acre.

Therefore, in 1873, the Scott brothers headed south, to Thorp Spring, where they had established AddRan Male & Female College—Add for Addison and Ran for Randolph, the brothers apparently wanting their names branded on the sheepskins of the youth they'd educate.

Now, Jeff Casey was a stove-up ex-cowhand who'd found himself a lawman. He could read and write, do his own ciphering if you gave him enough time, and even form a complete sentence or two— sometimes making sense—but he did not know much about colleges and universities. From what he had heard, however, AddRan brought in the best professors and taught some two hundred to four hundred kids. Boys and girls. Together. Jeff had never heard that a college could teach both boys and girls. Now for kids, sure, that was a given. Jess had stepped inside enough of those schools and could remember the schoolmarm asking him and Lisa Davis to do their readings—Lisa always could read better and clearer than Jess. But they'd been not even in their teens. That was one thing, to have nine-year-old boys mingle with eight-year-old girls and risk getting cooties. But colleges? Those were practically grown men and women. Together. Jess's ma would have frowned on such commingling.

Coeducational, folks called it, and AddRan was the first of its kind in the great state of Texas and one of the first established west of the Mississippi River.


He had broken his arm when a chuckleheaded horse had tossed him after they'd crossed the Brazos River with a herd of twelve hundred longhorns some years back, and Jess remembered the cook setting the arm. Pretty country down that way. Jess wouldn't mind seeing it again. Granbury had started as nothing more than a log courthouse, but these days folks from the Brazos to the Red bragged about the big opera house in town.

It would be a good excuse, he told himself. Ride south. See this Professor Vogt. He had cowboyed for the Rafter J, and that would be maybe fifteen or twenty miles south of Granbury. Maybe the boss man there was hiring.

He sighed. A nice dream. But he couldn't do it. Couldn't leave Fort Worth, not with Luke Flint dealing stud in some bucket of blood over in Hell's Half Acre, and not with Burt McNamara sitting in jail, guarded by only Hoot Newton, and Burt's three brothers somewhere in town. And not with the Butcher of Baxter Pass heading straight for the Panther City.

Stepping inside the telegraph office, Jess realized that he didn't have to ride forty miles southwest.

Bald-headed Clint Stowe sat in his chair, his

stocking feet propped up on the desk, head back, mouth open, snoring like a dog.

"Clint!"

He jerked up, pulling his feet off the table, dropping them to the floor, hitting the spittoon and turning it over, sending the brass cuspidor rolling toward the sidewall, which confirmed Jess's suspicion that the telegraph office did in fact lean toward the north.

"Marshal," Clint blinked.

"Sheriff," Jess corrected.

"Do somethin' fer ya?"

"Need to send two telegrams." As Clint yawned and scratched his bald head, Jess tore one of the blank slips from a pad, found a pencil that didn't need sharpening—the fourth he picked out of the dried bull scrotum Clint Stowe used as a pencil holder—and went to work.

He filled out the date, wrote Professor Mitchell Vogt, AddRan, Thorp Spring, and wrote:

*Requesting any information you might have on Baxter Pass and General Lincoln E. Dalton.*

He signed his name and title, slid the paper across the counter to the still-yawning Clint Stowe, and ripped off another sheet from the blank pad.

This one he sent to Paul Parkin, the Dallas city constable.

It read:

*What can you tell me about a gambler named Luke Flint? Got off the stage this AM from Dallas. Did you send him our way, too?*

*P.S.: No sign of Dalton yet. Guess he went back your way. Enjoy his company.*

Jess grinned, dropped the pencil in the scrotum, and handed the second flimsy piece of paper to Clint, who took it.

"You want me to send these two telegrams?" Clint asked.

"This is a telegraph office," Jess said. "Isn't it?"

Clint had to think for a moment.

"Uh-huh."

"Send it . . . like . . . today . . . now . . . *muy pronto.*"

First Clint nodded. Then he lifted his arms over his head and behind him and stretched long and hard. Finally he turned in his seat, laid the first telegram in front of him, and started making the telegraph wires sing.

Jess dropped some coins on the counter.

"When you get a reply, Clint," he said. "Come tell me. Just me. Not Stout. Not your grandmother. Just me."

Clint had moved to the second telegram now, and he tapped a few keys to make sure the line was still open and nodded. Then he frowned and said: "Grandma Stowe died when I was twelve. Grandma Parker . . ." He looked out the window. "Don't know whatever become of her after she taken off with that drummer . . . Like to broke Ma's heart, it did, as the drummer was an Eye-talian."

The keys started tapping again, and rolling his eyes, Jess Casey stepped outside.

He stopped for dinner two blocks down at the café

that had no name. Grover Wyatt ran it, never closed it, and never slept. It catered to schoolmarms and whores, gamblers and cowhands, bankers and lawyers. It served the best chopped beef in North Texas, with slices of toast cut three inches thick and beans seasoned with fatback and beer. You washed down the grub with bottled beer. Some folks never wanted to leave, and as far as Jess Casey could tell, a few hadn't since he had first arrived in the cow town.

Jess was lucky. There was a spot just vacated by a fat Mexican *vaquero* at the counter, and Jess slid onto the stool as Grover Wyatt swiped away the plate and empty brown bottle, wiped down the spot in front of Jess with a greasy rag, lifted the rag, blew his nose, then wiped the spot next to Jess as another patron left. A drummer quickly filled that seat, unaware of how unclean the area was in front of him.

You did not order at the café with no name. You sat down. Wyatt brought a plate and a beer. You ate. You paid. You left. Round the clock.

When Grover Wyatt came by moments later and dumped two plates on the counter, then opened two bottles of beer, Jess, remembering something, said, "Grover?"

Wyatt was a sour-faced man with close-cropped hair, arms the size of cottonwood limbs, no neck to speak of, and a gut and a face that said he had been living off his own food for some time now. He scowled. Jess figured the man hadn't washed that apron tied around his fat belly in six months.

"Could you bring me a couple of plates to go?"

The big man leaned forward. "You feedin' jailbirds my chow, Sheriff?" he growled.

Which gave Jess a moment's pause. He hadn't even thought about feeding Burt McNamara. He was buying two plates for Hoot Newton. "Better make it three," Jess said, then, upon further reflection and recalling Hoot's appetite, corrected himself. "Four."

Grover Wyatt left with a curse and a fart. Jess took a swig of beer. About one-quarter of the people filling the café without a name had been in Jess's jail cells before at one time or another.

He ate in silence. Few people dared to speak in Grover Wyatt's place, probably afraid that one of the thousands of flies buzzing inside would be digested in their bellies along with the chopped beef and beans. Jess had been in nastier places to eat than the café without a name—several cookhouses on the ranches where he had cowboyed came quickly to mind—but Jess couldn't recall ever going back to any of those places.

Grover Wyatt's joint, however, was different.

The place was hell, but the food was pure Texas heaven.

As soon as Jess swallowed the last bite, Grover Wyatt was there, ripping away the empty plate and bottle of beer, heading back to the kitchen, then returning. He deposited a brown sack already dripping with grease in front of Jess, and then turned toward the man sitting beside him.

The drummer was picking his teeth with a toothpick.

"Folks eat here, mister," Grover bellowed. "There's a tooth-puller four doors down." Unceremoniously, Grover Wyatt ripped the plate from underneath the drummer's nose and went back to the kitchen. At least he hadn't taken the man's beer, which the drummer quickly downed, dropped a quarter on the countertop, and hurried outside.

Jess took a final swallow of his own beer, found the dirtiest, grimiest, chewed-up dollar bill he had in his pants pocket, and left it atop the warped pine countertop. With a greasy sack of dinner for his jailer and his prisoner, Jess Casey stepped out of the café without a name and headed back to his office.

The bells at the St. Stanislaus Catholic Church pealed. It was noon.

That's when another sound reached his ears. He wasn't sure at first if he had actually heard it, but then he was turning, staring down Main Street, watching. One woman with a yellow parasol who was crossing the street at the corner had heard the noise, too. It stopped her dead in her tracks and she turned, lowering the parasol, watching.

A merchant in sleeve garters and a sweaty face pushed through the batwing doors of his mercantile, staring.

Two men stood up from the cracker barrel where they were playing checkers.

A cowboy had to rein in his horse, which was turning, ornery, scared, doing a little sidestep in the middle of the street.

"What in the blazes is that infernal racket?" the merchant said, now wiping his forehead with a handkerchief.

"It's a song," Jess heard himself answering, more to himself than to the mercantile's clerk.

But he had never heard anything so strange. Loud, but far away. Musical, yet jarring. It took him a moment before he recognized the tune, a song no one in Fort Worth, Texas, would sing. The lyrics came to him, slowly, and he remembered the last time he had heard the song had been back in 1880, when someone had the audacity to campaign for James Garfield for president of the United States.

*The Union forever! Hurrah, boys, hurrah!*
*Down with the traitors, up with the stars;*
*While we rally round the flag, boys,*
*We rally once again,*
*Shouting the battle cry of freedom!*

The clerk in the mercantile doorway spit, cursed, and said, "A damn Yankee song."

Which is when Jess Casey dropped Grover Wyatt's chow in the street, the sack missing the edge of the boardwalk and landing in horse droppings and dirt. Because Jess Casey knew what that song meant, who it meant, even before the obnoxious wagon came around the bend and into view.

He remembered that steam piano, the one Hank Joseph had been talking about, the one *"a body could hear ten miles outta town."*

Brigadier General Lincoln Everett Dalton, the Butcher of Baxter Pass, had arrived in Fort Worth.

# CHAPTER ELEVEN

*Monday, 12:03 p.m.*

The cowboy had to dismount. Otherwise that claybank gelding would have pitched him and taken off for parts unknown.

A team of four speckled gray Percherons—the smallest just shy of seventeen hands and every one of them deep-chested and bulging with muscles—pulled the damnedest wagon Jess Casey had ever laid his eyes on.

Two small, wide wheels on the front, and two slightly larger and a wee bit wider wheels on the back, the boxing, hub, and hub band painted red; the spokes alternating red, white, and blue; and the felloes red with white stars, though now caked with dirt and grime. Only the flat steel tire had been untouched by paint. The brake pads were white.

A black-mustached man, resplendent in a uniform of the Army of the Potomac, sat atop the high wagon, feet propped against a blue box, holding the lines to the Percherons with one hand and a red steering wheel that came up on a blue pole from the bottom of the wagon.

The wagon itself was ornate, with bas-relief moldings along the sides of Ulysses S. Grant, Abraham Lincoln, and William T. Sherman near the front wheels, their names underneath the sculptures in big gold letters. Toward the rear wheels were two other sculptures of a cannon and a Gatling gun. In the middle of the wagon was an ornate American flag made out of wood trim. Thirty-five stars, after West Virginia had been added to the Union. Above that was the name, trimmed in some Oriental design, the background white, the first letter of each word in scarlet, the other smaller letters in blue. All capitalized.

## GENERAL LINCOLN E. DALTON, U.S.A.

Behind that were more wild designs of red, gold, and black, above blue trim, while in the front of the wagon, in red trim, were carvings of crossed sabers, the cover of a Holy Bible, a few stars, and crosses in a rainbow of colors. A lantern hung on each side of the front of the wagon, and at the top, in more colors, were other gilded designs and the words in a floral script:

## The Union Forever

Red, white, and blue bunting draped the side of the wagon, or that had been the intention. The winds on the North Texas prairie between Dallas and Fort Worth had kind of destroyed much of that look, but unless someone was really studying that it would not be noticed. Probably because every eye on Main Street looked above the bunting and behind the driver at the Gatling gun mounted atop the wagon.

Hank Joseph had said Dalton himself had stood on that roof, cranking the Gatling gun, but that had been ten or twelve years ago. General Lincoln Everett Dalton did not stand. He sat in a rocking chair, his white beard flowing, his shoulder-length white hair tangled by the wind. Jess Casey couldn't tell if the old man was even alive.

Then there was the music, and as the wagon rolled past Jess, he saw something else even more spectacular than the garish contraption pulled by four giant draft horses.

Recessed inside the back of the wagon, sheltered from the wind and dust, was a calliope, its pipes rising behind the player, coming out at the roof, along with a circular chimney pipe, also painted red and blue with white stars. There had to be a boiler somewhere inside the wagon, burning coal or some fuel to provide the steam needed for the calliope. The tune—sounding like a bunch of train whistles blowing out the notes—was still the *Battle Cry of Freedom*, but Jess Casey no longer paid that much attention to the song. He stared at the woman playing the keyboard.

Her hair was blacker than a raven's wing, hanging in curls well past her shoulder. A silver necklace, adorned with turquoise and coral, hung around her thin neck. The wagon was so close to the boardwalk that Jess could even see her eyes, the lightest gray he had ever seen, highlighted by those perfect black eyebrows and an unblemished, peachy face. The lips, unpainted, were perfect, her neck thin. Her dress—which was all Jess could make out—was a blue French sateen, decorated with white dove patterns and a stand-up collar. Anywhere else she would be freezing, but the wagon served as a wind block, and Jess could only imagine how hot it must be with the calliope's boiler somewhere behind her. Every now and then she would look up and smile, but then return her focus to the organ's keys.

"Excuse me."

Mesmerized, Jess pushed through the crowd that had emerged and stepped off the crowded board-walk. He started to follow afoot but then remembered the sack of food he had dropped. So he picked it up. The dirt had soaked up much of the grease leaking through the sack. With the sack swinging at his side, Jess followed Brigadier General Lincoln E. Dalton's circus wagon.

There was one other man aboard the wagon. His legs dangled over the back. His pants were kersey blue wool with red stripes—identifying him as a member of the artillery—but his boots weren't army, but black with white corded stripes up the sides and blue stars inlaid in the uppers. He wore a wide-brimmed, low-crowned black hat and a gray greatcoat covered with brass buttons. He held a Centennial Winchester model 1876—one of those massive repeaters that fired a .45-75 cartridge, and since the greatcoat wasn't buttoned, Jess could make out a couple of belts strapped across his waist. Each belt, Jess figured, held a holstered revolver.

The blond-headed man wore a walrus mustache and had pale eyes that missed nothing. He'd be the protector, because from the looks of the old man in the rocking chair with a feeble hand on the Gatling gun, the Butcher of Baxter Pass couldn't protect himself anymore.

The gunman's eyes lighted on Jess, saw the star, then searched the crowd, the rooftops, and the streets. He was a professional. That much was clear.

When the wagon reached the Trinity River Hotel, the driver pulled on the lines, stopped the team, and set the brake. Immediately, the woman playing the calliope stopped and went through the back door, disappearing inside. A door on the side of the wagon Jess hadn't seen, but equally decorated in brassy colors and grotesque gild, ornate carvings, and wind-blown bunting, opened, while the gunman pulled himself up, holding the big Winchester, still searching the crowd for trouble.

"Ladies and gentlemen!" the driver of the conveyance was saying, speaking through a megaphone and sounding just like all those hawkers Jess had heard at probably a dozen dog-and-pony shows that were, literally, dog-and-pony shows he had seen as a kid. "General Lincoln E. Dalton, the Butcher of Baxter Pass, is here to entertain and enlighten you. Tickets will go on sale this evening, right here in the lobby of this grand old hotel. The general's lecture will be tomorrow night—"

"Now wait a dad-blasted minute!" Mayor Stout had

stepped into the street. "That Texas man-killer ain't welcome in Fort Worth. And you sure ain't settin' up no show in my fair city."

Jess had to turn, hold up his hands, and stop the crowd from coming any closer to the wagon. Behind him he heard the metallic ratcheting as the gunman worked the lever on the Centennial. That sound— more than Jess's arms and his voice or badge—did the job.

The barker wasn't listening to Mayor Stout's protest. By now he was lifting something from the rooftop, fastening a bolt, bringing up some rigging, which he swung over the side, and Jess realized it was a pulley system. In a matter of minutes, he had hooked the general's rocking chair and began lowering the chair, with the white-haired old general still sitting in it below, turning the crank carefully.

By then, the woman had come out of the side door. She was tall and wore a brace of Navy Colts, converted to take modern brass cartridges, around her slender waist. Reaching up, she grabbed the arms of the rocker, steered it to the ground, then freed the hooks and cable and helped the old man to his feet.

"Are you all right?" she asked.

The old man's wind-chapped lips moved, but Jess couldn't hear. The woman lifted the rocker and put it inside the coach, shut the door, and turned to face a crowd that likely wasn't as friendly or interested as the one Hank Joseph had missed back in Council Bluffs, Iowa.

"Please give us room, ladies and gentlemen," the driver was saying. "The general needs to rest after that arduous journey from Dallas. But this evening, while we sell tickets, he will perhaps be able to sign an autograph or two."

*If he's still breathing,* Jess thought, and he moved to the side of the wagon. He held out his arm, gently nudged one cowhand back to the boardwalk, and started to stop another man from getting too close to Dalton, only to realize it was Mayor Harry Stout.

"You take this carnival act and this butcher out of my town!" The mayor glared at the wagon driver, who had come down from the top and now stood on the other side of the general.

"We have an engagement here . . . I don't believe I have your name," the barker said.

"Stout. Mayor Stout. I said—"

"Ah, yes, Mayor Stout." The man reached inside his tunic and pulled out a few papers. "We have rooms reserved at this grand old hotel. And here are the papers. We will be speaking tomorrow evening at your opera house."

He slid the papers into Stout's hands, and Jess wasn't that blind. He saw the thin greenbacks beneath the contracts and notices. He hoped that Mayor Stout wouldn't take the bribe, but he knew he would. Stout's fingers had always been sticky like honey.

"Well, if it's just for two nights, one show." The mayor returned the papers after a glance and surreptitiously slid the cash into his coat pocket.

"And I'm sure," the driver said, "we can arrange a front-row seat for you, Mayor Stout. Complimentary, of course. And even for you." The man grinned and held out his right hand toward Jess Casey. "We are law-abiding people, Sheriff. I see you have your hands full keeping this town safe and clean."

That prompted at least a couple of chuckles from the boardwalk, and Jess grimaced, wishing he had left the sack of chow for Hoot Newton and Burt McNamara on the street a few blocks up. The beautiful calliope player, Jess noticed from the corner of his eye, was also staring at the greasy, dirty sack in his left hand.

That also reminded Jess of Burt's three brothers—and the fact that, if he could believe the young punk in his jail cell, the McNamaras' father had been killed by the Butcher of Baxter Pass.

"My name is Clarke," the driver and barker said, but Jess was only half-listening. "Jedediah Clarke. Major Clarke of the 75th Ohio Infantry."

Jess saw no signs of Big Dan, Tom, or Neils McNamara in the crowd, and, just a wee bit more relieved, looked at Major Clarke, saw the proffered hand but ignored it. Not to be rude, but he just thought he might need to keep his gun hand free, probably for the next two days.

The hand lowered, but Clarke never lost his smile. The smile of a trained thespian, Jess figured.

"We shall be checking in now, Mayor," said Major Clarke, who Jess figured had never served in any army regiment and who looked far too young to be a major, especially a major more than twenty years ago during the War Between the States. "General Dalton needs his rest."

*More likely an undertaker,* Jess thought.

"Make way for the Butcher!" the gunman with the Centennial Winchester yelled, and like Moses parting the Red Sea, the crowd cleared a path to the front door of the Trinity River Hotel.

That's when Jess saw the cowhand storm through the door, jerking an old Remington .44 from his waistband, and yell, "Die, you damned Yankee son-of-a—"

# CHAPTER TWELVE

*Monday, 12:21 p.m.*

In Fort Worth, everybody who knew him, and had seen him in action, said Jess Casey was faster than a prairie rattler with a six-shooter, yet even Jess knew he could never beat that cowhand. The .44 was up, cocked, and the man's finger was tightening on the trigger.

If anyone had asked him about it—and, later, some-one would—Jess would not have been able to say exactly why he had done it. He just had. Hadn't even thought about it, because he had not a moment's time to spare to think. He just reacted.

He dived to his left, felt his shoulder crash into the feeble-boned Brigadier General Lincoln E. Dalton, and fell toward the beautiful woman in the blue sateen dress as the bullet buzzed and burned a path across Jess's neck. The general was falling, and Jess was rolling off him, as he pawed for his own gun. Even before he hit the dirt, he heard Dalton mutter a little groan, and Jess recognized the roar of the Winchester from atop the circus wagon. People screamed. Hoofs and boots sounded as men and women and mounts sought safer climes.

His neck burned, but he felt no blood, and he could still move, because the Colt was in his right hand. He didn't even remember drawing it, but as the big rifle roared again from above, Jess had found his knees and was leveling the .44-40 toward the doorway. He saw the cowboy, his white shirt now blossoming red, stagger down the boardwalk. The man's hat had fallen off, and pain masked his tight face, but he still held the long-barreled Remington in his right hand. The finger tugged on the trigger once more, but all the dying waddy managed to do was blow a hole in his own right foot.

Again, above Jess, the .45-75 repeater boomed, and this time the bullet struck the cowboy in the center of his forehead. His head slammed against the bulletin board nailed to the front of the hotel, staining the dinner and supper menus and the stagecoach and train schedules with blood and disgusting bits of bone, hair, and brain matter. That third shot, Jess thought, had been a waste, but so had the second. The first bullet the gunman had fired would have done the job.

The cowhand slid down the wall and slumped over on his side in a pool of his own blood and urine.

"That's one!" the gunman atop the wagon bellowed. "How many more?"

Jess saw at least one. An old man with a silver mustache and beard stubble had palmed a massive Colt—a dragoon by Jess's best guess—and had stepped around a corner, holding the old horse pistol with both hands.

The gunman atop the circus wagon hadn't noticed him but Major Clarke did. Jess saw the Remington derringer in his right hand. Apparently, the man had the gun rigged up his sleeve for handy access.

Jess fired quickly, and the old man dropped to his knees, an instant before the derringer roared. Jess's shot had nicked the old-timer in his left thigh. Major Clarke's bullet would have drilled the man plumb-center if Jess hadn't fired first.

The old man rolled over, gripping his bleeding leg with both hands, but his gun had skidded a good three or four feet down the boardwalk, well out of his reach. Nobody else in the crowd—those who hadn't skedaddled into some building or dropped behind a water trough or rain or garbage barrel—showed any inclination to pick up the big old cap-and-ball pistol.

By that time, Jess had come to his feet, stepping toward the boardwalk, turning toward the wagon, and raising his revolver at the sound of the levering of the Winchester. Jess drew a bead on the gunman.

"He's down," he yelled. "Leave him be, or you join him."

The man stopped the movement of the rifle, and his finger eased off the trigger, but his eyes glared with intense hatred. A man like that didn't care much for a gun barrel trained on his stomach. Few men did.

Jess didn't lower his Colt. Nor did he take his eyes off the gunman.

"That goes for you, too, Major," he told Clarke.

Still looking at the gunman on the wagon's rooftop,

he noticed the major slip the derringer up his sleeve.
The girl, he saw through the corner of his eye, hol-
stered the two Colts and lowered herself beside
Brigadier General Dalton.

Mayor Stout let out a few choice curse words and
ordered Jess to "clean up this mess," then rushed
down the boardwalk toward his office.

Jess lowered the hammer on the Colt but did not
lower the barrel until the gunman butted the Winchester on the roof. He hooked one thumb inside one
of the belts and used his left hand to hold the warm
barrel of the big rifle.

"You're fast," he complimented.

"So are you," Jess said.

"I have to be."

"So do I."

"Name's Bodeen. Lee Bodeen."

"I've heard of you," Jess said. Bodeen was a man-
killer who hired out, mostly up around Paris, Texas,
but he'd range into the Indian Nations and Arkansas.
Jess decided Bodeen was not a regular with the
general's traveling circus, but likely a local gunman
Major Clarke had hired for this Texas tour.

A tour that so far had left one man dead and another with a bullet in his thigh.

Bodeen was waiting.

"Jess Casey," Jess told him.

The man nodded. "I haven't heard of you."

"You have now."

He holstered the gun and knelt beside the woman,
who had helped the old general until he was sitting
now, his eyes flashing this way and that, leaning
against the colorful front rear wheel of the wagon.

She had picked something from the dirt and was wiping it off with a rag.

"Here you go," the beautiful woman said, and held out a set of false teeth for General Dalton. Then she said something that caused Jess to lean back.

"Father."

General Dalton took the teeth, but his hands shook so much the woman had to help him slip the teeth back into his mouth. They clicked and he smiled.

His beard came down to the middle button on his coat and his hair hung down like Wild Bill Hickok's or Buffalo Bill Cody's. If he weighed a hundred pounds in his heavy coat and boots, Jess would have been surprised. The pale face was so tight, like a wet rag wrapped over a skeleton, but his eyes burned with an intense light.

"Thank . . . you . . ." he said in an ancient whisper. "Do I . . . know you, miss?"

The head turned from the woman and locked on Jess.

"Young man," he said, and paused for breath. "You almost . . . broke . . . every bone . . . in my . . . body."

"Thank you," the woman was saying, and Jess realized she was looking at him with those beautiful gray eyes, but the eyes had filled with tears. Perhaps because for a moment, the old man had not known her. "Thank you, Sheriff," she repeated.

"It's my job," Jess said, but nodded his thanks and pulled himself up. By then, Lee Bodeen was on the ground, and he and Major Clarke were helping the old Butcher to his feet. Caroline Dalton stood on her own and moved up the boardwalk, through the open door, making a beeline for the registration desk.

"I assume," Bodeen said as he followed Jess toward the dead cowman, "there will be an inquest."

"Imagine so," Jess said, and looked up and down the street for Mort Thompson, the county solicitor, but that rapscallion was nowhere to be seen. "But it was self-defense. No doubt about that."

"Murder!" someone shouted.

Jess sent a glare into the crowd but heard another hiss that stabbed him in his gut.

"Low-down Yankee-lovin' sheriff."

He ignored that, and moved down the boardwalk, loosening the bandana and kneeling beside the cowboy.

Without speaking, he wrapped the bandana over the bullet wound, tightened it in a hard knot, while Bodeen picked up the .44-caliber dragoon.

"You protected that damn Yankee cur, Sheriff," the old trail hand said.

Jess could have replied that he had actually saved the old cowboy from being blown apart with a .45-75 rifle slug or taking a .41-caliber derringer bullet in the heart.

"I'm sworn to uphold the peace," he said, "and you were breaking it." He hooked his thumb toward the dead man. "So was he."

"Murderin', mad-dog killer like him." The old cowhand, his face weathered and covered with three days' growth of whiskers, spit. "He don't deserve to live. Not after what he done at Baxter Pass."

"That was twenty-five years ago," Jess said.

"Not to me. To me it was yestiday."

Jess sighed. A voice came from behind him, and he pushed himself up as Doctor Amanda Wilson hurried through the crowd, her black satchel at her side. She stopped by the dead man, her face paling at the ugly sight, but she quickly recovered and dropped to her knees, not even caring that the hem of her dress soaked up some of the blood. Her fingers found the man's throat, and then she rose, wiping her bloody fingers on her dress.

Major Clarke had helped General Dalton into the hotel. Amanda came to see the cowboy, and she did not speak or even look at Jess Casey or Lee Bodeen.

"How bad are you hit, sir?" she asked.

"Ask the sheriff. He done it."

"Didn't hit the bone," Jess said. He sighed again. "Send me the bill, Doc. County will take care of it."

It was a job for the town law and should be coming out of the town coffers and not Jess Casey's billfold. He was moving away now, shedding his jacket, and covering the dead man's face and upper torso. And that should have come off Lee Bodeen's person, not Jess's, but he knew a man like Lee Bodeen would not care one whit about protecting innocent eyes from an unholy sight.

Jess glanced through the doorway. The woman, Caroline, was at the desk, signing the register. The general sat on a settee in the lobby, head on his chest, maybe asleep. Ever the protector, Major Clarke stood beside him.

Jess stopped Willie Duncan as he left the hotel's restaurant.

"Fetch old Mr. Stokes, will you, Willie?" he said, and tilted his head to the corpse partly covered with

Jess's own Mackinaw. "Got a customer for him. Tell Mr. Stokes to bill Kurt Koenig." He was done paying for burials on his own dime.

"Will do, Jess," Willie said, and went down the boardwalk at a fast clip.

"Where's a decent livery, Sheriff?" Lee Bodeen asked.

Jess motioned across the street.

"I'll hire some boy to take the horses there, then," he said. "The wagon stays where it is . . . if that's all right with you."

"Is that Gatling gun loaded?" Jess asked.

Bodeen laughed. "No." He pushed back the tails of the greatcoat, revealing the two revolvers holstered and tied down on his hips. Ivory handled. Nickel plated. New model Remingtons. "But these are. No one will bother that Gatling. Or the general."

Two days, Jess thought. What were the chances that nobody else would get killed in two days?

Jess picked up the sack of food and walked back to his office without another word.

# CHAPTER THIRTEEN

*Monday, 1:45 p.m.*

"He's here, ain't he?" Burt McNamara said as he accepted the plate of brisket and beans. "The Butcher of Baxter Pass . . . the man who murdered my pa . . . he's in town, ain't he? I know he's here."

Without answering, Jess Casey left the jail, slamming the door shut and cutting off the prisoner's words: "When my brothers find out—"

In his office, he moved to the coffeepot, and poured a cup. "Want a cup, Hoot?"

At Jess's desk, Hoot Newton spoke only a few snorts and grunts, and he devoured the three plates of food Jess had picked up at the café without a name. The old cowhand sounded like a hog or a hungry dog. Jess stood by the stove, holding the cup in his hand, watching Hoot Newton eat. It was not an appetizing thing to see. Two plates were now empty, and the third would be gone in a moment or two, with nothing but gravy. Nope. That's what the thick slices of toast were for. Already, Hoot was mopping up the remnants, shoving the big chunks of bread into his mouth, chewing with his mouth open.

When Hoot had finished, he wiped the palms of his hands on his thighs, belched, and noticed Jess for the first time.

"You say something, Jess?" he asked.

Jess sipped the coffee. "Nah. Get enough to eat?"

Now, Hoot picked his teeth with his fingernails and shook his head. "Remember how the cookie at the Double 3 used to make that vinegar pie?"

Jess sighed.

"Always loved vinegar pie."

"I'll remember that, Hoot," and the door to the office opened.

Clint Stowe came in, waving the flimsy piece of yellow paper as if it were on fire.

"Professor Vogt?" Jess asked hopefully, which stopped Clint Stowe in his tracks. His brow knotted in puzzlement, and he frowned, and then looked at the telegram, back at Jess, over at Hoot Newton, and again at the telegram, as if he were reading it for the first time.

"Uh . . . no . . . Marshal Casey . . . uh . . ." He held out the paper to Jess, who took it, and frowned.

"Nothing from that college man at AddRan?"

"No, suh. Not yet. Maybe I should go back to the office in case it comes in."

"Maybe," Jess said, and glanced again at the reply from Paul Parkin, Dallas city constable.

NO KNOWLEDGE OF LUKE FLINT STOP
AND YOU CANT FOOL ME STOP TELL
THE BUTCHER I SAID BYE

Well, Jess didn't really think his telegram to Dallas would fool the city constable, but it was worth a try. He wadded up the paper, tossed it in the trash can, and as soon as Clint Stowe was out the door, it opened again. Jess stood, watching the old-timer who had been wounded in the fracas outside the Trinity River Hotel hobble in, using a broomstick as a crutch. His thigh was bandaged, the pants cut off just above the wound, and he still wore those scuffed-up old boots.

Doc Wilson followed him in, closing the door behind her and answering the question before Jess could ask it.

"Mort Thompson said hold him for a grand jury inquest. Public intoxication. Carrying a firearm in the city limits. Unlawful discharge of a weapon. Attempted murder. Resisting arrest." She tossed her black satchel on the desk, followed by the gun belt and revolver the old man had been carrying when he had tried to gun down General Dalton, and pointed at the coffee. "You got more of that?"

The old man had moved toward the gun case but made no move for one of the weapons. By then, Hoot Newton was standing, and the big man undoubtedly put the fear of the law in the wounded man.

"Discharge of a weapon?" Jess said. The old-timer hadn't even gotten off a shot.

First things first, though. Jess filled a cup with what passed for coffee and handed it to the doctor. He then moved to his desk, opened a ledger, grabbed a pencil, and looked at the wounded man. His legs were thin, and pale except for the stains of blood that

Amanda Wilson had not cleaned up. He looked ridiculous in his one-legged pants.

"You got a name?" Jess asked.

"'The Man Who Killed Lincoln Dalton.'"

"Not even close, old man," Jess said. "You want to try again?"

He spit in the cuspidor.

"Then I'll write your name as Lincoln Dalton." He started to scratch something in the ledger underneath Burt McNamara's name.

"Pete Doolin," the man said.

Jess wrote it down, opened a drawer, withdrew an old flour sack, and tossed it to Hoot Newton. "Give any valuables to my jailer," he said. "You'll get them back when you're free to go. Hoot. Search him."

"Huh?"

"Never mind. I'll . . ." Jess was already moving toward the prisoner. He took the suspenders because Kurt Koenig demanded that no prisoner was going to hang himself with a belt or socks or suspenders while he was town marshal, and as sure as there was a God, if Jess let the old man wear those, he'd hang himself. Probably could use his pants—what was left of them—or shirtsleeves, or even his socks, but Jess wasn't going to have a bunch of naked men in his jail while he was in charge of the city.

When it was all said and done, Jess had put a rabbit's foot, three dollars and seventeen cents, a gun belt, old revolver, and a pair of spurs in the sack, which he deposited on the desktop. "Put him in the cleanest cell we got, Hoot." He shot Doc Wilson a quick look.

"Clean wound. I can come by every day to change the bandage."

He nodded and sank into his chair as Hoot guided Pete Doolin into the cells.

Amanda found the chair opposite him, frowning at the empty plates Hoot had piled up over a couple of wanted dodgers.

"Jail's filling up," Jess said.

"No jury in Fort Worth. No jury in *Texas* will indict that old man for anything," Amanda said, "not even the firearms ordinance violation."

"Yep."

She sipped the coffee.

"I would have run him out of town," Jess said. "He didn't even get off a shot."

He shook his head, and then added, upon reflection. "But . . . I guess maybe it's better to have him off the streets . . ." He did not trust Lee Bodeen.

The thought of Bodeen gave him pause. He also thought of Caroline Dalton. He'd go back to the Trinity River Hotel. Lee Bodeen couldn't pack a revolver, nor could that carnival barker Major Jedediah Clarke and his hideaway derringer. For that matter, he should also take away Caroline Dalton's matched set of Navy Colts.

"I can't believe . . . after all this time . . ." Her voice faded away, and she stared at the cup that she now held in her lap.

"He's an old man," Jess said.

"He's still the Butcher of Baxter Pass." She lifted the cup, started to drink, and then slid it on the desk. Her eyes found his. "And that major . . . that man makes my skin crawl . . . he has asked me to . . ." She leaned her head back and let out a laugh, but there was no humor to be found in either her laugh or her eyes.

The door to the jail cells opened, and Hoot Newton came out, closed the door, slid the bolt, then, with a heavy yawn, and moved over to the stove. Amanda Wilson handed him the cup as he passed. "Here," she said.

He stared.

"There are only two cups," she told him, "and I'm finished." She rose, finding her bag, and locked her eyes on Jess Casey's again. "Major Clarke asked me if I would come to the general's room."

"Is he sick?" Jess asked.

"He's an old man, like you said."

Jess considered this, but mostly, he considered Amanda Wilson.

"Don't worry about me, Sheriff Casey," she said. "I am a doctor. I know my duty. I also know my conscience . . . unlike that butcher."

And she was gone, slamming the door as she left, leaving Jess Casey alone with a cup of coffee that suddenly tasted bitter, and Hoot Newton, who belched again and slurped his own cup.

"That gal mad at someone?" Hoot asked.

Jess shrugged. One thing kept puzzling him. Amanda Wilson's story had the prisoners gunned down inside the prison camp at Baxter Pass, Ohio. Burt McNamara had the Texas boys, by then mostly skeletons, walking through the gates before being caught in the maelstrom of lead from Gatling guns. Yet the story he read said the prisoners were on a steamboat about to head down the Ohio River before they were massacred. That's one reason Jess wanted to hear back from that college teacher at AddRan Male & Female College down in Thorp Spring. Hank Joseph had told him that the professor had been imprisoned at Baxter Pass.

Not that it really mattered. No one had ever denied that some two hundred prisoners of war had been gunned down by General Dalton.

He couldn't count on actually hearing back from Mitchell Vogt down at AddRan, though. Fort Worth had no library, although a bunch of women in town kept threatening to start one, even if they had to get in touch with that Yankee Andrew Carnegie to foot the bill. Yankee money was good in Texas . . . sometimes. Of course, no one had gotten up the nerve to ask the philanthropist for money for a library.

Jess rose, moved to the window, and looked outside. The streets were quiet but busy, typical for this time of day on a Monday. Some dirty little urchin stood across the street, waving a newspaper over his head, shouting out to passersby, though Jess couldn't hear the words. Too soon, though, Jess realized with relief for any of the newspapers to be informing their readers about the arrival in town of Brigadier General Lincoln E. Dalton and his Gatling gun.

But the newspapers. . . .

Jess turned, thinking. A journalist might be able to steer him toward the truth of what had happened at Baxter Pass. Fort Worth still boomed and boasted a number of newspapers: *Daily Reporter, Evening Mail, Fort Worth Gazette, Fort Worth German Gazette, Fort Worth Guide,* the *Advertiser, Commercial Reporter, Livestock Journal, Fort Worth Standard.*

"Be back in a little bit, Hoot," said Jess, grabbing his hat and hurrying out the door.

# CHAPTER FOURTEEN

*Monday, 2:30 p.m.*

His first stop, however, was at the Trinity River Hotel. He didn't even have to ask the clerk for the room numbers for the Butcher's coterie. Major Clarke and Lee Bodeen were sitting in the lobby, smoking cigars, and sipping brandy. With the exception of the clerk, no one else was inside. Nobody stood outside, either. No one even gawked at the circus wagon with the Gatling gun affixcd to its top.

The streets of Fort Worth were busy—except here on Main Street. Texans seemed to be avoiding this place like the plague, and usually, immediately after a gunfight, a body could make a small fortune if he could have sold tickets.

Jess glanced at the clerk, and made a beeline toward Clarke and Bodeen. Both men laid their cigars in ashtrays but did not rise. Nor did they extend their hands in a friendly greeting.

"Sheriff," Clarke said.

They had changed their trail duds into gray Prince

Alberts, pinstriped pants, blue silk shirts, and ties—
a red polka-dot cravat for the major and a black ribbon
tie for the gunman. Bodeen also wore a vest, double-
breasted, of dark gray worsted wool. A brown bowler
rested on Clarke's knee. Lee Bodeen had not bothered
removing his black hat, the one piece of wardrobe
he had not changed, though he must have brushed
the dust off the brim and crown up in his room. The
Centennial Winchester was nowhere in sight, though
the two revolvers on his hips remained in plain view.

"I should have thought of this earlier," Jess said.
"But we have an ordinance in our city that prohibits
the carrying of firearms. I'll take yours now." He
held out his left hand toward the major. "Yours, too,"
he told Bodeen.

Jess kept his right hand on the butt of his .44-40.

Actually, the city ordinance allowed men to check
their weapons at saloons or hotels, or merely leave
them at their hotels, homes, or boardinghouses, but
Jess didn't trust these two galoots.

Wordlessly, Clarke and Bodeen looked at one
another before Clarke, a sudden smart-aleck grin
beaming across his face, set down his snifter and
reached inside his coat. Jess waited, keeping his eyes
on both men, ready for anything, though he doubted
if either would make a play. Major Clarke withdrew
an envelope and held it out for Casey.

Jess just stared, not moving his right hand off the
butt of the Colt.

Shaking his head in amusement, Major Clarke
opened the envelope and held out a letter. Jess
moved closer and took the letter, while Clarke picked

up his snifter and swirled the dark liquor around the rim of his glass.

Immediately, Jess recognized the seal of the governor of the state of Texas. Frowning, he read:

> *To Whom It May Concern:*
> *The Bearer of this letter is Jedediah*
> *Clarke, late of the 75th Ohio Infantry*
> *and a friend of Texas and this office.*
> *He is to be given any consideration,*
> *including the possession of concealed*
> *weapons, tolls for ferries and pikes, and*
> *minor offenses that might arise in defense*
> *of his person, or to protect his cargo and*
> *employer, Brigadier General Lincoln Everett*
> *Dalton, U.S. Army.*
>
> > *Sincerely,*
> > *Lawrence Sullivan Ross*
> > *Governor*

Sul Ross himself. Jess could scarcely believe what he had just read, but the seal was official. Sul Ross had grown up in Texas during the republic years—his folks, Jess recalled, had even founded the town of Waco down on the Brazos River. He had fought Indians . . . and Yankees. In fact, Sul Ross had joined the Confederate army almost as soon as Texas had voted to secede. He had fought at Corinth and Thompson's Station and countless scrapes in Mississippi. In fact, the story Jess had heard countless times at campfires was how when the Yanks had captured Sul Ross at Brown's Mill in Georgia in the summer of '64, his men had immediately launched a counterattack—simply to free their general. He had been one of the youngest generals to wear the gray.

In 1886, Ross had won the election for governor in a landslide, but now Jess remembered a few details about that election. Although he was a Texas Democrat, folks said Sul Ross pandered to Green-backers, but mostly to Republicans. Apparently, holding this letter and seeing Lincoln Dalton's name in Ross's flowery script, there had been some truth to those charges. Jess decided he wouldn't vote for Sul Ross ever again, unless he ran against Mort Thompson for Tarrant County solicitor.

He handed the letter back to Clarke, who took it with that impish grin and began to fold it and return it to the envelope.

"I suppose you have one of those letters, too," Jess said, staring at Lee Bodeen.

The gunman did not smile, nor did he lower his brandy snifter. Casually, he brought his free hand to his Prince Albert and slowly pulled the frock coat away just long enough for Jess Casey to see the badge pinned to the lapel of his fancy vest.

"Reckon I can do better'n a letter, Sheriff," Lee Bodeen said.

The badge was small but unmistakable: a circled star cut out of Mexico's version of a silver dollar, a five-peso coin. Folks in Texas called it the *cinco pesos* star.

It was the badge of a Texas Ranger.

"That good enough for you, Sheriff?" Now, Lee Bodeen grinned.

Jess said nothing. There was nothing to say, but now he remembered something else about Governor Sul Ross. Shortly before the War Between the States had broken out, Sul Ross had joined the Texas Rangers down Waco way. The captain had made Ross a lieutenant, and later Ross had been appointed by Governor Sam Houston to form his own Ranger battalion, so Ross had gone chasing Kickapoos and Comanches. In 1860, Ross's boys had surprised a Comanche village on the Pease River, killed the war chief, and rescued a white woman captive. The woman was Cynthia Ann Parker, who had been taken by Comanches during a raid at Parker's Court back in 1836. As a young woman, Cynthia Ann Parker had become the wife of the chief killed by Ross's Rangers. She had given birth to at least one son, and that son had grown up to become Quanah, the greatest Comanche chief of them all. Now Quanah went by his full name, Quanah Parker, and was courted by governors, presidents, but mostly by Texas ranchers for that rich grazing land up north of the Red River on the Comanche reservation.

Sul Ross, Jess figured, had given Lee Bodeen a badge.

No. Jess would definitely not vote for Sul Ross for anything, even if he ran against Mort Thompson.

His eyes moved to the staircase and the balcony, and suddenly he forgot all about his troubles and Lee Bodeen and his dislike for the current governor of the state of Texas. His right hand left the handle of the Colt in the holster, and he swept off his battered cowboy hat. Bodeen and Clarke might have looked stupid, or questioned one another, or merely turned, saw, and stood. Jess couldn't have said one way or the other.

Caroline Dalton stood by the balustrade, her dark hair shining, her face angelic. She was staring right at him, right through him, and now she moved, one hand gripping the railing as she moved to the stairs and descended like an angel coming down from the heavens.

She had changed her outfit, too, now wearing a kilt-pleated skirt of black velvet with a cutaway basque of red velvet, the collar and cuffs trimmed in black, and mother-of-pearl buttons on the tightly fitting front. Her hat was of black lace with a Chantilly net, pearl beads on one side, and a shirred rim.

He sucked in a deep breath and did not move.

Caroline Dalton did not wear her brace of .36-caliber revolvers, but even if she had, Jess wouldn't have asked to see her Rangers badge or a letter from Governor Ross. *Hell,* he thought, *she probably has letters of introduction from President Benjamin Harrison, Queen Victoria, and Porfirio Díaz.* If she asked, Jess Casey would have given her a letter or badge himself.

She crossed the floor and came directly to Jess Casey, extending her slender, ungloved hand. He started to take it in a handshake, then remembered himself and brought it up slowly to his lips, which tingled as he kissed her hand.

"Ma'am." Then he remembered his hat, and swept it off his head, wondering if his hair resembled a rat's nest.

"I wanted to thank you again for all your help earlier today," she said. "And I apologize for any unfortunate problems that have arisen from our arrival."

*Such as one dead man and one man in jail with a bullet hole in his thigh. And another prisoner in jail who'd love the chance to put a bullet in General Dalton's brain.*

He thought that. He said: "It's my job, Miss Dalton."

She looked for the longest while. He stared into those beautiful, big, haunting gray eyes, until he realized what he was doing, and he made himself look up to the second floor and gestured lamely with the hat in his hand.

"I hope your father is well."

She looked down. "The doctor is with him now."

"Alone?"

He hadn't meant to blurt it out, and he half-expected to hear the muffled report of a pistol from that second story as Amanda Wilson avenged the death of her cousin.

"Lee." Jess turned toward the major and the gunman, saw Lee Bodeen rising at Major Clarke's order. Bodeen hitched his two gun belts and started for the staircase, but Caroline Dalton stopped him.

"It's all right, Bodeen," she said, and faced Jess again.

"She's a doctor."

"She's also a Texan, ma'am," Major Clarke said.

Neither of them knew the half of it. Had they known that Amanda Wilson's cousin had been killed during the massacre at the Ohio prison camp all those years ago, this troupe probably would have kept right on west to Weatherford or Belknap . . . maybe San Angelo or even El Paso.

"So is my father," Caroline Dalton said.

Jess dropped his hat. His old joints cracked as he bent to lift it off the floor, and he could see the surprise in the faces of Bodeen and Clarke. Even the desk clerk, who had been eavesdropping as he always did, knocked over the inkwell.

"He's a . . . Texan?" Major Jedediah Clarke sank deep into his sofa and quickly polished off the snifter of brandy.

"Well, he was born in Memphis," she said. "But came to Texas during the Revolution. Fought at San Jacinto under Houston. Fought at the Battle of the Knobs, and that's why he moved to what's now Decatur before there was a Decatur or a Wise County."

Jess had cowboyed up in Wise County for a season or two, so he had heard about the Battle of the Knobs. He had even found some old arrowheads near the site. It had happened in November of '37, when eighteen soldiers of the Republic of Texas, under the command of some lieutenant whose name Jess could never remember, had engaged one hundred and fifty hostile Indians. Outnumbered, those old Texans refused to retreat and held their ground, killing fifty of the hostiles and driving off the rest. Only eight of the soldiers survived.

"He was one of the first men to settle in that county," Caroline said.

Which sounded right, too. The old rancher at the Rafter J said he had come to what had been Wise County back in the spring of '38.

Another bit of history rang true, too. Wise County bordered parts of Tarrant County and butted against Jack County to the west. Jack County had voted against secession. So had Wise County, as did most of the counties just north of there that bordered the Red River. Like Cooke County, where Hank Joseph had said he hailed from and had had to flee when things became unpleasant for anyone who was thought to favor the Union during the War Between the States.

"Your father left during the war," Jess said. "Wise County had a lot of pro-Union men."

Caroline Dalton stared at him, partially amazed. Sometimes Jess surprised himself. He did have a brain and could reason a few things out—unlike a lot of cowhands he had worked with.

"That's right," she said. "When the war broke out, he said he could never fire against the Stars and Stripes."

"He wasn't alone," Jess said. "Sam Houston felt the same way."

"Which is why they kicked him out as governor," she said.

Jess nodded.

"So Father returned to Memphis and then to Cincinnati. That's where his brothers lived."

"And joined the Union army," Jess said.

She nodded. "But he never stopped loving Texas."

That, Jess might have to question. If he loved Texas, why had he murdered two hundred Texas soldiers after the war had ended?

"So," Jess said, "why return now?"

# CHAPTER FIFTEEN

*Monday, 3:05 p.m.*

"Because," Caroline Dalton said, "Father came home to die."

Jess Casey didn't have time to react to that, because Mayor Harry Stout ran into the lobby of the hotel, sweating despite the coolness of the afternoon, laboring for breath, but just managing to choke out Jess's name.

Jess turned, half-expecting the mayor to drop dead from an apoplexy, but, alas, Jess had no luck that Monday. The mayor bent forward, hands on his knees, until he could finally straighten and manage to say between gasps:

"Gary . . . Custer . . . he's . . . dead."

Gary Custer—no relation to the boy general who, as a Yankee killed by Indians years ago, wasn't popular in Fort Worth, either—had managed the Fort Worth Opera House on Calhoun Street for the past seven years. He had brought the Jersey Lily,

Miss Lily Langtry herself, to the cow town to wow the theater patrons with her dazzling performance as Kate Hardcastle in *She Stoops to Conquer*, the play she had made her own in London. *The Wild Duck* . . . *Dr. Jekyll and Mr. Hyde* . . . *The Pillars of Society* . . . *An Enemy of the People* . . . *Les Érinnyes* . . . *Cinq-Mars* . . . *The Battered Bride* . . . *The Pirates of Penzance* . . . and just about everything Shakespeare had penned had been performed in that brick building. Jess knew that because of the placards that hung in the windows and on the walls of the opera house and from what he had read in the newspapers. He had only seen three or four plays himself, on a dare or a whim, but didn't remember too much about *Hamlet* or *As You Like It*. A lot of John Barleycorn had led to those dares and whims.

Still, Jess knew that countless thespians, locals, traveling troupes, and famed actors had treaded those boards. And now, if Harry Stout knew what he was talking about—and by the way he looked, Jess Casey figured he wasn't exaggerating—Gary Custer was dead.

"Mur-derrrrreed," Stout said, before staggering to a chair and collapsing onto it.

It felt a little creepy, inside a dark theater in Hell's Half Acre, alone except for Mayor Harry Stout, who had recovered thanks to some brandy poured by the desk clerk at the Trinity River Hotel, Major Clarke, and Lee Bodeen. Bodeen came as a duly appointed

Texas Ranger. Jedediah Clarke said he had a significant investment and a letter from Governor Sul Ross.

Stout pointed, and Jess led the way down the aisle and onto the stage, followed by three quiet men. Their boots echoed eerily as they crossed the theater stage and slipped between the curtains.

"To be or not to be," Lee Bodeen said, and laughed at himself.

"Shut up," Major Clarke said, expressing Jess Casey's sentiments to a T.

Only Caroline Dalton had not come. After hearing what Mayor Stout said had happened, she had gone back upstairs to her father's room, but she had insisted that Clarke and Bodeen come along with Jess.

"This could be a trap," Bodeen had warned her. "To get us away from your father."

"I can protect my father," she had said, and her tone let everyone know she would not tolerate any further argument. Jess figured Caroline Dalton would be more than a match for anyone who went upstairs with murder on their mind.

"His office . . ." Stout's voice echoed in the cavernous theatre. "It's . . . back . . . there."

They moved, past chairs, an old makeup case, sandbags, and other things Jess didn't recognize, until they were heading down some steps and into a dark hallway; so dark, in fact, that Jess had to stop to light a candle. They walked past dressing rooms until they reached the end of the hallway and saw a door cracked open, a light shining from inside.

"That's his . . . office . . ." Stout said. "Where . . . I . . ."

Jess pushed the door open and saw the Congress gaiters, the plaid britches, and the pool of drying blood.

Gary Custer lay on his side, eyes and mouth open, skewered with a . . .

"Sword," Jess said aloud.

"Rapier," Major Clarke corrected.

Jess looked at the cramped office, the overturned chair, the gas lamp burning above the desk, and papers strewn about the top and floor. If he were a detective, Jess would have reasoned that the killer opened the door, having found a sword . . . um, rapier . . . in the room they had passed that had a PROPS sign painted on the door, and Gary Custer, who had been working, had risen quickly, sending papers and the chair every which way, and then felt the sword . . . rapier!—pierce him right beneath the sternum.

No footprints in the blood. If the killer had stayed after his crime, he had been careful. Only a small chain of some kind in the blood between the elbow of the dead man's left arm and his torso.

Behind him came the mayor's moan, and Jess looked at Stout, usually a bellicose, arrogant, back-stabbing fiend and liar but now a pale, sweating, haggard-looking politician. He leaned against the doorjamb, mopping his brow with an already soaking-wet calico rag.

"What were you doing here, Mayor?" Jess asked.

Harry Stout wet his lips and returned the wet rag into his coat pocket. "I came to talk to Custer about . . . them." He gestured to Clarke and Bodeen. "The performance."

Which sounded reasonable. And Jess didn't think Stout had the gumption to run a man through with a little rapier. He turned his attention to Jedediah Clarke.

"Did the general arrange this little engagement?" Jess asked. "Or did Custer contact you?"

"It was General Dalton's idea," Clarke answered readily enough. "His last lecture and performance. Decatur, where he desires to rest till Judgment Day, has no opera house worth speaking of."

"Why would anyone want to kill Custer?" Stout said. "With . . . that?"

Oh, Jess had a pretty good idea. Anybody on the street when that circus freak show came parading down Main Street could have heard that Gary Custer was responsible for bringing the Butcher of Baxter Pass to Fort Worth. Somebody apparently had decided they didn't want to hear General Dalton's lecture.

That was a motive, Jess reasoned. And why use the sword . . . rapier? Well, that was a whole lot quieter than a revolver.

"His watch is missing . . . Sheriff."

Jess looked at the smiling Bodeen, and then down at the corpse. Again, Jess studied the broken chain, gold plated, lying in the tacky blood, which he had seen earlier. Only now, he examined the chain and the dead man a little more carefully. He could tell from the dead man's vest that the watch had been snatched from it, likely after he had fallen. His coat pocket, Jesse now observed, was inside out. He knelt, reaching inside, then patting the dead man's body. No wallet. No watch.

"Robbery?" Major Clarke suggested.

Jess pursed his lips, then sighed. "Or someone wanting us to think it was robbery." He looked back at Harry Stout. "Do you know what kind of watch Custer carried?"

"Just a watch," he said. "Gold . . . I think. But . . ." He shrugged.

Frowning, Jess looked at the body again. He fingered the blood, sticky, not even what he would call warm. Jess could only fathom a guess, but he figured that Gary Custer had been dead for an hour or so. Death had not been instantaneous, but he probably had bled out pretty quickly.

"But he had a diamond stickpin," Stout said.

Jess looked. There was no stickpin in the dead man's loose cravat.

"Is there a safe here?" Jess asked. "Money box? Anything like that?"

"I wouldn't know," Stout said.

Jess let out a long breath and pushed himself to his feet. He might as well leave, fetch the undertaker, and find out if Custer had any next of kin that should be notified.

"I guess this cancels your show, gents," he told Clarke and Bodeen.

"Oh, no," said Clarke, who had likely been waiting for someone to challenge that. "We rented the facility. Paid in advance. I can show you the contract."

He grinned like a man holding a full house. "And that letter from my dear old friend, Sul Ross."

Jess let it go because the mayor was pointing at the dead man.

"But . . ." Stout said. "I remember the watch fob."

He waited, listening as Stout told about the hand-carved bone fob. The killer must have taken it, too, along with the watch, leaving the chain, since it had fallen into the pooling blood. The piece of bone had been carved into a Federal eagle icon, the head of the bald eagle, and the stars—Stout couldn't remember how many—and the red and white vertical stripes. Or course, on the bone, the stripes were just white, like everything else.

"He said he carved it at Salisbury," Stout said. "Prisoners could exchange carvings like that for food, privileges, money . . . bribe the guards . . . or keep for themselves. Custer had carved that one, but then the war ended, and he was free to go. Or something like that."

"Salisbury?" Jess asked.

"Prison camp for Yanks," Bodeen answered. "In one of the Carolinas, if I recollect right. Maybe Georgia."

"He fought for the Union?" Jess asked.

Clarke snorted. "With the 22nd Iowa. Why else would he let General Dalton rent his opera house?"

"Best send word to the undertaker," Bodeen said. "We'd like to get this place cleaned up before tomorrow night."

Jess let the comment slide. Bodeen had said it merely to rankle him some more, and Jess wasn't playing any games with this man-killer. Since the Butcher had arrived in Fort Worth, two men were dead and another wounded. He stepped out into the hallway, heard the blast of a small-caliber pistol, saw the muzzle flash and the silhouetted figure move down the darkened hallway, and felt the bullet tear a seam through the left side of the crown of his hat.

Over the ringing in his ears, Jess heard some strange shout down the hallway.

Next he heard Stout yelping like a struck puppy, and then heard, but did not see, as the mayor lost his balance and fell into the small office, landing in the blood and on the dead man who felt no pain. Jess had dropped to his knees, palmed his gun, bringing it up and cutting loose—though he had no memory of anything. He blinked away, trying to see something other than the orange, blue, and gold flashes pounding his eyeballs. Bodeen came to the open doorway, and one of his pistols roared three times.

Jess knew better than to look at the gunman, knowing those muzzle blasts would just hurt his eyes more. Besides, now he could see, but he saw just an empty corridor.

"The coward ran!" Bodeen said.

Jess knew that because he was already running after him.

Up the stairs and through the door, into the darkened stage of the theater. He swung his revolver barrel this way, then that, looked at the curtain, and heard a bottle crashing to his right, a curse, footsteps, and . . . the jingling of spurs. Jesse ran toward the sound. Stage left. Or so he thought.

He almost tripped over a rope, or wire, or something, then heard a door opening, closing, catching that brief glimpse of light. He leaped down the steps, not even touching one, landing on the floor, hearing his knees pop as he bent and came up. His left hand found the knob, and he jerked the door open, waited, then dived into the alleyway, looking toward the street. Nothing. He rolled over, bringing the Colt up, and saw a hat disappear behind a wall of wooden pickets. He fired . . . once . . . twice . . . three times, seeing the wood splinter, but hearing no screams or grunts from behind the wall.

Back to his feet, cocking the .44-40 as he ran, but now carefully removing his finger out of the trigger guard. He wasn't about to shoot his own foot off. He leaped onto a trash bin, came up, and looked over the wall, gun at the ready. The alley ended ten feet away. He saw nothing, not even a passerby on the opposite boardwalk, but he climbed onto the top of the picket wall, dropped down, and moved to the intersection.

He looked down the street one way, then the other. Nothing. Holstering his Colt, he moved back toward Main Street, stopping the first three people he saw, asking if they had seen anyone, but knowing the answer he would get even before they shook their heads.

With a curse, Jess Casey walked back to the opera house.

# CHAPTER SIXTEEN

*Monday, 4:30 p.m.*

Here's what Jess Casey knew about the latest killing in Fort Worth:

Nobody had seen Gary Custer that day. The janitor had been sweeping up from the previous night, but Custer had not been around. In fact, the janitor said he thought his boss had said something about taking the train to Dallas to play some poker, and that had been Friday afternoon. Stout did say that Custer enjoyed a game of paste cards and frequented the mayor's own saloon to try his hand at poker, sometimes Spanish monte, but usually faro. He loved to buck the tiger.

At the depot, no one remembered seeing Gary Custer that weekend, but Fort Worth's train station was one busy place, and, hell, who even knew what the owner, operator, and general manager of the Fort Worth Opera House even looked like? He wasn't Lily Langtry or Edwin Booth.

Stout said the front door to the theater had been

open. That's how he had entered. The back door, the one the person had entered who had come within a few inches of blowing Jess Casey's head off, had been busted open from the outside. Jess figured the gent with the small-caliber pistol had come in that way.

Which led to Major Jedediah Clarke's theory that that was the killer, who had returned to the scene of the crime to make sure that Gary Custer, indeed, was dead.

Jess dismissed that idea. Criminals did not return to the scene of their crimes except in sordid melodramas that often played at the Fort Worth Opera House, which was another reason the late Gary Custer probably tried his luck with the paste cards. Unless Lily Langtry or some fancy Shakespearian troupe was performing in the Panther City, the theater business didn't quite rank up there with the White Elephant Saloon, the myriad cribs, the railroad, or the stockyards in drumming up a good, steady, profitable business. The killer had taken time to take a hand-carved bone fob, a golden pocket watch, a diamond stickpin, and a wallet that likely held some cash. Jess figured Gary Custer was dead by the time the killer had finished his robbery.

"Did you see what the man who shot at you looked like?" Lee Bodeen had asked.

Jess had shaken his head. "Too dark. But . . ." He squinted, wondering if he had imagined that shout. "Didn't he yell something after he pulled the trigger?"

"Indeed," Major Clarke had answered. *"'Sic semper tyrannis!'"*

Jess had pursed his lips. "I've heard that before . . . I think," he had said.

"John Wilkes Booth," Lee Bodeen had answered. "It's what he yelled when he jumped off the balcony at Ford's Theater in Washington City. After he'd put a bullet in Mr. Lincoln's head."

"Followed by 'The South is avenged,'" Major Clarke had said, "which that fellow might have shouted, too, but by then your and Bodeen's guns were booming in that hallway."

"That's Latin, right?" Jess had asked. "That *sic* something?"

*"Sic semper tyrannis?"* Clarke had nodded. "Yeah. It means 'Ever thus to tyrants.'" He had grinned, mentioning something about the irony, a murder in Fort Worth, an assassination in the nation's capital. Both in theaters. Both with similar motives, perhaps, separated only by thirteen or fourteen hundred miles and pushing twenty-five years.

Jess didn't think much about irony, but that had led Jess to come up with a theory, and a pretty decent one to his way of thinking. Two men with murder on their minds had entered the Fort Worth Opera House that day. One had succeeded, killing and robbing Gary Custer. The other had failed, but it had been his intent to assassinate the man who had brought the Butcher of Baxter Pass to Fort Worth. He had seen Jess step out of the office into the darkened hallway and assumed that was Gary Custer. He had fired. Luckily, he had missed.

By the time they had returned to the Trinity River Hotel, Caroline Dalton was upstairs with her father, the lobby and saloon were filled with people, and the eavesdropping desk clerk had said that Doctor Wilson had left an hour or more earlier, shortly after Mayor Stout had ran into the lobby with his cries of murder.

Clarke and Bodeen invited Jess into the adjoining saloon for a beer or shot of whiskey, but Jess made that lame excuse that he was on duty and needed to get back to his office. Which is where he was headed when he passed the newspaper office, saw a couple of men with their sleeves rolled up and working on some printing press, and went inside.

A bell chimed over the door and both men turned.

*"Kann ich dir helfen?"* the bigger of the two men asked. He wore green-striped britches, sable tip boots, and a yellow-striped cotton shirt, the paper collar removed, the sleeves held up by gold garters and sleeve stockings pulled up over his forearms. The stockings were black. So were his fingertips, and Jess couldn't tell where the ink ended and the cotton began.

Jess looked at him blankly. The man repeated the question and then removed his glasses, which he handed to his smaller assistant.

"May I help you?" he said, speaking English, although his accent remained thick.

"Ummmm." Jess felt like an idiot. He had stepped inside the office of the *Fort Worth German Gazette*. German. Of course. For Germans living in the cow town, many of whom had proven quite handy at the stockyards. German. The paper was printed in German.

"Ya are da *Wachtmeister, ja*? The . . ." He shrugged, and gestured at Jess's gold badge.

"Sheriff," Jess guessed. "Lawman. Yeah."

"Vat do ya vant?"

The big man went through the swinging gate, leaving the thinner man with his eyeglasses and the printing press. He wiped his hands on a towel and bowed slightly. "I am Aldabert Armbrüster, editor."

"Jess Casey, Tarrant County sheriff." They shook. The German's grip almost crushed every bone in Jess's hand. "Listen," Jess said, "I don't know if you can help me or not, but . . ."

So he explained about the various stories he had heard about the murder of those Texas prisoners at Baxter Pass, Ohio, about the arrival of General Dalton in town.

"Ya need not tell us dat," Armbrüster said with a laugh that led the other German printer to laugh, as well. "Ve are da press. Ve know ever-thing."

"Right," Jess said, and went on talking.

Turned out that Armbrüster and his assistant, a tramp printer, Markus Gloeckne, had been working on their story for Wednesday's edition—the paper was a weekly—about the arrival of the Butcher, so they had already been digging in their files about General Dalton's history. Armbrüster was a native of Burnet County, down in Texas's hill country west of Austin, which also had been predominantly Unionists during the vote for secession.

They had pulled big folders filled with newspapers, not only papers from Texas but across the country. As a tramp printer, Markus Gloeckne had made his rounds, working at papers from New York and Oregon to California and Louisiana. They had found stories about Dalton's lectures, a few profiles of his life. . . .

"What I'm curious about," Jess said, "is what actually happened at Baxter Pass."

Which stopped the two Germans.

Gloeckne blurted out something in German, and he and the editor carried on a conversation for about three minutes. Finally the editor said, returning the spectacles to his face. "Ven vas dat?" he asked.

"May," Jess said. "Of '65. I can't give you the exact date. But I remember a story in the *Dallas Mercury*."

Which caused the two Germans, now loyal Fort Worth promoters, to curse Dallas, Dallas newspapers, and anyone who was foolish enough to live in that wretched city.

Gloeckne pulled out a few more binders of papers, paused, and asked something in German.

Armbrüster looked at Jess. "Do ya remember dat . . ." He held up his hand, snapping his fingers, trying to find the word. "Name of da ship?"

Snapping one's fingers must be like yawning. See one person do it, you do it yourself. Jess's fingers snapped. "Filly . . . no Belknap . . . no . . . no . . . no . . . Fancy. Fancy something!"

*"Phantasie,"* Armbrüster told the printer.

"The *Fancy Beltre*! No, *Fancy Belpre*. That's it. The *Fancy Belpre*." Jess said at last, wondering how in the blazes he had managed to pull that name from his memory after all those years.

Which stopped Aldabert Armbrüster, who removed his glasses, began muttering something in German, and moved to his desk, opening a drawer, closing it, then moving to a cabinet on the wall.

Jess glanced at Gloeckne, who shrugged. Both

men watched the editor as he pulled out one big binder, cursed, said something that sounded like, *"Nicht, nicht, nicht."*

Slamming the cover to that binder, he went back to the cabinet, tossed one aside, found another, looked at it, cursed, found another, and finally brought out one, laid it on his desk, overturning a pencil holder, and knocking a book of some kind onto the floor. Armbrüster did not care. He was so focused, so absorbed with this task that he turned page after page, until at last, he stood erect and bellowed: *"Ich habe festgestellt! Kommen Sie schnell."*

The printer was hurrying across the floor, so Jess followed.

"Dere!" The editor pointed a thick finger at the left side of the page. "Read. Please. Read."

Jess squinted. He couldn't read German, but he moved over to the desk, and his eyes widened. He saw the title of the newspaper: *Kokomo Commercial*.

In smaller type: *"All the News of Indiana and the World."*

He saw Armbrüster's finger on a small article in the lower right-hand corner, just above an advertisement about Kokomo Liver Pills.

### Steamboat Tragedy

Jess sucked in a breath and looked back at the top of the paper. He found the date: June 2, 1865.

That would have been just about right. Leaning forward, welcoming the moment when the German editor moved his massive finger off the small type, Jess read:

> BAXTER PASS, OHIO (MAY 31)—The storied old stern-wheeler *Fancy Belpre*, with able master Penrod Ebersbacher at the helm, burned and sank shortly after departing for New Orleans here tonight.
>
> The veteran packet, a trusty transporter of cargo and passengers for a number of years, had just backed out from the landing near Cincinnati when the boiler exploded. Among the passengers were several recently paroled Rebels from the prison camp near town.
>
> Eyewitnesses report that the ship went up like a tinderbox and was blown in half. She sank quickly. Only a handful of passengers and crew appear to have survived.
>
> Among the dead, we sadly report, was Captain Ebersbacher himself, who had been steering down the Ohio River since the waters first opened to steamboat travel.
>
> We are reminded of the *Sultana* disaster.

And that was all there was to it.

# CHAPTER SEVENTEEN

*Monday, 5:20 p.m.*

Jess sat at another table in the *Gazette* office, one clear of binders filled with old newspapers but with a few copies of last week's edition, and, more important, a bottle the printer had fetched from his lunch pail. Sipping the strongest coffee he had ever tasted, chatting with Aldabert Armbrüster, editor of the *Fort Worth German Gazette*, and even managing to converse with Markus Gloeckne, tramp printer from Niagara Falls, New York—as long as Armbrüster translated—Jess tried to figure out what the Indiana newspaper story meant.

"There's no mention of General Dalton," Jess said, stating the obvious.

With a shrug, Armbrüster said, "Conspiracy?"

Jess cocked his head. The editor grinned. "Dat be vat ya Rebels vud think."

He didn't believe that, of course, but he figured more than half of the population in Fort Worth would likely agree. The *Kokomo Commercial* was a Yankee newspaper, so the editor would automatically cut out any facts that might be damaging to the Union cause—even if the war had ended.

The printer started speaking in that harsh language, and Jess freshened up his coffee with a splash of the whiskey. He wasn't sure what it was—the label was in German—but it was brown and malty. Not Scotch. Maybe something like bourbon. The coffee cut out most of the taste. Jess glanced outside the window. It was getting dark, and when the sun set, that's when Hell's Half Acre truly came to life. He told himself: No more whiskey.

With the Butcher of Baxter Pass in town, this could be a long, long night.

Aldabert Armbrüster turned from his printer and began to explain to Jess about their conversation. "Markus vork at *Commercial* dat time."

And Markus Gloeckne, tramp printer with hundreds of newspapers and thousands of miles behind him, had an iron-trap memory.

A Kokomo salesman, advertiser in the newspaper, and stringer had been bound for Cincinnati and had stopped to make a few sales calls in Baxter Pass. He had witnessed the *Fancy Belpre* disaster, talked to a few locals, hurried to the telegraph office, and sent a wire straight to Kokomo. That's how the *Commercial* was the first newspaper in Indiana to get the story.

Not that many people living in the middle of the state would have cared about something that had happened on the Ohio River, but . . . it was news.

"What was the reference to the *Sultana*?" Jess asked.

Armbrüster removed his eyeglasses, amazed at

the Tarrant County sheriff's ignorance. "Ya never heard of da *Sultana*?"

Jess could only shrug. "I was only a kid back in '65. I didn't read newspapers often back then."

"No vunder," the editor said, smiling. "Booth . . . da assassin . . . he vas killed vun day before. End of da var, da murder of our president, Booth's death . . . many people have forgotten da *Sultana*."

She was a side-wheeler on the Mississippi River, usually hauling cotton from St. Louis to New Orleans but often carrying federal troops since New Orleans had fallen into Union hands early in the war. She was steaming south toward New Orleans when word reached the captain of Lincoln's assassination, so the captain bought every newspaper he could find and continued his journey, bringing news to all the stops he made. She made it to New Orleans, then steamed north, stopping at Vicksburg for its biggest load.

Fourteen hundred Union soldiers, recently freed from prisoner-of-war camps, were to be loaded onto the *Sultana*. That was the deal the ship's captain had made with a Union officer in charge of getting those soldiers home. Many of those men were half-dead already, having spent an eternity in the hellholes of the prison camps at Cahaba, Alabama, and Andersonville, Georgia.

Fourteen hundred. To be loaded on a steamboat that could carry, safely, fewer than four hundred. But that was the deal, and both the Yankee in charge of the prisoners and the captain of the *Sultana* figured they could get rich. The federal government promised to pay the *Sultana*'s captain five dollars for each enlisted man and ten dollars for each officer carried home. Naturally, the *Sultana* captain would give a little bit of that cash back to the Union officer in charge of the paroled prisoners.

Only instead of fourteen hundred, more than twenty-one hundred boys in blue had been loaded onto the ship. A deckhand could hardly make his way from bow to stern without stepping on one of those poor boys. Decks sagged so much that supports had to be constructed. The entire ship stank of human waste and rot.

But the *Sultana* steamed north, on a river flooding from recent rains. On the night of April 26, she reached Memphis, Tennessee, unloaded a load of sugar, added some coal, and pulled out around midnight. Two hours later, seven miles north of Memphis, three of her four boilers exploded. Fire raced across the deck. Men leaped into the water, but most of them were too weak to stay afloat long.

The *Sultana* burned and sank.

A southbound steamboat came upon the scene, and the crew began pulling what they could onto her decks. Hours later, men floated past Memphis, calling out for help. Union warships and others quickly steamed out to save what they could, but few—very few—managed to live through the night. By most accounts, eighteen hundred people died that night in the Mississippi River.

For a long while, Jess stared at the cup of coffee in his hand, but he did not feel like drinking. What a waste. Finally, he looked at the *Gazette* editor.

"The *Sultana*'s captain?"

"Ach. He died, too."

"And the Yank in charge of getting those boys home?"

Armbrüster shook his head. "He resigned. Da army could do nothing. No vun vas ever charged."

Shaking his head, Jess put the coffee cup on the table.

"Dere is vun more thing ya should know," Armbrüster said.

He waited.

"Last year, a man in St. Louis . . . on his deathbed . . . he said he sank da *Sultana* with a coal torpedo. He vus a Rebel spy, a . . . how do ya say . . . saboteur?"

"Why would he have done that?" Jess asked.

"Vhy vould Booth kill Lincoln?"

"Do you believe him?"

The editor shrugged. The printer said something. Armbrüster smiled a grim smile and nodded at Gloeckne, before turning back to Jess Casey.

"Markus," Armbrüster said, "he say da var never ends."

Jess could only agree as he rose, shook both men's hands, and walked out of the newspaper office.

oblivion by 1880. Instead, she had blossomed and boomed. These days, more than twenty thousand people lived here—and more were coming every day.

And Jess was alone this night, unless he counted Hoot Newton. One man . . . and the most hated man in the South was spending the night in the Trinity River Hotel.

First, he stopped at Dean's meat wagon and bought a sausage, and then he went inside a bakery for a dozen day-old doughnuts, a fresh loaf of bread, and a cherry pie to bring to Hoot and the prisoners for supper. He made sure to get a receipt from the street vendor and the clerk at the bakery, because he was fed up feeding prisoners on his own dime— especially seeing how he would have kicked both men free and run them out of town had he gotten his way.

When he stepped inside his office, nothing had changed. Dirty dishes remained on his desk along with the gun belt and revolver belonging to the new prisoner, Pete Doolin. Leaning back in a chair, feet propped up on the edge of the gun case, snoring as loud as a braying mule, Hoot Newton woke at the smell of sausage and fresh bread.

"Good, Jess," he said, yawning and bringing

Jess sat behind his desk Well, he thought, there's another dead man, a regular citizen, with a sword—*rapier*—through his body. An ominous night about to begin. Two gunmen in the lobby of the Trinity River Hotel that Jess couldn't do anything about. A gambler that gave Jesse a queasy feeling, a beautiful woman with a brace of Navy Colts, and her father, the most despised man in the South, in town . . . dying . . . and Jess hoped he wouldn't die here, on his watch. Not to mention three brothers of one of his prisoners maybe in town, maybe on their way home to Stephenville.

Jess opened the bottom drawer of the desk and started to slide Pete Doolin's holster, shell belt, and massive horse pistol into it but stopped and looked up at his deputy, who was still yawning.

"Hoot," he said. "What happened to the gun rigs that were in here?" He looked beyond Hoot Newton at the gun case. The Winchester carbine belonging to the McNamara boys was missing.

"They took 'em," Hoot said.

"They?"

"That fella's brothers. Big one and the two not big ones." Big Dan, Tom, and Neils.

"They were here?"

"Uh-huh."

Carrying on a conversation with Hoot Newton wasn't the easiest job.

"They can't carry firearms in the city limits," Jess told him. "That's why their guns were here."

"But they said they was goin' home."

For a moment, Jess felt a little relief. Then he asked: "Did they see their brother?"

"Uh-huh."

Relief left Jess at that moment. Burt McNamara would have been certain to have informed Tom and his siblings that the Butcher of Baxter Pass had arrived. Well, hell, Jess decided, all twenty-something-thousand people in town by now knew that General Dalton was staying at the Trinity River Hotel. Burt could have confirmed that, but seeing a circus wagon on Main Street with a Gatling gun on the top would have been proof enough.

"You sure they left town?" Jess asked.

Hoot had at last risen from the chair. "They said they was," he said.

Sighing, Jess dropped Doolin's revolver and gun leather into the empty drawer. The McNamara brothers had even taken brother Burt's weapons with them.

"They say anything else?" Jess slammed the drawer closed.

"Just that they was goin'." Hoot stopped, went back to the gun case, and picked up an envelope. "This come for you whilst you was out."

Jess waited as the big man crossed the room. Hoot extended the envelope, which looked tiny in those meat paws he called hands, and then brought it back to his side.

"Well . . . one of 'em boys did says somethin'. Not the big cuss, but one of 'em other ones. The one who ain't called Tom."

"Neils," Jess said.

"I reckon. We didn't bother with no introductions. But the one who is called Tom, he said, as they was bucklin' on their belts and the big one was gettin' that carbine. Tom, he says, 'Tell the law we'll be

# CHAPTER EIGHTEEN

**Monday, 6:20 p.m.**

"Smells perty, don't it?" Hoot Newton grinned.

"The dishes, Hoot," Jess said, although he didn't care if the prisoners ate off dirty dishes or clean ones. And Hoot was right. The note smelled even better than that Sweet Bye & Bye cologne he had bought for that gal who worked in the dance hall down around Pleasanton so many years back. That little bottle had cost Jess twenty cents. He figured what he smelled right now had to be worth at least a dollar. Maybe more, if you considered inflation.

*Jess Casey, Sheriff* had been written in a beautiful cursive. Practically art. No return address, but the back of the envelope read *Trinity River Hotel, Fort Worth*.

Eagerly, Jess opened the note with a pocketknife, although he felt like ripping it open to get at it immediately. But a note like this deserved preserving. He was careful with the knife blade and gingerly withdrew the folded piece of hotel stationery.

goin' home.' And that one, the one that you call Neils, he says, 'As soon as we pay a Yankee-lovin' cur dog opery house owner a visit and deliver him a reminder 'bout folks he shouldn't be bookin'.' Or somethin' like that."

Jess had to smile.

"Now I know who took a shot at me in that hallway," he said.

Hoot said. "Huh?"

Jess said. "The note, Hoot." And pointed at that tiny envelope.

the Tarrant County sheriff's ignorance. "Ya never heard of da *Sultana*?"

Jess could only shrug. "I was only a kid back in '65. I didn't read newspapers often back then."

"No vunder," the editor said, smiling. "Booth . . . da assassin . . . he vas killed vun day before. End of da var, da murder of our president, Booth's death . . . many people have forgotten da *Sultana*."

She was a side-wheeler on the Mississippi River, usually hauling cotton from St. Louis to New Orleans but often carrying federal troops since New Orleans had fallen into Union hands early in the war. She was steaming south toward New Orleans when word reached the captain of Lincoln's assassination, so the captain bought every newspaper he could find and continued his journey, bringing news to all the stops he made. She made it to New Orleans, then steamed north, stopping at Vicksburg for its biggest load.

Fourteen hundred Union soldiers, recently freed from prisoner-of-war camps, were to be loaded onto the *Sultana*. That was the deal the ship's captain had made with a Union officer in charge of getting those soldiers home. Many of those men were half-dead already, having spent an eternity in the hellholes of the prison camps at Cahaba, Alabama, and Andersonville, Georgia.

Fourteen hundred. To be loaded on a steamboat that could carry, safely, fewer than four hundred. But that was the deal, and both the Yankee in charge of the prisoners and the captain of the *Sultana* figured they could get rich. The federal government promised to pay the *Sultana*'s captain five dollars for each enlisted man and ten dollars for each officer carried home. Naturally, the *Sultana* captain would give a little bit of that cash back to the Union officer in charge of the paroled prisoners.

Only instead of fourteen hundred, more than twenty-one hundred boys in blue had been loaded onto the ship. A deckhand could hardly make his way from bow to stern without stepping on one of those poor boys. Decks sagged so much that supports had to be constructed. The entire ship stank of human waste and rot.

But the *Sultana* steamed north, on a river flooding from recent rains. On the night of April 26, she reached Memphis, Tennessee, unloaded a load of sugar, added some coal, and pulled out around midnight. Two hours later, seven miles north of Memphis, three of her four boilers exploded. Fire raced across the deck. Men leaped into the water, but most of them were too weak to stay afloat long.

The *Sultana* burned and sank.

A southbound steamboat came upon the scene, and the crew began pulling what they could onto her decks. Hours later, men floated past Memphis, calling out for help. Union warships and others quickly steamed out to save what they could, but few—very few—managed to live through the night. By most accounts, eighteen hundred people died that night in the Mississippi River.

For a long while, Jess stared at the cup of coffee in his hand, but he did not feel like drinking. What a waste. Finally, he looked at the *Gazette* editor.

"The *Sultana*'s captain?"

"Ach. He died, too."

something that sounded like a Dubonnet, tasted like syrup. Way too sweet. Jess liked the wine better.

Those Frenchies didn't eat much, Jess thought, and was saddened that the meal hadn't lasted long at all. He started to reach for his hat when the waiter came back, but he wasn't bringing a check. He had more food.

This one was more fish—and not the fried catfish with corn dodgers Jess usually chowed down on over at Harry's Fish Shack on Throckmorton—with some squash (Jess had never cared much for yellow squash) and pumpkin, which was pretty good. Now they ate and talked.

"How long have you been a lawman?" she asked.

"Not long. Still figuring out how to do this job." He dabbed his lips with the napkin and discreetly spit out the squash.

"What did you do before?"

"Cowboyed."

"Really?"

"Yes, ma'am."

"And before you were a cowboy?"

He smiled. "That's it. I was a thirty-a-month-and-found drifter, Miss Dalton."

"Call me Caroline," she said. "And I'll call you Jess."

He did not object.

They finished up the fish and vegetables, and the waiter quickly took away their plates. They sipped more wine.

Jess wanted to ask her about her father, about Baxter Pass, and the *Fancy Belpre*, but every time he summoned up the nerve, he would look into those wonderful gray eyes. So instead, he answered her questions about trail drives and broncs, cattle yards and branding irons, chuckwagons and St. Elmo's fire, that glowing light during thunderstorms that cowboys feared more than rattlesnakes and stampedes. He even had to tell her about prairie oysters, what they were, how you got them, how they tasted. Her eyes brightened.

"That is so amusing, Jess," she said.

"Not if you're a new steer," he told her.

She giggled, sounding just like a regular girl, and Jess laughed with her.

By then the waiter had returned with what Jess assumed was dessert. Lime sorbet, he called it, but to Jess it tasted partly like ice cream—Fort Worth having its own ice cream parlor, too, though it didn't do much business in the dead of winter.

"How long have you been playing the calliope?" he asked.

"Mother taught me," she said. "She played piano." She set her spoon on the dish. "She loved the piano, and I loved hearing her play. The calliope . . . well . . . she didn't enjoy that, and I don't blame her, but she did it for Father." She picked up the spoon, chipped away at the ice cream—sorbet!—and smiled at either the sweet dessert or the memory.

"And your mother . . . ?" Jess broached.

"She died in '79. I was just fifteen."

"I'm sorry," he said, while mentally doing the math in his head. That meant Caroline would be twenty-six or twenty-seven, though she didn't look a day past eighteen. "Didn't mean to bring up unpleasant memories."

"There are no unpleasant memories about Mother," she said. "Or Father."

Which came out as a bit of a challenge.

"You were born in . . . ?" he tried.

She told him: 1863. Then she added, "I did not meet my father until after the war's end."

The waiter returned, and Caroline told him that he could take her plate, even though she had scarcely touched the sorbet. Jess quickly finished his and let the nice fellow take away those dishes, too. He wondered if she expected him to pay for this meal. It would likely set him back a month's salary. She had invited him, but that wasn't the way a gentleman did things. He wondered if the waiter or that mean cuss with the mustache and tails would let him hock his spurs. Or if he'd be doing dishes the rest of the night.

Hell, the rest of the month.

"Why did you save his life?" Caroline Dalton asked.

Jess studied her. He had to think, which he had not done when he had snapped that shot at Pete Doolin.

"I'm paid to uphold the law," he said. "As far as I know, General Dalton isn't wanted for any crime."

*He'll face his judgment on Judgment Day.*

She looked as if she could read his mind. She probably had. But she smiled sweetly. "You're good with those guns."

"I get too much practice," he told her. "Might surprise you, but I don't like using my revolver."

"It won't surprise you that Lee Bodeen does."

"No, ma'am. I'd heard of him long before you and that wagon came to town."

"He was Major Clarke's hire. Father lets the major attend to that part of business."

"How long have you . . ." He had to stop. Damn him if that waiter wasn't bringing back more food.

This was antelope, and not some tiny portion, but a big chunk of meat that left Jess's mouth drooling. Some green stuff on the side—garnish, Caroline Dalton called it—and some carrots glazed with honey and pepper. The waiter also brought out another bottle of wine, let Jess taste it first, as if he knew what good wine tasted like. Jess nodded his satisfaction, and the waiter filled two new glasses, taking the old ones away. He left the bottle.

"You were asking?" Caroline Dalton reminded him.

"Oh." Jess had forgotten that he wasn't supposed to be hungry, but that antelope was calling his name. "How long have you been touring with your father?"

"All my life," she answered. "Well, since the end of the war. Father tried returning to his business." She looked away. "Not here. He wanted to open a hardware store. He just wasn't good at business. That's what Mother always told me. And he had to face the Senate hearing in Columbus. That wore him out."

# CHAPTER NINETEEN

*Monday, 7:20 p.m.*

"Senate hearing?" Jess asked.

"Yes." She had picked the knife and fork up off the table, but now she laid both on the plate of wild game, carrots, and garnish. "The stories you have heard in Texas we heard in Ohio. Especially after Major Wirz was hanged."

"Wirz." Jess nodded. "Andersonville," he said.

"Right."

Henry Wirz was a native of Switzerland who had come to America in the 1840s, eventually hanging up his shingle as a doctor in Kentucky and Louisiana before the war broke out. He had joined the Confederate army as a private, but within a year he was a captain. Then a minié ball had shattered his right arm at the Battle of Seven Pines, and the fighting war was over for Henry Wirz.

For a while, he had served as Confederate president Jefferson Davis's special minister to Europe. Probably because he could speak French and maybe

other foreign languages. Jess wasn't sure what the
Swiss spoke. Didn't matter. Wirz had returned to the
South by 1864, and that spring assumed command
of a prisoner-of-war camp deep in Georgia. It was
officially called Camp Sumter. It was known as
Andersonville, the nearest town—if it actually could
be called a town.

It was, in fact, hell.

In an enclosed stockade that covered sixteen
acres, Yankee prisoners crowded the filthy pesthole.
Thirty-two thousand were imprisoned there by
August of '64—not that many more lived in Fort
Worth today—and they died by the hundreds from
dysentery, scurvy, and other diseases, but mostly,
from starvation. Or they were just sick of living like
animals, freezing in the winter, sweating in the
summer, living off rats, with nothing to drink but the
wretched water that flowed through the compound.

When the war was over, Major Henry Wirz was
captured and taken all the way to Washington City.
The Yanks charged him with war crimes, and he was
brought before a military tribunal. Major General
Lew Wallace was the presiding judge. These days,
Wallace was known more for a novel he had finished
while serving as territorial governor of New Mexico:
*Ben-Hur: A Tale of the Christ*.

According to testimony, Wirz hadn't just con-
spired to kill Yankee prisoners. He had beaten at least
one bluecoat to death with a pistol, shot some,
kicked one poor man to death, and left others to rot
in stocks. He had sicced dogs after some men who
had tried to escape, and those dogs had killed plenty.

The tribunal found Wirz guilty, and he had been

hanged by the neck at the Old Capitol Prison in Washington. The Yanks botched the execution. The drop through the trapdoor didn't break the major's neck. He twisted, turned, and kicked until he choked to death. Some Southerners said the Yanks did that on purpose.

Guilty? Jess didn't know. He did know that not many people were eating well in Georgia after Sherman's bluecoats had marched their way through, burning, ransacking, and pillaging. Food had been scarce throughout the Confederacy. But what about those Southern boys confined in hellholes up North? Many of those had died, too. Some of them had been murdered.

"Father answered the questions, and the Senate sent him home. He never faced another day in court, but there were always those questions about what had happened at Baxter Pass."

"And how did he answer?"

She smiled, and picked up the knife and fork. "You'll have to come tomorrow night, Jess. Hear it for yourself."

Thinking of Wirz . . . of Andersonville . . . and of two hundred Texas boys gunned down at Baxter Pass, Ohio, after the war had ended spoiled Jess's appetite. He barely made a dent in the antelope, even though it was delicious. He only took a few sips of the wine.

Eventually, the waiter took away their plates . . . only to return with more. A green salad with a vinaigrette. Jess wondered where in blazes the headman at Café Lavendou had managed to find fresh greens at this time of year. He made himself eat a couple of bites.

"And the Gatling gun?" Jess asked.

"The one on our wagon?" Caroline smiled. "For years, Mr. Richard Gatling paid Father a tidy annual sum to display his weapons. Sometimes, when Father was younger, he would even fire a round. For three months, we even charged ten dollars for people to get to turn the crank one entire revolution. You'd be amazed how many people would be willing to part with that much money to shoot a weapon like that."

Jess almost told her that she'd be amazed to see how many men had been killed in Fort Worth for much, much less money than ten bucks. But he didn't want to interrupt her. She had a lovely voice, musical, not like that calliope.

"We had to stop that, though," she said. "After a gentleman in his cups shot up the side of a livery stable in Faribault, Minnesota."

"So the Gatling isn't loaded," Jess said, praying that she would confirm.

She did. "It's just part of an act. We are a circus, more or less." She hadn't exactly answered Jess's question, but he didn't pursue.

Instead, Jess asked, "How did your father manage to get a Gatling gun at Baxter Pass? That wasn't standard issue for prison camps. If my memory's right, those fast-shooting weapons weren't even standard issue for most Union armies."

"They weren't," she said. "Very few guns made their way into that war. The War Department considered Mr. Gatling a copperhead. He lived and started his company in Indianapolis, but that city

wasn't entirely loyal to the blue. If you asked the War Department. And Mr. Gatling had family, everyone said, from South Carolina. Or was it North? Yes, North Carolina. Anyway, General Butler bought a few of those guns, and Admiral Porter got one. The U.S. Army didn't come aboard until the year after the war ended."

Jess waited. She had not answered his question.

Realizing this, Caroline smiled at him again. "Most of those guns," she said, "were manufactured at a plant in Cincinnati. Just down the river from Baxter Pass. Have you been to Cincinnati?"

Jess shook his head.

"It's beautiful. Just beautiful."

"And Baxter Pass?"

Her smile vanished and her eyes darkened. "I've never been there, but I hear it's nothing more than a ghost town these days. Most people left for Cincinnati. Or just moved. There's little left there today."

Except, Jess thought, a forgotten graveyard.

"In 1870," Caroline said, "Mr. Gatling sold his interest in his patents to Colt, but he's still president of the Gatling Gun Company. The weapon we have now came from Colt, though. They used to send a new one every two years, but we've had that one for five years now."

She frowned. "People have forgotten about Father. Maybe that's for the . . ."

She stopped. The waiter came to take away the plates. Good. Jess figured he wouldn't be hungry for another week—if he lived that long. He made himself sip some wine and tried to think of something pleasant to talk about, but his mind kept focusing on

Baxter Pass and the Butcher who was up in a room in the Trinity River Hotel.

"How old is your father?" he asked.

"He'll be seventy-four if he lives to see June." Her head dropped. "I doubt if that will happen." He heard the click of her purse and saw her hand disappear, but it came up with a silk handkerchief and not a .36-caliber Colt or a Remington over-and-under derringer. She dabbed her beautiful gray eyes and lowered the handkerchief.

"It's the carcinoma," she said.

"Ma'am?"

"Carcinoma. Cancer. The doctor in Dayton gave him six months. That was ten months ago. That's Father, of course." For a moment, she seemed cheerful, but then the gloom returned, and she said softly, "I really think he stopped living when Mother passed on."

Jess knew then why Caroline Dalton had invited him to supper. It wasn't to thank him. It was to get out. To see someone other than Jedediah Clarke, Lee Bodeen, or even her own father, the Butcher of Baxter Pass. He felt flattered. Then ashamed of himself for bringing up those awful memories.

He decided to tell her about Fort Worth . . . maybe not the sordid dealings in Hell's Half Acre . . . but how the bluebonnets looked in spring. He'd tell her that as he walked her back to the hotel.

Nope. Maybe now. Because the waiter had returned with a plateful of cheeses, grapes, and peaches.

* * *

Three and a half hours. Jess was used to eating supper in three minutes, but one of the church bells was sounding out ten o'clock as he walked back to the hotel. This part of town was dead—at least, this block on First Street was—but as soon as the church bells ceased, he could hear the noise, the laughter, the curses, and the pounding hoofs or pounding fists from inside Hell's Half Acre.

After the cheese and fruit, they had indulged in chocolate—white and black (Jess would never have believed that chocolate could be white)—with a demitasse of café, which tasted a lot like coffee, only better than anything Jess had ever consumed—which wasn't saying that much.

Despite the massive meal, Jess felt light. He was, naturally, a little lighter. Oh, Caroline Dalton had insisted on paying for the meal, but Jess said then he would have to leave the tip. That's why she had showed him the bill. So he'd know how much money he should leave. He made sure she didn't watch him and wondered if that nice little waiter would be mad at all those pennies he had deposited on his squash-soaked napkin.

The coffee had helped. He didn't feel quite so tired, and the temperature had dropped substantially over their three and a half hours inside Café Lavendou. The cold air made him alert.

When they neared the Trinity River Hotel, Jess studied the shadows. The saloons here were noisy—just not quite as raucous—and a few horses lined the hitching rails. He recognized a few of the local drunks staggering down the boardwalk across the street, but Jess didn't think of them as threats. Then again, he probably wouldn't have given Pete Doolin a second thought after one glance, and Doolin was now in the jail with a hole that Jess had put in his thigh.

When they reached the hotel, Caroline Dalton turned, pulling away from Jess's loose grip. He figured she would send him on his way, but she said, "Would you like to meet Father?"

He thought she'd say over breakfast, but she said, "Now."

"Now?"

"Yes. He doesn't sleep much."

Hell, Jess thought, General Dalton had slept through much of the gunfire earlier this afternoon, slept in his rocking chair.

"He'll be upstairs now," she told him, "reading Dickens. He loves Dickens. Always has. And preparing his speech for tomorrow evening. You should meet him," she said, her voice almost pleading.

No screams were sounding from the tenderloin. The McNamara brothers were nowhere to be seen along Main Street. Hoot Newton could handle two prisoners in jail.

"I'd love to meet the general," Jess said, knowing *love* was the wrong word.

She bounced up the steps into the hotel, and Jess followed, adjusting his eyes to the light, looking into the restaurant and saloon but finding no suspicious characters at the bar. He followed her up the stairs, and as soon as they had reached the second floor, the door opened.

Lee Bodeen stepped out. The man probably had heard Jess's spurs. He frowned, and then stepped

aside as the Butcher himself, General Lincoln Everett Dalton, came out of the room, still in his fancy Union duds, wobbling on two canes, cursing at Bodeen when the gunman offered to help.

As soon as he stepped out of the hallway and onto the balcony overlooking the lower lobby, Jess saw the movement on the street.

"Get down!" he yelled.

# CHAPTER TWENTY

*Monday, 10:10 p.m.*

The plate glass window in the lobby blew apart in a shower of glass shards and buckshot as Jess grabbed Caroline Dalton's shoulder and pulled her to the floor while his right hand found the Colt and fired at the muzzle blast below. The balustrade would not offer much protection, but a shotgun like that had minimum range—and shooting through a window, uphill, was a tough shot for even the best sharpshooter.

Below, people screamed. The shotgun roared again, but this time the shooter aimed at Jess, not General Dalton.

The ornate woodwork splintered from the shot, and Jess felt something tug on the collar of his coat. He fired again and saw the killer take off toward the river.

Jess was up, glancing only a second at the people on the second floor balcony. Lying prone, Caroline Dalton had pulled a Smith & Wesson pocket pistol

from her purse, had it cocked, and was drawing a bead below, but holding her fire. Lee Bodeen lay atop the Butcher, who was cursing him as a fool, telling the gunman to get off him. Bodeen rolled over, a revolver in either hand. A couple of other people had poked their heads out of the doors to their rooms. That was all Jess had time to see, because he bounded down the staircase, taking the steps three at a time.

"Stay back!" he yelled at some brave souls who started out of the restaurant. They obeyed. The clerk, his face whiter than the tablecloths at Café Lavendou, pulled himself up from behind the registration counter, his mouth agape.

Jess stepped onto the boardwalk, his boots crunching glass. A man lifted his head from behind the water trough, recognized Jess, and pointed north. "Th-th-that w-w-w-way, She-she-riffff," he managed to say, but Jess knew that already. Boot steps sounded behind him, but Jess didn't look back. He knew it would be Lee Bodeen. Jess didn't wait. He took off down Main Street.

Past Second and First streets and toward Weatherford, where a reporter from the *Fort Worth Standard* came bolting out, pencil in his mouth as he hurriedly pulled on his coat. He raced down the boardwalk toward the sound of the gunfire, not even noticing the Colt in Jess's hand, ever the diligent ink-slinger.

He stood at the corner of Main and Weatherford, staring across at the big lawn and the Tarrant County Courthouse. To the west, yellow lights shined from the windows and open door of the saloon and billiard hall, but no one stepped outside. Two shotgun blasts and a shot or two from a revolver weren't going to interrupt a game of pool. A wagon loaded with hay had been parked on the lawn, and behind that the courthouse sat dark, looming.

By then, Lee Bodeen had caught up to Jess.

"You see him?"

Before he had started shooting, yes, Jess Casey had seen the gunman. He had been leaning against a wooden column, rolling a cigarette, chatting with the man Jess had seen hiding behind the water trough. He wore a big black greatcoat, but now Jess realized that the coat had kept that shotgun concealed. A brown bowler hat. A silver mustache and underlip beard. Jess didn't know the man by name, but he had seen him often enough in town.

Jess's office and jail lay over on the far side of Belknap Street, near Rusk Street a block to the east. He didn't think the shooter would go that way. But he could have turned down Weatherford, moved west, toward Houston and Throckmorton, toward the saloons and billiard halls, dropped in there, and mingled with the crowd. Or he could have kept running toward Belknap, even Bluff Street.

On a hunch, Jess crossed the street, stopping beside the wagon full of hay and looking at the courthouse.

It was on this bluff that the original army post had been established by the 2nd Dragoons back in 1849. The first courthouse had gone up here in 1860, but had been destroyed by a fire back in '76. The new courthouse had been completed in '78, two stories, but a renovation four years later had added a third story for offices. The courthouse's most famous feature was the clock tower but only because of all the bullet holes in the clock face, which was expected in a cow town like Fort Worth.

Mayor Stout and other city big shots kept talking that it was high time for a new courthouse, maybe something made of pink granite, something that would rival the Capitol building down in Austin. After all, this city had water lines, some electric lights, hundreds of artesian wells, a telephone service that only a few people used, and Main and Houston Streets had been paved all the way from the courthouse to the Texas and Pacific depot on the other end of town. Of course, those paved streets were typically covered with dust, dung, dirt, or mud.

"We are a civilized city," Stout was fond of saying.

Yet here stood Jess Casey, with a gun in his hand, and a gunman behind him, staring at the darkened courthouse.

"What do you think?" Bodeen drawled.

Jess motioned with his revolver barrel, and the killer with the Ranger badge understood. In a crouch, he angled his way across the lawn, heading toward Belknap and Houston. Jess went the other way.


Lee Bodeen found Jess across from the courthouse, halfway toward Bluff Street, kneeling. It was a new moon, and the streetlamps, electric or gas, did not reach this far. Jess struck a lucifer on his thumbnail, holding it down toward the ground.

Bodeen saw what was lying in the dead grass.

"He reloaded that shotgun," he said. "Or tried to."

The remains of two drawn brass shells lay on the

ground beside one shell that the man had apparently dropped and not tried to pick up. It was brass, too, with the overshot card wad and rolled edge. Stamped ten-gauge, Parker Brothers. A mean, well-made shotgun.

Nodding, Jess pointed at the print of the heel of a boot. "Ran that way," he said, nodding north.

"Can he swim?"

Jess grinned. Beyond Bluff Street flowed the Trinity River. He shook out the match and pushed himself up. "We're civilized," he said. "Bridges and everything now. Let's go get our horses."

"What for?"

Now Jess could place the man with the greatcoat and silver hair—and the shotgun.

"Man who shot at the general works at the stockyards," he said. "That's more than two miles north of here, and I'm an old cowboy. I don't walk when I can ride."

When the railroad had finally arrived in Fort Worth back in 1876, things changed dramatically. Cattle didn't have to be driven all the way to Kansas, although many Texas drovers had done that anyway until the shipping rates dropped and made things more reasonable. A few years back, plans to build massive stockyards north of the Trinity River began to be discussed. Plans were drawn up, construction of cattle pens began, and a rich Yankee from Boston named Greenleif Simpson had been invited to Fort Worth. That wealthy Yank saw more cattle than those pens could hold, so he decided to invest. Not only that, he had returned to Massachusetts and gotten a couple more rich Yanks to put their money in Fort Worth's stockyards and a packing plant to go along with it. Simpson's neighbor, Louville V. Niles, eagerly put up some money as he had made his fortune in meatpacking and saw a chance to make even more millions.

Now, the practically brand-spanking-new Union Stockyards had become the talk of Texas.

Before the Union Stockyards opened for business last summer, four stockyards had been used for shipping down south near the railroads, but the Union dwarfed those four rickety old pens. The Union spanned more than two hundred and fifty acres. It was a veritable maze of wood, cow dung, and bawling beeves—though not at this time of year.

The stockyards were practically deserted, and only a few lights shined from the office buildings as Lee Bodeen and Jess Casey rode down Main Street, past the rickety buildings and huts, even a few tents that served as homes for the poorer side of Fort Worth, a picket house that served as a saloon, a ramshackle boardinghouse for some of the packinghouse workers, dugouts, and constructions that resembled lean-tos more than homes.

A man yelled at a woman. The woman cursed the man. Somewhere, an infant wailed. Dogs barked. A cat screeched. The hoofs of the horses clopped, and then they were at the stockyards. The smell of cow droppings was pungent in the night air. A few lanterns glowed on posts near the entrances to the shipping pens, and yellow light shined out of a window. That was all the light there was at this time of night, this time of year.

"This guy you saw works here?" Bodeen asked in a hoarse whisper after they had reined in their mounts.

"Yeah. Night manager. Watchman. Something like that."

"You didn't suspicion him while he was standing out in front of the hotel?"

"No reason to. He had the shotgun hidden in his greatcoat."

Jess slid from his horse, tethering the reins around a hitching post. Lee Bodeen did the same.

"I thought Yanks built this place. Why'd a Yank want to kill Dalton?"

"Yankee money built the stockyards," Jess said. "But it's Texas muscle that keeps it running." Texas. Black. Irish. Mexican.

"You reckon that man'd come back here?"

"Just long enough to pack his traps and skedaddle." Jess pointed to the mule in front of the office. "He hasn't skedaddled yet."

A shadow moved behind the window then disappeared.

Jess motioned down the street. "Stay off the boardwalks," he told the Ranger. "Go low, quiet, get a good position behind that water barrel. I'll come up on this side, place myself in that little alley near his office. When he comes out of the office to throw his war bag on that mule, I'll take him." He stared hard at Lee Bodeen. "Alive."

"It's your town," Bodeen said. "Your play. Just remember . . . that shotgun'll blow you in half at close range."

"I'll remember that," Jess said, and knelt to unfasten his spurs.

He let Bodeen go first, until the shadows covered him. Jess wiped his palms on his britches, pulled up the collar of his Mackinaw, and moved past the outer buildings, the feed shed, the privies, a couple of lean-tos. The mule's ears jerked up, and the big molly mule pulled at the reins, turned her head, and brayed.

Jess dropped, bringing up his revolver at the front door to the office. The shadow was back. Then the light went out.

Again, the mule called out, but neither Jess's horse nor the gelding Lee Bodeen had borrowed answered. Both animals had been trained not to.

Jess hadn't gotten into position yet, and from where he squatted, he'd be a sitting duck if the night man with the shotgun saw him. That wasn't likely, because the assassin had blown out the lamp inside the office. Now the only lights came from those lanterns on the posts in front of the stockyards. But buckshot from a shotgun didn't have eyes, didn't need light. A lucky shot, as Bodeen had reminded Jess, could just blow him in half.

# CHAPTER TWENTY-ONE

*Monday, 10:55 p.m.*

The door to the office squeaked open. Jess couldn't see the door, just hear the hinges, and make out the vague outline of the office building. Silently, he managed to get down into a prone position, making himself as small of a target as possible. He brought up the .44-40 revolver, aiming it toward the noise of the door, fighting the urge to glance over at where Bodeen should be, but knowing not to take his eyes off the general direction of the office.

A board squeaked and instantly stopped. The mule stamped one of its hoofs.

Jess decided to give the would-be assassin a chance.

"You missed Dalton!" he yelled, and heard the board squeak again, probably as the watchman jerked back inside the office. "Didn't kill anyone. Didn't wound anybody. Give it up, mister. No sense in anybody else getting hurt or killed."

He waited. Nothing. Which felt a whole lot better

than having double-ought buckshot fly over his head in the middle of the night.

After wetting his lips with his tongue, Jess tried it again. "I'll talk to the solicitor. Get you charged with only unlawful discharge of a weapon. Plead guilty. Pay a fine. Replace the window at the hotel. Be free to go." Not that Mort Thompson ever listened to him, but this time, Jess would make him. Mayor Stout might even go as far as backing Jess on this one and stand up to that carpetbagging lout Mort Thompson, because it meant easy money and no bad publicity for Fort Worth.

A strong wind picked up, followed by a low rumbling of thunder. Which was not exactly what Jess Casey needed. Thunder didn't happen often during the dead of winter, but that was the joke about weather in Texas. Stick around a minute, and it was bound to change.

The door squeaked again, and the wind must have caught it because it slammed hard against the inner wall of the office. Instinctively, Jess lowered his head, holding his breath, his finger tightening on the trigger.

"I . . . am . . . coming . . . out!" the man inside the office yelled. There was another squeak—this one from a loose board on the walk, as Jess could make out the outline of the man as he stepped from the office—and a gunshot followed.

"Damn it!" Jess rolled to his left, seeing a second muzzle flash and hearing the report from Lee Bodeen's position. The shotgun roared once, and then the man was running from the office. Jess fired, saw orange flame spit again from the shotgun's second barrel as the man ran. Bodeen cursed, fired. Jess felt like sending a shot toward Bodeen, who had botched this whole evening now. Instead, he fired in the general direction of the man, but that was a warning shot.

"He's used both barrels, Bodeen!" Jess yelled when the gunman with the Ranger star shot again.

Something popped. Jess saw the flash near the loading pens and felt a bullet whistle past him.

"He's got a pistol now, Casey!" Bodeen snapped back.

Jess heard wood smash against wood, and then a soft grunt. The wood slammed again, and he knew that the man who had shot at General Dalton—and now Lee Bodeen and Jess Casey—had made his way into the stockyards.

He came up to his knees, lowering the hammer on the Colt and started toward the water trough. "I'm heading your way, Bodeen!" he yelled, and took off running, sliding the last several yards, and coming up into a half-seated position, his back resting against the wooden trough. He tried to catch his breath while he shucked out the empty casings and reloaded the revolver. From the noise he heard on the other side of the trough, Lee Bodeen was doing the same.

"He was coming out, Bodeen," Jess told him over the trough. "Giving himself up."

"How do you know?" Bodeen's voice was tight.

"Didn't you hear me?"

"Couldn't make out any words," Bodeen said. "Wind and all."

Jess filled the last empty chamber with a cartridge

and snapped the loading gate shut with another curse. Most times, he kept the chamber under his hammer empty, but his gut told him not to worry about safety right now. As far as Lee Bodeen's excuse, he didn't believe him but dropped the subject.

"He's got only that peashooter now," Bodeen said.

"Unless he reloaded the shotgun," Jess told him.

Now, it was Bodeen's turn to curse.

Jess brought himself up, staring at the mostly empty stockyards.

The pens went on for acres, loading chutes off to his left. Most likely, the watchman would have to climb over the high wooden fences or open some heavy gates. Jess didn't know how many pens there were, but there had to be plenty. Once he got through this maze, beyond the stockyards lay mostly empty prairie. Thunder rolled again, but the sound came from the distance, and Jess saw no flashes of lightning.

"Well, Sheriff?" Sarcasm laced Bodeen's voice.

The safe bet would be to wait until daylight. Send out a posse. Jess looked at the lanterns along the top walkway on the side of the pens near the loading chutes. They seemed to be spaced out about every four pens, and the light wouldn't cover more than two pens away from the chutes. Several more pens would remain in complete darkness.

If the watchman were smart, he would stay in the darkened pens. He knew this place. Had to. Anyway, since the Union Stockyards were practically brand-spanking new, having operated for only one season, the watchman would know the lay of this land a lot better than Lee Bodeen or even Jess Casey. On the other hand, staying in the light from the lanterns, or at least on the edge of the light, would make his traversing of these corrals a lot faster.

Somewhere in the pens, a steer bawled.

Jess pushed himself up, pointing with his gun barrel. "Let's go," he said. "When we get inside, stop."

In a crouch, he hurried to the gate, which the wind had slammed open. He came through, stepped to his left, and waited until he heard Bodeen go to the right. The night remained so dark, he could see nothing. They stood in the darkness closer to the chute side of the pens.

It was a dangerous risk, but Jess found a lucifer and struck it with his thumb, cupping his hands to protect the blaze and waiting till the wind died down. As soon as it stopped, as if in answer to Jess's silent prayer, he raised the burning match.

"There," he said, nodding. "You see that?"

"The opening?" Bodeen asked.

"Yeah." Jess shook out the match, returning the pair of lawmen—*lawmen* being a loose term—into darkness.

"You go through that. Slow. Careful." He started to gesture toward his left, only to realize that would be a waste of effort since Bodeen couldn't see him. "I'll go to the walkway. You're low. I'm high. You should be able to see me with those lanterns. So don't shoot at me."

"That guy who cut loose with that double-barrel will be able to see you, too, Casey."

Jess nodded grimly. "Yeah. Don't I know it."

"I think your way makes a beeline straight through the stockyards. Fellow we're after might be nearer you, at the edge of the light. Might also be in those other pens, in the darkness. Watch yourself."

"You, too, Casey."

Jess grinned. "Watch your step, Bodeen," he said. "They run cattle where you'll be walking."

Bodeen snorted a laugh and was gone.

Revolver in his hand, Jess moved along the wooden fence, past the empty pens, then came up the steps eight feet until he was under the first lantern. His eyes adjusted to the new light, and he stepped away, gun pointing at the empty pens. Two pens over he could see Bodeen, though only as a shadow, as the gunman crept along. Jess backed against the wooden rails at the edge of the walkway and moved carefully toward the next pen. In a moment he was out of the light, heading toward the next lantern, aware of the sound of his boots on the wooden planks. In darkness, a steer snorted and skedaddled from the sound of Jess.

Jess almost shot the animal.

He sucked in a breath, exhaled, told himself to settle down, and stepped closer to the light.

At the third pen, he stood underneath a wooden structure and realized it led to more pens to his left. He peered through the slats, into darkness, and smelled the odor of old cow dung, mud, and his own rank stink from sweat and nerves.

The watchman could have gone that way, Jess thought, sneaked back toward the street, waited for

Jess and Bodeen to disappear inside the maze, then go for his mule and hurry out of Fort Worth.

No. Quickly, he dismissed that idea. The watchman would have to climb up, out of the pens, and onto the walkway. He'd be in the light from the lanterns, easy to spot, easy to shoot. No, he'd stay in the dark, over toward Bodeen or beyond him.

Jess walked, gun ready, seeing the figure that had to be Lee Bodeen again, a few yards ahead of him.

He moved on, now with more intent, and when the next pen loaded with a few cows started bawling, Jess did not come close to shooting them, although he did look at the animals—just to make sure the watchman wasn't doing that startling.

Nice looking beeves, thought Jess, ever the cowboy. Probably bring thirty-five a head at market.

He kept going, farther into the darkness again, deeper into the abyss, heading toward the next lantern and its warming, though possibly deadly, light.

How much time had passed, he had no idea. He glanced skyward, but clouds blocked any stars. Jess kept moving, in and out of darkness, past more pens that now remained empty. The wind blew. Thunder rumbled. He saw nothing but Bodeen's shadowy figure and the glowing light from distant lanterns.

Something stopped him, and he crouched, bringing the hammer back on the Colt and looked back. He couldn't place the sound. Maybe he had just imagined it, but he looked back a few pens, toward the blackness near the pathway Lee Bodeen had taken. A number of pens went beyond that path, and Jess had thought the night watchman might have gone that way, taking advantage of the dark.

Holding his breath, he listened, not wanting to take his eyes and ears away from that direction, not looking to see if Lee Bodeen had stopped, too.

The noise sounded again, a soft thump from behind Lee Bodeen. Cattle? Possibly, but Jess didn't think so. He couldn't see anything but blackness in those cattle pens. Now, he heard nothing but the wind, but a few moments later, came the soft faint sound, maybe, of iron hitting wood.

That's when Jess knew, and he sprang up, and ran, back down the walkway above the shipping pens, toward the street, the offices, and Jess's and Bodeen's horses and the night watchman's mule. It was a guess, actually, more of a hunch. The watchman was smarter than Jess had figured, had hidden in the darkness in those far pens and waited for Jess and Bodeen to pass. Now he was moving back to get his mule—or better yet one of the horses—and flee Fort Worth.

Jess wasn't sure if Bodeen would understand, follow, and didn't want to shout. He heard nothing except his own footsteps and breath, but had to guess that the watchman would hear the noise, too, would understand that Jess had guessed what was afoot. Yet Jess wasn't even sure if his hunch was right, until the gunshot sounded, the orange flash appeared over one of the pen walls, and the lantern above Jess exploded.

His back burned, and he felt the heat, smelled the singeing of his Mackinaw, saw more flames flying past him. He ran a few more feet, and then realized that flaming coal oil had landed on his coat, ignited the wool, and he was merely feeding the flames. Instantly, he dived into the pen, just as another bullet whistled past him.

# CHAPTER TWENTY-TWO

*Monday, 11:20 p.m.*

Landing on the hard, frozen ground, Jess Casey immediately fell to his back, rolled over and over and over, putting out the flames licking the woolen coat on his back. Cattle scurried about, and Jess realized that his luck had put him in one of the few pens that held beef. He came to his feet, moving toward the wall, leaping, hoping to find wood and not the sharp point of a longhorn's horn.

Next, he began climbing up out of this pen, over the top, and dropping down into the adjoining cattle pen. His gun remained in his hand. He smelled the stink of burning wool but not burning flesh.

Behind him and to his left came the sound of footsteps in a hurry, but that would be Lee Bodeen. Jess moved across the pen to the next fence of wooden planks and climbed. Ahead of him came the sound of the night watchman as he raced toward the street to get out of this death trap, this dark dungeon of wood, dust, and frozen and fresh cattle droppings.

He heard the gunshot, saw another flash of orange, and heard the bullet smack into the top plank several feet to Jess's right. His finger squeezed the trigger, and the .44-40 bucked in his hand. Over on the street, the mule brayed. Jess came down into the next pen.

This time, he slipped on ice but kept from falling and moved. Wood slammed, followed by footsteps, and he realized that the watchman had reached the end of this abyss and that he had to be hurrying for a horse. By then, Lee Bodeen had shot past Jess, which Jess had expected. The gunman had a straight shot down a path, not obstructed by high wooden fences that separated the holding pens.

Jess had considered climbing over the pen wall and dropping into that walkway but didn't want to risk it. Bodeen might mistake him for the watchman and kill him. Or the watchman might be waiting for Jess to do just that and kill him. He came up, dropped over, and realized he was in the outer yard. A gunshot roared—this time from a shotgun—and beyond the yards, Lee Bodeen answered with a shout and a shot. A horse screamed. Hoofs danced, and Jess found the opening and dived out, landing on his stomach.

He sensed the presence of Lee Bodeen, crawling on hands and knees in the darkness toward the water trough. He heard the mule snort and bellow, and Jess came up, thumbing back the hammer on the Colt, moving. He fired, low, intentionally toward the mule and heard the bullet whine off a rock. Then the mule snapped its tether, the watchman cursed, and the mule's hoofs clopped on the dusty street as it ran toward Main Street, away from the shooting.

Which left the watchman afoot. One horse—Jess prayed it wasn't his—lay on the ground, kicking, squealing, in its death throes. The other horse, Jess's own mount, he could sense more than see, had pulled loose and hurried back toward Fort Worth proper.

Now came other sounds. Dogs barking. People shouting. Lanterns began to be turned up, but none so close as to light up the stockyards. A shadow slipped one way and vanished.

"In the alley!" Jess shouted toward Bodeen, and ran toward the watchman's office. He slammed against the side of the wall, saw the door, and stepped inside. Striking a match, Jess found the lantern, lighted it, and came outside, lantern in his left hand, Colt in his right.

He was careful not to look into the glowing light. Bodeen hurried past him and stepped toward the lean-to across from the office. The alley separated the two men.

There was one thing Jess remembered about the layout of the Union Stockyards business buildings. The alley was a dead-end. Oh, there was a high wooden fence that butted between the office and a warehouse full of hay and feed, but that fence had to be ten or twelve feet high—too far for the watchman to climb, and the man hadn't slipped past the lean-to. He had a picket building on his left and a brick warehouse on his right. Nowhere to go.

"Give it up!" Jess yelled. "It's finished! You're trapped!"

The pistol popped twice, one bullet whistling through the lean-to, the other slamming into the picket wall of the watchman's office.

Jess swung the lantern back behind him, then let it fly, seeing it arc upward—the watchman, unnerved, even took a futile potshot at it—and landing on a bale of hay where workers would sit during their dinner breaks to eat, smoke cigarettes, and wear out chewing tobacco.

It burst into flames, lighting the alleyway, but also giving the watchman a clear shot at Jess and Bodeen when they showed their faces.

If the watchman hadn't reloaded, and Jess couldn't figure how the panicked man would have had time, he had a couple of shots left in the revolver and one barrel full of buckshot in the scattergun. Jess nodded at Bodeen, and motioned with the Colt's barrel low and then nodded again.

Bodeen would go low. Jess would go high.

Now!

He moved, saw the watchman, the pistol tucked in his waistband, the shotgun held at his hips with both hands. The man had a clear shot, but the wicked flames of the burning haystack would distort his vision. He swung the barrel at Bodeen, then back at Jess, and three shots sounded almost as one.

Jess felt the kick of the Colt in his right hand as he watched the watchman stagger backward against the high fence at the end of the alley. The shotgun had discharged, but a bullet had caught the man in his chest, and the buckshot fired toward the clouds overhead. Jess knew he had aimed low, not to kill, but more to discourage. Bodeen had no sensibilities.

For the gunman shot again. And once more.

"He's finished!" Jess yelled, stopping the man-killer from putting another bullet into the watchman.

Bodeen had cocked his revolver, but now came the metallic clicks as he lowered the hammer.

Jess Casey did the same. Both men stood in the alley now, watching the night watchman slide down the fence, then topple over onto his side. He did not move. The flames licked savagely at the dry hay.

While Lee Bodeen put out the fire, walking back and forth to the water trough with a bucket, Jess walked down the alley toward the dead man, his greatcoat spread out like a blanket beneath him, head resting on the ground, mouth wide open, eyes locked in eternal surprise. He wore no hat. Likely, he had lost it somewhere in the stockyards.

The empty shotgun, still smoking, was indeed a Parker Brothers ten-gauge, its thirty-two-inch Damascus barrels with two-and-seven-eighths-inch chambers. Jess picked up the gun, which had to weigh nigh ten pounds. The handgun in the waistband was a little .22-caliber Smith & Wesson, silver-plated with rosewood grips, probably one of those No. 1 second issues with a seven-shot cylinder.

What caught most of Jess's attention were the three bullet holes in the center of the dead man's boiled shirt. There was little blood seeping through any of the holes. All three rounds must have struck the gent's heart. Jess figured a Morgan dollar would have covered two of the holes. Two dollars would have covered them all.

The light died, as water made the hay bale hiss, and Jess sighed and searched his pockets for a match, but he had used all of what he had. Boot steps sounded behind him, and then Lee Bodeen brought a match to life, lowering to his knees while holding out his left hand toward the dead man.

The watchman did not see the flame that reflected in his dead eyes.

"Little off in my shootin'," Bodeen said. "Need to get in some more practice." He laughed at his own sick joke.

The match died as the killer shook it out, and Jess rose.

"Horses are gone," Bodeen said. "One I rented is dead. That'll probably irritate that old sop who rented that nag to me."

Nag? That was as fine a horse as you'd find in any Fort Worth livery, Jess thought, but he kept those thoughts to himself.

"Guess the major and Miss Caroline will have to pay that damned Mick off." He began reloading his revolvers. "Mule taken off after your mount, I figure. I guess we got us a long walk back to town."

"We'll get a horse," Jess said as he walked back toward the smoldering hay bale and toward the street.

Dogs barked and lanterns and torches began to shine in the darkness, coming eerily toward the Union Stockyards. Jess could make out Irish brogues and Mexican whispers as the workers cautiously approached the street and the shipping pens.

"I'm the sheriff," Jess called out to the lights. "Jess Casey. Everything's all right here." He repeated that in Spanish, and let out a heavy sigh.

*Everything's all right here?* That was a bald-faced lie.

Thunder rolled, but only slightly closer now, and

the wind picked up, chilling Jess and his burned Mackinaw to the bone.

The dead man's name was Banan Bainbridge.

No one who came to the Union Stockyards that night could say why the watchman would have wanted to kill General Lincoln Everett Dalton. As far as they knew, Bainbridge hadn't fought in the War Between the States. Fact was, Bainbridge had likely just stepped off the boat from Ireland maybe ten years back. He had worked some in New York City before moving west. Wasn't married. Kept to himself. No one at the stockyards would have called him a friend, but he hadn't made many enemies. He drank a wee bit of Irish every day and more than a wee bit every night, though the liquor never seemed to hinder his work. On the other hand, what work did a watchman have to do at the stockyards? It wasn't like he was guarding a bank or express car on a train.

On the other hand, he often bragged that folks would be hearing about Banan Bainbridge one of these days, that this job would be only temporary, that he was going to be a big man.

Maybe that's why he had cut loose at General Dalton with the shotgun. He wanted to be a big name, and the man who killed the Butcher of Baxter Pass would likely be heard of across these United States.

Big man. Instead, he was a dead man lying in the back of an alley with three slugs in his heart.

Jess told the gatherers to leave the body where it

was and that he would send the undertaker to fetch the corpse tonight as soon as they got back to town.

A quiet Mexican in duck trousers pulled up over his nightshirt agreed to carry Jess and Bodeen back. Jess thought about asking the man to bring the body back, as well, since he had a rickety old buckboard, but he didn't want to push his luck. Banan Bainbridge wasn't going anywhere, and none of the men in the crowd looked like they'd rob a corpse.

No one spoke on the wagon ride south, until Jess found his horse grazing near the bridge across the Trinity River. He mounted it and rode along beside the wagon. They didn't spot the mule that had belonged to Bainbridge, but Jess figured it would show up sometime—unless someone stole it, which was highly possible this close to the acre.

They crossed the Trinity River to where Hell's Half Acre had sprung to its wild, lust-filled life. They stopped at the undertaker's place on Calhoun Street—Jess had to wake up the crotchety old goat and bribe him with two greenbacks—then cut down Fifth Street over to Main and worked their way back to the Trinity River Hotel.

After hitching his horse to the rail, Jess paid the kindly driver a silver dollar for his troubles and watched him head back toward the stockyards.

A tarp had been nailed up over the busted plate glass windows, and the newspaper reporters had given up on getting a story in time for the morning papers, had gotten as much information as they could, and had hurried back to their presses. Some had heard gunfire in the direction of the Union Stockyards, but none of them had the inclination or courage to head across the Trinity River at that time of night. News could wait till daylight.

Lee Bodeen had already disappeared inside the hotel—Jess figured he would wait until morning, if at all, to inform the livery stable owner what had happened to his horse. The major, however, was standing beside the door smoking a cigar.

"The general," Major Jedediah Clarke said after withdrawing the potent, long black cigar from his mouth, "will see you now, Sheriff."

As if Jess Casey had been waiting for an appointment all day with that damned old Butcher.

# CHAPTER TWENTY-THREE

*Tuesday, 12:45 a.m.*

"How many men do you reckon I've killed?"

Jess stood in front of the dresser, hat in his hand, staring at Brigadier General Lincoln Everett Dalton, who sat rocking in the chair that had been atop that old gaudy circus wagon parked out on Main Street in front of the Trinity River Hotel.

He thought: *Well, you didn't pull the trigger, but there are three dead men already with the undertaker waiting to get planted, and you haven't been in town a full day.*

The Butcher of Baxter Pass didn't look like he had when he had arrived. Gone were the flashy outfit and even the wig and makeup that made him look half alive. He wore a nightshirt that hung over his body like an ill-fitting shroud. The shirt was yellow cotton, which matched his jaundiced face.

Now he sat in the rocking chair, an unlit cigar in his mouth, the end soggy from his drooling. His hair—what was left of it—was stark white, the top of his pate bald unless you counted the liver spots, and his brow knotted tight against his waxy skin. Sideburns ran down to his chin, which was covered with beard stubble. White hair sprouted out of both nostrils, and his eyebrows were thicker than anything Jess had ever seen, combed upwards, it appeared, and slicked back with bear grease, maybe half an inch up toward the first crease in his forehead.

Just behind him sat his lovely daughter, Caroline, on the bed. She still wore the velvet outfit from the evening dinner, though now she looked much, much more tired. Jess couldn't see her eyes, yet he had to wonder if she had been crying.

Beside the armoire leaned Lee Bodeen, thumbs hooked in his gun belts, just standing there like the cock of the walk. Next to Jess, Major Clarke sat on a stool, poring over stacks of paper on a writing table, not making any noise and definitely not looking over at General Lincoln Dalton. Trying to keep a low profile, Jess figured, and he couldn't blame Clarke for that.

"Go on, boy. Guess."

His nose jutted out and down like a hawk's beak, and his eyes were gold, heartless, soulless—unlike his lovely daughter's stunningly beautiful gray eyes. The general's fingers were long, bony, and his hands seemed like the only part of his body that had retained any muscle. The rest looked like dying skin with the bones about to poke through.

Jess wished that the general would light that cigar,

because the hotel room smelled like death, and Jess knew he was looking at a dead man.

What was it that Caroline had told him? Carcinoma? The cancer? Eating away at what had once been a virile man. He didn't know what kind of cancer and didn't want to know. It was an ugly way to die, even for the Butcher of Baxter Pass.

"Well?" Dalton repeated.

Jess shrugged. "I don't know, General."

Dalton ripped the cigar out of his mouth. "That's another thing. I am no general, boy. My rank was major. Some fools in the War Department decided I should be brevetted a brigadier, and that's what they done. But the money the army paid me was what they paid any major. General? Balderdash."

Jess turned the hat around in his hands in a circle, fingering the brim.

"Two hundred men? That be your guess?"

"I don't know, Mr. Dalton." He figured that would pass muster, but it didn't.

"Don't *mister* me, boy. In my day, I could have whupped the tarnation out of you. With one hand tied behind my back."

"Father . . ." Caroline pleaded behind him. She started to rise from the bed, and now Jess could see that, yes, she had been crying—though he doubted if she would have let Bodeen or Clarke see her lose control. That's how strong she was. She just wasn't any match for her father.

Few women, and few men, could hold up against that old codger. Jess wasn't certain how long he could stand it.

Lincoln Dalton raised his right hand. "Hush, child.

This is between this Texas boy and me." Caroline settled back onto the bed and stared at Jess, those gray eyes apologizing for that cantankerous man in the rocking chair at the foot of the bed.

"Say two hundred, boy," the Butcher barked, as if he were ordering his guards back at Baxter Pass. "Say that you think I killed two hundred men."

"You said it," Jess said. He was growing tired of this game and had been pretty much since he had stepped into the room.

Jess was bone tired and sick of having this lot—with the exception of the general's daughter—in his town. Men were dead. Men were wounded. And instead of Marshal Kurt Koenig handling this, Jess had to. With no help from anyone in town, except another stove-up cowboy watching the jail.

"But I want you to say it," Dalton said.

"I'm a lawman," Jess said, choosing his words with caution and speaking them carefully. "I'm supposed to find out the facts. I didn't fight in the late war. I've never been to Ohio, never seen Baxter Pass. I've read articles, heard people talk, but I don't have any proof that you ever killed anyone. Lawmen are supposed to deal with proof, with facts. And I'm not paid to judge. That's for the courts to decide. Sir."

The man stared for the longest while, so long, in fact, that—as he did not blink—Jess Casey wondered if General—er, *Major*—Dalton had just died.

At last, the unlit cigar returned to the Butcher's mouth. Jess now realized that the old man had no teeth. He gummed the cigar. His wooden dentures sat on a plate by the washbasin.

"I reckon that's a fair answer, coming from a Texas Reb."

Jess considered correcting the old-timer, reminding the Butcher again that Jess had not fought in the war. Instead, he just stood there twisting his hat in his hands.

"He saved your life, Father," Caroline reminded him. "Twice."

"I know that, Daughter. I haven't lost all of my faculties."

Major Clarke muttered something under his breath, which the Butcher heard and changed the direction of his attack.

"The hotel, I imagine, will ask for us to pay for that window that fool shot out. Is that right, Clarke?"

A few papers slid across the desk as Major Jedediah Clarke whirled around on the stool. "Sir? General? Um . . ." He ran his hands through his hair and looked as if he were about to start sweating. "No . . . no one . . . it would be . . ."

Clarke's frightened eyes found Jess. "It would be up to the man with the shotgun to pay for damages, isn't that right, Sheriff?"

"Man's dead," Jess said, but this time he looked at Lee Bodeen. "Thanks to your Texas Ranger."

Bodeen no longer looked bored. He smiled a mirthless grin at Jess and nodded his head in appreciation.

"Well," Clarke said, stopping to wet his lips. "Still . . . be that as it may . . . it's . . . well . . . it's . . ."

The Butcher stopped him by raising his hand. "Don't worry yourself sick, Clarke. I can afford to pay for a plate glass window in a hotel like this. Or maybe I'll tell them I consider it a wash, considering the bedbugs that infest this wretched place. Go back to your financials, Clarke. Let us men discuss manly affairs."

Clarke sucked in a deep breath and looked as if he might even argue with the general, only to lose his resolve and return back to the writing table, gathering the papers.

"You'd think," Lincoln Dalton told Jess, "that a man with a double-barreled shotgun could have killed me. What kin of his did I put under?"

"None that we're aware of," Jess told him. "Right now, it looks like he was just trying to make a name for himself."

"Like Bob Ford when he sent Jesse James to Hades?" The bony head bobbed in satisfaction. "That's a good reason, I guess."

A brief respite of silence held for just a few seconds.

"I just want to know . . ." Dalton leaned forward, those cold eyes burning all the way through Jess. ". . . *Why*? Why'd a Texas boy like you save a damn Yankee like me?"

"I'm paid to keep the peace in Tarrant County. And I don't believe anyone has the right to commit murder."

The Butcher grinned his toothless grin. "Like how I committed murder all those years ago?"

Jess didn't answer.

"You know why I came back to Texas after all these years," Dalton said. "You likely think I figured a bullet would be an easier, less painful way to go to my maker than"—he tapped his chest with the soaked end of his cigar—"than rotting like I am."

At that, Caroline Dalton bowed her head, which the Butcher, his senses highly alert, must have realized. "Come on, Daughter. Remember you're a Dalton. Daltons don't cry. Don't grieve." The cigar returned, but only for a moment, as a sudden coughing fit sent the old man almost toppling out of the chair and catapulted the cigar toward Jess, landing and rolling to a stop just in front of his boots. Major Clarke started for the old man, as did Caroline, but the Butcher's right hand went up, stopping them both. Lee Bodeen, Jess noticed, did not move a muscle. The gunman just stood there, looking bored.

When Lincoln Dalton straightened a moment later, he turned and spit phlegm into the empty Folgers coffee can by his rocker that had been turned into a spittoon. After wiping his mouth with the sleeve of his nightshirt, he again looked up at Jess Casey.

"So how many men have I killed, Sheriff?"

"I don't know."

"You glad you've saved my life?"

"It's my job. My duty."

"You hate my guts?"

"I don't know you."

That's when Brevet Brigadier General Lincoln Everett Dalton slapped his thigh and cackled. The laugh—and even now the dying man's eyes— seemed full of life. He shook his head, turned to spit again, and rocked contentedly in the chair.

"I like you, Casey. You don't rile. You're good with a gun, but you aren't keen on using it." The rocker stopped, and the old man turned his head, glaring at Bodeen. "Unlike some rapscallions in this room."

Then, Dalton faced Casey again.

"They say I killed two hundred Texans at Baxter Pass."

Jess nodded. "That's what they say."

"Shot them down like the dirty rotten traitors to the flag that they were."

Jess twisted his hat.

"Two hundred men."

Jess waited.

"Nah." Dalton pulled out his cigar, studied it, frowned, and dropped it into the spittoon. His fingers moved toward his mouth, but stopped, and he laughed once more, this time briefly, and shook his head as his hands folded across his lap. "Reflex. Was going to pick the flakes of tobacco from my teeth. But my teeth is over yonder." His jaw tilted toward the dresser and the plate holding his dentures.

"I didn't kill two hundred men, Casey." He leaned forward and dropped his voice into a whisper. "It was twelve hundred and seventy-four."

# CHAPTER TWENTY-FOUR

*Tuesday, 1:05 a.m.*

That's when Lincoln Everett Dalton looked frail, regretful, even halfway human. His head dropped onto his bony chest, his hands clasped at his lap—not in prayer but as close as a butcher like Dalton could possibly come—and he repeated that number. Only this time the words did not come out in the creaking but forceful voice full of challenge and courage, but as a weak, dying whisper. He sounded remorseful.

"Twelve hundred and seventy-four."

The room fell silent again. Even Jedediah Clarke stopped with his papers and turned respectfully, staring at the Butcher of Baxter Pass. Everyone in the room looked at the old man, except Caroline, whose head had also bowed, only the dying man's daughter brought her hands up as if in prayer.

After a lengthy pause, Lincoln Dalton looked up. "Twelve hundred and seventy-four," he said again. "And that was before the two hundred shot down on the decks of the *Fancy Belpre* or swimming for the banks of the Ohio River."

Now Jess took an interest in what the Butcher was saying. He'd mentioned that steamboat, the one he had read about, had heard about. And, indeed, it sounded as if Brevet Brigadier General Lincoln Everett Dalton was admitting to what should have been considered a war crime.

"May thirtieth," Dalton said softly. "A day this nation should always remember."

May 30, 1865, when two hundred paroled prisoners had been shot down aboard a steamboat that was supposed to have been taking them home. Home. To Texas.

Jess waited.

"It's the others . . ." Dalton's head shook. "It's the twelve hundred and seventy-four . . . it's their deaths . . . that haunt me."

"Father," Caroline Dalton said, and now she left the bed, kneeling on the Butcher's right, and taking one of his long, bony but strong hands in her own. She brought it to her lips and kissed the hand that had killed so many. "You did all you could."

Anger fueled his voice. "I did *nothing*!"

He stared up at Jess, who thought he might be imagining the tears that welled in the Butcher's eyes.

"God has damned me," Dalton said. "He has cursed me. That's why I have the cancer. To rot. Like those twelve hundred and seventy-four."


Some died, eventually and slowly but surely, from the wounds they had sustained in battle. A few—no more than a dozen that could be confirmed, but no Yankee at Baxter Pass knew for certain—had been murdered in prison—by their fellow prisoners. Some of those, Lincoln Dalton said, were understandable. They were traitors, informing the Union guards of escape plans or where tunnels were being dug. Dalton did not regret those deaths. Traitors got what they deserved.

But others had been murdered for money or the brass buttons that could be used as money or the bone carvings—which reminded Jess of the hand-carved fob the late Gary Custer, manager of the opera house, had most likely carved at the prison camp in Salisbury. Or they had been murdered for a blanket, an ounce of cornmeal, a rat to be roasted for supper, or the wax of a candle many prisoners had to eat to survive.

Maybe a dozen more had been killed trying to escape. A few drowned, trying to swim across the Ohio and touch ground on Kentucky soil, then make their way back to Confederate lines. But far too many others had been shot by trigger-happy guards for the best men, the best soldiers, they were fighting to preserve the Union and/or free the slaves. Good soldiers were not sent to guard prison camps. Major Lincoln Everett Dalton commanded the dregs of society.

"He would have made a fine guard," Dalton said, and hooked a thumb back toward Lee Bodeen.

Most of the prisoners, however, died. Scurvy. Small-pox. Dysentery. Consumption. Influenza. Typhoid.

"They starved to death," Dalton said. "Because we could not feed them."

That had been the story in the South, at Andersonville, Cahaba, and Salisbury and those other horrible pestholes. Yet the South, even when the war was fresh, new, and long before the war was lost, could barely feed its own troops. Civilians left behind starved. Prison camps had little enough food for the guards.

It was an excuse Major Henry Wirz had tried during his military tribunal in Washington. A plea to escape the hangman's noose for all he had done, or not done, at Andersonville. The officers in charge had not bought it, and Wirz had hanged.

Wirz had been on the losing side, though. Lincoln Dalton's army had won.

"They don't talk about that when the Grand Army of the Republic reunites," Dalton said. "Or when generals and politicians remind us of the blood that has been shed to preserve our Union, to make us strong. Oh, they point to Andersonville, the slaughter of our colored troops at Battery Wagner and Fort Pillow. No one talks about Elmira . . . Rock Island . . . Camp Chase. We starved Southern soldiers to death, just as they did at Andersonville and other hellholes. But we did it because our people, our brave Northern people, did not care."

"You tried to get food, Father. Mother baked all day—"

"Which could have kept, what, Caroline, five, ten men from dying?"

"You wrote letters—you pleaded. Mother told me . . ."

"I did nothing." His head shook weakly. "Oh, sure. I wrote to the governor, to the mayor, to the good citizens of Cincinnati, Dayton, even into Kentucky. I begged for corn. Bacon. Anything. Nothing came." Suddenly, he laughed. "Except for those old ladies who sent me . . . me, not my men, not my prisoners—a box of lemon cookies. I brought them to the sergeant in charge of the prisoners, a burly man with a graying red beard, Brandt was his name, from Galveston. Gave him the cookies."

He paused. Jess waited. Thunder rolled again, closer now.

The old man sucked in a deep breath, then exhaled. Yet there were five or six more minutes before he resumed his tale.

"Sergeant Brandt was found dead the next morning. Murdered for lemon cookies by his own, God-loving men." The Butcher's head shook. "The sugar in the cookies gave his killers dysentery—that's how weak their bodies were—and I expect most of them died. That's what a fool I was. Trying to help the prisoners I was guarding, killing them instead."

"Father . . ." Caroline bowed her head, and now wept, unashamed. Even Major Clarke fished out a handkerchief and blew his nose. Only Lee Bodeen looked unmoved.

The thunder sounded closer, and Jess glanced toward the window, but the curtains were pulled down, the window shut to keep the night's chill out of the room.

Suddenly, Lincoln Dalton's hands clapped loudly, almost sending Clarke spilling from his chair, and lifting Caroline Dalton's head up in rigid shock.

"There you have it, Sheriff!" the Butcher sang out. "Confessions of an idiot. My deathbed statement, or should I say my death-rocking-chair confession. That good enough for you? Tell me, Sheriff. What do you think?"

Jess waited a moment before answering.

"People died in prison camps all across the country," Jess said. "North and South. No one blames you for that. Well, maybe some do. But not most of them. You didn't become the Butcher of Baxter Pass for what happened during the war, sir. It was May the thirtieth, after Lee, after just about every Confederate general had surrendered. And after your prisoners had taken the oath to the Union. They were paroled when they died, sir. The war was over."

With a weak smile, Lincoln Dalton shook his head. "The war is never over, Sheriff. It wasn't over when Lee called it quits. It wasn't over when the *Fancy Belpre* exploded and sank. It isn't over now, more than twenty years after the last battle."

"So," Jess said, "what happened that night? What happened to those two hundred Texans?"

Again, the old coot laughed and slapped his knee. "That's the question, isn't it, Sheriff? HA! Yeah, that's the one I've been asked for twenty-something years. The one I've never answered. Until now. Tomorrow. In my farewell performance, I will admit all, tell all. If my mind does not falter, as it often damn does." He looked at his daughter. "Isn't that right, Daughter?" Back to Jess. "Don't you feel lucky that I've chosen your fair city, Sheriff? Admit it. Don't you feel lucky?"

He waited, and Jess knew he wanted an answer.

"I wish," Jess said, "you'd picked Dallas."

This time, the old Butcher's eyes beamed with amusement, even though Jess had been dead serious with the statement.

"Bully for you, you Texas brush-popping badge-toter. Well, tomorrow, you'll learn the truth." He held up his hand, and snapped his finger. "Major Clarke!" Only now, he sounded just like the general, his voice firm, robust, and his eyes full of fire and vinegar. "Give Sheriff Casey a pass for tomorrow night's show. No, wait. Not tomorrow. By thunder, it's well past midnight. Tonight. Tonight's show."

Dalton looked at Clarke. "What time is my farewell performance, Major?"

"Five-thirty, sir. Right about sundown."

"Good show, Clarke. Yes, as the sun sets on Fort Worth, as the sun sets on my storied legend, I give my final performance." He turned quickly to face Jess Casey. "Free of charge, Sheriff. You'll be there, I know."

Jedediah Clarke busied himself searching through papers until he found whatever he needed, and he began writing on it.

Jess stared at the Butcher. "I have to be there, Major Dalton," he said. "It's my job. Remember? To protect the peace?"

"Good luck with that, boy," Dalton said with a crazed smile as Major Clarke handed Jess Casey a pass and he glanced at it:

**ADMIT ONE**
*J. Casey, Tarrant County Sheriff*
Front Row Seat, Back Stage Access.

***An Historic Evening***
***For All Ages:***
*The Final Lecture of the Butcher of Baxter Pass,*
**BRIGADIER GENERAL LINCOLN EVERETT DALTON**

5:30 P. M., Tuesday,
The 21st of January.
**Fort Worth Opera House,**
500 Throckmorton, Fort Worth, Texas.
☞ *Compliments of the General.*
[Signed]
*Jedediah Clarke, Major, Manager*

**God Preserve Our Glorious United States !**

It felt great to be outside again, breathing fresh, but cold, air. Jess sniffed the air, wondering if that might be rain—even snow—but couldn't get the stink of the Butcher of Baxter Pass's room out of his nostrils.

He pulled up the collar on his burned Mackinaw, which reminded him that he would need a new coat to get through this winter. He would also need a new shirt and a new bandana, but those he could fetch out of his war bag.

After finding his horse, he tightened the cinch and swung into the saddle. Sounds of laughter, of bad fiddle players, and out-of-tune pianos told him that

Hell's Half Acre was at its wildest worst, but he felt too tired to show his badge among the gamblers and prostitutes. Besides, this wasn't cattle-shipping season, so maybe it would be a quiet—by the Acre's standards—night.

He rode down Main, past a few of the more respectable saloons, and the morning newspaper offices that were busy printing today's papers, toward the courthouse, and half considered just riding right across the bridge of the Trinity River, past the Union Stockyards, all the way through the Indian Nations and into Kansas . . . Nebraska . . . maybe the Dakotas or Montana. Try cowboying again.

Instead, he left his horse at the livery on Belknap and walked back to the jail and his office.

The lights were off, but at least Hoot Newton hadn't locked him out. He opened the door, closed it, patted his pockets before remembering he had used all his matches earlier, and tried to make his way toward a lantern.

That's when he tripped over the body and landed flat on his face.

# CHAPTER TWENTY-FIVE

***Tuesday, 2:40 a.m.***

Jess rolled up and over, the Colt revolver practically leaping into his hand, covering the dark office.

"Hey!" a voice, muffled by the heavy door, called from the jail cells. "Is that you, Sheriff? Let me out of here! I don't like the dark!"

Jess backed up to the body and felt a massive bicep. That's all he needed and with a savage curse, he spun around, holding his free hand over the man's face. He felt the breath and let out a sigh of relief. Figuring whoever had coldcocked Hoot Newton would be long gone by now, Jess holstered the .44-40 and fumbled in the darkness until he found the lantern and a box of lucifers. Once the room was lit, he grimaced at the sight of Hoot Newton, lying faceup, with copious amounts of blood already congealing on the side of his head, his nose crooked and also darkened with old blood, and bruises already forming on his cheeks and throat. His knuckles were cut and chafed.

"Let me out of here!" the voice cried from the jail cell.

Jess Casey had a pretty good idea that he'd find one prisoner in the jail and that man would not be Burt McNamara.

"In a minute!" he yelled, and moved to the wreck pan, found a towel, and soaked it in the water.

The office was freezing cold. The fire in the pot-bellied stove had gone out, so Hoot had been lying there for quite a while. Jess heard a buggy outside, and he moved fast, stepping through the door onto the boardwalk and stopping the startled driver. He recognized Bob Winfield, a deacon with the Baptist church and owner of the ice cream parlor—probably coming from an evening of gambling in the Acre, which he thought to be a secret as he was well-respected, when in fact everyone in Tarrant County knew his fondness for the paste cards and whiskey, but no one said anything about it. Bob Winfield was a decent man, and his ice cream tasted fabulous.

"Bob," Casey called out. "I need you to ride over to Doc Wilson's. Tell her to come quick. Hoot Newton's been beaten up. Lying there. Half-dead."

"Hoot Newton?" The ice cream man looked perplexed. "Somebody beat up Hoot Newton?"

"Hurry, Bob. Tell her to come quick."

He returned to his office before Bob Winfield's whip cracked, and the horse took off down Belknap.

Inside, Jess knelt, and began wiping the blood off the big cowboy's face. With a slight groan, Newton flinched and turned his head away from the wet towel. Jess wasn't sure how clean the towel was, but it was all he had—and he had to do something. He kept at it, as gently as he could, ignoring Pete Doolin's protests from his jail cell.

Finally, Hoot's eyes fluttered, opened, and after a start, landed on Jess Casey.

"Sorry . . . Jess." He sighed heavily.

"Don't fret over it," Jess said, relieved that the big man had regained consciousness. "It was my fault."

"Jumped me . . ."

"The McNamara brothers?" Jess asked, though he knew the answer.

"Big one. Fellow you whipped." His eyes squinted. "How come you whupped him, and he whupped me?"

"I used a singletree on him," Jess reminded Hoot.

The cowhand smiled. "Yeah." His right hand gingerly moved toward the wicked cut and knot over his ear. "Think one of his brothers used something like that on me."

Rifle butt, Jess guessed.

"Jess?" Hoot asked.

"Yeah, Hoot?"

"How 'bout some whiskey?"

Jess rose, found the new bottle of rye, and opened the door to the jail cells, where he lit a lantern on the wall. Pete Doolin cursed and screamed and did not even thank Jess for ending the darkness that had turned his face ashen. The iron-barred door to Burt McNamara's empty cell remained open.

"Shut up, Doolin," Jess told the old-timer. "My deputy's lying on the floor, alive but hurt bad, and I'm in no mood. You savvy?"

The curses stopped, but Doolin pleaded, "But I wanted to help your big jailer, Sheriff. I told 'em cur dogs that if they'd let me out, I'd whup ever' one of 'em. I did. Swear on the Good Book. That's what I tol' 'em. And I ain't et no supper."

Jess glared and shut the door behind him.

"He's lyin', Jess," Hoot said after Jess returned to dab the towel on his battered head.

"About supper?" Jess grinned. "I knew that. He got some sausage and stuff that I brought in earlier."

"But he didn't get none of that cherry pie." Hoot grinned. "No, he begged them McNamara boys to let him out. One of 'em, can't recall which one, he said somethin' 'bout this bein' strictly family. That's 'bout all I recollect, though. Somebody then put my lights out."

Hoot sighed. "Guess those boys didn't ride home after I let'm have their guns back."

Jess went to his desk, and pulled open the bottom drawer. The McNamaras had taken Pete Doolin's old horse pistol with them. He wondered if they would go straight to the Trinity River Hotel and try to gun down the Butcher of Baxter Pass—and anyone, including Caroline Dalton, who got in their way. He knew he should head over there, right now, but he was not going to leave his friend here on the floor until Amanda Wilson showed up. Besides, Lee Bodeen was in the hotel, he got paid to protect Lincoln Dalton, and he had already proved to Jess how mighty handy the Texas Ranger could be with his six-shooters.

Doctor Amanda Wilson took the towel from Jess's hands and tossed it immediately into the wastebasket. She opened her satchel and began caring for

Hoot Newton, while Jess got the fire going again in the stove and decided to make fresh coffee.

"Concussion," she said as she worked. "How long ago did this happen?"

Jess waited for Hoot. "Ten I reckon. Ain't exactly sure."

Doc Wilson had already set Hoot's busted nose, and propped up both nostrils with cotton balls, so the big man sounded nasally when he spoke.

"He was unconscious when you found him?"

"That's right," Jess told her.

Her shoes, a rich cognac color with three-inch heels, had been laced up only halfway, and she had thrown on a cream-colored day dress, thin cotton, with mother-of-pearl buttons, though she had missed a couple of buttons. That was a dress for summer, but she had tossed on a gray and black-checked woolen cape, fastened at the top with a pewter clasp. When she had arrived, she had unfastened the cape and dropped it on the gun case. Her hair was a mess of tangles and bangs that went every which way but loose.

She looked like a total wreck. She looked like a million.

"I think this will require a few stitches," she said. Her eyes were rimmed red from a lack of sleep. "But I don't think the skull has been fractured."

He stood by the door, watching Amanda Wilson work on Hoot Newton, but listening to Fort Worth. At any moment, he expected to hear gunfire from the Trinity River Hotel.

\* \* \*

He looked pretty bad, with some plaster over his nose, cotton balls sticking out of his nostrils, and white strips of bandage wrapped around that big noggin of his. But Hoot Newton did manage a smile when Jess handed him a tin cup that held more rye whiskey than coffee.

He was sitting in the chair at Jess's desk, and Amanda Wilson handed him a bottle.

"This is for pain," she said, "and you will have a wicked headache for a few days. Two tablets as needed. No more than four times a day." When Hoot reached for the bottle she pulled it back. "And not to be chased down with whiskey."

She tossed the bottle to Jess, who caught it and placed it on the gun case.

"Don't let him sleep very long," she told him. "People with injuries like that have been known to fall into a coma. I don't think that'll happen. He's strong as an ox. But . . ." She accepted the coffee cup Jess slid toward her but shook her head when he held up the whiskey bottle.

After a sip, she studied Jess for a moment.

"You look exhausted," she told him.

He blew on his steaming cup, which he had not doctored with rye, either. "I am exhausted."

"You should get some sleep."

"After Dalton leaves Fort Worth."

He paid Doc Wilson three dollars and seventy cents. When she had gone, he dropped her cup in the wreck pan and pulled off his burned Mackinaw. It went into the trash basket on top of the dirty towel Amanda Wilson had thrown away in disgust. What was left of his bandana and shirt also went into the basket, and Jess found a relatively clean shirt in the cabinet underneath the gun case. The bandana he wouldn't miss, but the bib-front shirt had been new and had set him back a whole dollar and forty-five cents. A shirt like that, and at that price, Jess had expected to have lasted him till spring and then the following winter.

The old shirt he found was red and tan plaid with a rounded collar, no pockets, and he slipped it over his head and buttoned three buttons, leaving the one at the collar open. The bandana was blue and white stripes, which clashed with plaid, he had been told, but he didn't care about that. His vest would be at the room he rented, a tan duck coat trimmed with corduroy collar and cuffs hung on the rack, so he could use it for the time being. He pinned the badge on his shirtfront and finished his coffee.

"How's your head, Hoot?"

The big cuss lifted his tin cup. "Better now, Doc."

That made Jess grin. He wasn't worried about Hoot Newton slipping into a coma. He'd be fine, and the McNamara boys would pay for what they had done here this night.

The smile died instantly. Gunfire roared in the night.

Hoot Newton tried to stand, but must have dropped back into the seat after a spell of dizziness. He had turned pale, dropped his elbows onto the desktop, and lowered his aching head into his big hands.

"Stay here," Jess told him. But it seemed obvious that Hoot Newton was not going anywhere right now.

Moving quickly, Jess didn't have time to pull on the coat, but he grabbed a Colt shotgun and checked

the breech, and then stepped onto the boardwalk.
More gunfire barked in the night. This wasn't some
drunken cowhand shooting at the clock at the courthouse. Jess almost felt relieved. Those shots weren't
coming from the direction of the Trinity River Hotel,
either.

Jess ran down the boardwalk toward Hell's Half
Acre.

# CHAPTER TWENTY-SIX

*Tuesday, 4:25 a.m.*

It was a long damned run.

More than a dozen blocks to the Third Ward. Jess was glad no cowboy he had ridden with had witnessed him, a cowboy, running instead of riding, but by the time he could have fetched and saddled his horse at the livery . . . well.

This was why the Scott brothers had moved what was now called AddRan Male & Female College out of Fort Worth. The college had been just a couple of blocks over, between Calhoun and Jones streets, until the professors and parents of the college kids decided that being butted against the worst red-light district in Texas, or maybe the West, was not conducive to higher education.

Jess found himself in the middle of Hell's Half Acre, directed by one pockmarked hurdy-gurdy girl and a staggering drunk in a stovepipe hat to a bucket of blood known as Gabe's Place.

Gabe Pryor didn't own the place anymore. He had

lost it to Luke Short back in '77, and Luke had sold it to a gambler named Pacific Knight in '79, and Pacific Knight had been shot dead while bucking the tiger in '82, and Jim Hanson had bought it at the courthouse for back taxes the following year. Jim Hanson had then gone under with a knife in his belly in '85, and maybe one or two others had owned the place since Hanson's demise. Nobody had ever bothered to change the sign out front, though.

With the shotgun pointed straight ahead, Jess Casey walked into the combination saloon and gambling parlor.

"Drop it," he said.

The shotgun in his hands was an 1883 Colt, a hammerless twelve-gauge with its Damascus barrels sawed down to eighteen inches. The checkered hard-rubber buttplate pressed against Jess's stomach, and his fingers lay gently on the twin triggers. A shotgun like that, in the hands of a lawman, usually held persuasive powers.

The man standing over a table, holding one of those fancy European pinfire revolvers in his right hand, glanced at Jess and the badge. He did not lower the double-action revolver with a lanyard ring affixed to the walnut butt. But he did not threaten Jess with it, either.

He wore the same black broadcloth coat and the fancy gold vest that he had been wearing when he had stepped off the stagecoach yesterday. Jess remembered him, and now he remembered that he still had the tinhorn gambler's Remington derringer in his back pocket. He suddenly felt the .41's weight.

Lantern light reflected in Luke Flint's shaded

spectacles. Gamblers often wore shades, even in dark saloons in the dead of night. They didn't want anyone reading their eyes.

Slowly Jess moved through the doorway toward the center of the saloon, keeping the double-barrel trained on the gambler at the table. He kept his legs wide apart, ready.

"No cause for that, Sheriff," Luke Flint said in an ugly drawl. He still did not lower the revolver. "Tell'm," the gambler barked to a girl, who stood in her flimsy attire against the bar, a shot glass trembling in her left hand, her face white, her right hand covering her mouth.

Jess listened to the girl, but he did not take the Colt shotgun's aim off Luke Flint's belly.

"It happened so fast," the girl at the bar said. So did the bartender. And two other gents, a graybeard local who made his rounds through the Acre's poker tables and a cowboy Jess did not know, supported her testimony.

Five men had remained at the poker table in a game that had started at Gabe's Place around five-thirty that afternoon. The game was five-card stud. The cowboy folded after the first bet. The graybeard lasted until his straight had been busted on the fourth card. That left Luke Flint and the two dead men, one crumpled over the table, the other lying in a pool of blood against the wall. The man on the table had been called Joe. The one on the floor was Herb Blackwell, the latest owner of Gabe's Place to meet an unfortunate, untimely end.

Raise followed bets, and then came a series of raises before Blackwell folded. The man named Joe called Luke Flint, and when Flint turned over his hole card to reveal he had a full house—treys over deuces—beating Joe's ace-high flush, Joe called him a cheater and jerked a Colt Lightning from his belly.

The Lightning is a .38-caliber double-action with a two-and-a-half-inch barrel. Luke Flint grabbed Joe's right arm with his left hand, and the revolver went off—six times in fact—every bullet slamming into poor old Herb Blackwell, who fell dead on the table. Then Luke Flint slammed the man's gun hand on the edge of the table, dropping the Colt to the floor. Simultaneously, Luke Flint broke the whiskey bottle that the dying Herb Blackwell had knocked over and rammed the jagged edge into Joe's throat. He shoved Joe away, and Joe likely bled out before he had slid to the floor.

"Self-defense," Luke Flint told Jess Casey.

Jess kept the shotgun on the gambler. He remembered what he had told the cardsharp when he had stepped off the stagecoach from Dallas.

*Gamblers are welcome in Hell's Half Acre. As long as they don't deal from the bottom.*

"Maybe," Jess said, and tilted his head—though never taking his eyes or shotgun off the gambler—toward the bar. "But what about him?"

*Him* was a burly man with balding red hair, a railroad worker by his striped denim britches, cap, and bulging biceps, who lay in front of the bar, facedown, three bullet holes in his back. His right hand still clutched a billy club.

"Now I didn't kill him, Sheriff," Luke Flint said.

Which made sense, in a way. The man appeared to have been coming from the bar toward the poker table. The bullets were in his back, and Luke Flint would have been facing him.

The voice behind Jess Casey said, "I shot him, Sheriff."

Jess didn't turn around, though. He kept the shotgun on Luke Flint.

"And you are?"

"Ira Flint. Luke's big brother."

Jess nodded. "Bullet holes are in his back, Ira."

"He was goin' after Luke. Didn't have no choice. Self-defense. Or maybe to protect my dear kid brother."

"He was a long way from your brother, Ira." Thirty feet, by Jess's estimate. "And your brother was armed—in violation of the city ordinance."

"I'm armed, too, Sheriff," Ira Flint said. "In violation of the city ordinance."

"Then I guess I'll have to take you both in."

The girl with the shot glass and the shaking body recovered long enough to walk around the bar and drop behind it. The graybeard and the cowboy moved into the corner of the building, as far from Luke Flint, the poker table, and two of the three dead men as possible. Batwing doors made a racket as other patrons of Gabe's Place left the saloon for fresh air. The bartender joined the shaking hurdy-gurdy girl on the floor but not before taking the two good bottles of actual single-malt Scotch with him.

"No, Sheriff," Ira Flint said. "Here's the way this morning will play out. Luke'll collect the money owed him. We'll borrow a couple of horses out front.

Leave your fair city. But first . . ." Now came the click of a revolver being cocked. ". . . first, you'll drop that scattergun."

Jess wasn't sure if it would work. The Colt twelve-gauge was hammerless but set ready to fire, so he tossed the shotgun, hoping it would hit at the right angle and discharge one or both barrels. With added luck, if the angle was just right, the blast might tear off Luke Flint's head. Then all Jess would have to worry about was Ira Flint, and the shock of the gun going off—and seeing his kid brother's head torn apart—would give Jess the advantage. And if the shotgun just went off and didn't kill Luke Flint, both men would still be stunned by the blast, and Jess could gun them both down.

Of course, it didn't work. The shotgun landed on the stock, flipped up, fell on its side, and slid underneath an abandoned faro layout. It did not discharge.

"Good," Ira Flint said, and now Luke Flint was moving, filling a carpetbag with the assortment of gold, silver, greenbacks, watches, and other plunder into the open satchel. He had laid the big pinfire revolver on the table.

"The Colt, Sheriff," Ira Flint reminded him. "Let's not leave that revolver of yours too close. Toss it beside the shotgun."

Jess started for the pistol, slowly, but now he felt the barrel of Ira Flint's revolver against his spine.

"Just to be safe. Use your left hand, Sheriff. And just thumb and forefinger, if you please."

Jess brought his right hand back and crossed his midsection with his left hand. Luke was watching him now, the carpetbag on the table next to Herb Blackwell's dead head. He had not picked up the big revolver, though. He just stood there, watching, enjoying himself.

Jess slowly drew the .44-40 from his holster and dropped it by the spittoon next to his boot. It was a lot harder than it looked, pulling a Colt out of a holster with only a thumb and forefinger.

"Kick it toward the shotgun, Sheriff," Ira Flint said.

Jess obeyed.

"That's fine." Jess felt the pressure removed, heard Ira Flint take a few steps back, then swing a wide arc around the sheriff.

Ira Flint was uglier than his kid brother. They were of the same build, with the same greasy hair, only Ira did not dress as flashy as Luke. He wore Wellington boots, plaid britches, a tan bib-front shirt, and moth-eaten black woolen vest. His hat was a Stetson Boss of the Plains. The gun was a single-action 1873 Colt, and the hammer remained cocked.

"Hurry up, Luke," Ira instructed his brother.

Luke let out a little sigh and gave Ira a wry smile. He backed up a bit, telling the man with the .45-caliber Colt, "Just going to the bar. For support. It's been a long day."

When he reached the bar, he leaned against it and sucked in a deep breath.

Ira Flint laughed. Luke Flint moved to other abandoned card tables, collecting coins and currency.

"Texas ain't been friendly to us," Luke said. He

even dropped a corked bottle of whiskey in the carpetbag.

"Then let's head back to Kansas," Ira Flint told him.

"There better be good horses outside," Luke said.

"Don't worry," Ira said. "The sheriff won't be comin' after us."

Jess smiled. He had reason to. While the brothers were bantering, he'd moved his right hand to his back pocket and fingered out the little derringer—ironically, Luke Flint's over-and-under Remington.

Which he brought up and put the first bullet right between Ira Flint's eyes.

The uglier and older of the Flint boys spun around in a complete circle, sending his long-barreled Colt skidding across the floor. He stood there for a moment, blood leaking from the purple hole just above his nose, eyes open but no longer seeing, mouth open, and surprise chiseled into his face until Judgment Day. This took only a few seconds, even though to Jess Casey it seemed as if it lasted for hours. Time had stood still until the dead Ira Flint collapsed in a heap.

Even before the killer had dropped to the saloon's sawdust-covered floor, Jess had dropped to a knee, turning his attention to the other killer. He brought the little hideaway gun up and only half-aimed as he sent the derringer's second and final bullet toward Luke Flint. Even before he pulled the trigger, Jess understood that it would have taken a scratch shot to hit the younger gambler. A Remington .41 was meant for targets across a card table, not across a darkened saloon against another man with a bigger, better, deadlier pistol in his hand.

Yet that little piece of lead from the derringer had done its job, which was all Jess could have hoped for.

The shock of his brother's unexpected death and the firing of a bullet toward his own head startled Luke Flint, who had swept up the pinfire revolver in his hand but jerked at Jess's second shot. Yelping, Luke Flint dived to his left, knocking over the neighboring card table.

Jess was moving himself. He thought about going for his shotgun, or his Colt revolver nearby, but changed his angle and went for the single-action .45 that the late Ira Flint had dropped. It was closer to him and a bit farther away from Luke Flint.

The skid over the floor tore at Jess's flannel shirt. Deftly, he snatched up the Colt .45 and rolled over, just as two bullets from Luke Flint's double-action pistol dug up chunks of wood and sent sawdust flying.

Jess rolled again, firing once and seeing the wall behind the overturned table splinter.

The circular table rolled back and forth, just a bit. Jess thought about shooting through the green felt cloth and wood but didn't want to waste a shot.

Outside, dogs barked throughout the Acre, and somewhere a rooster crowed.

Jess rushed for a potbellied stove in the center of the floor. Hearing the movements, Luke Flint came up over the top of the table and fired again, the bullet whining off the cast-iron stove. Jess found his knees, faked to his left, and then moved to his right, squeezing the trigger just a second after Luke Flint had dived back behind the table for cover.

Now Jess sprang to his feet and charged, cutting loose with a third shot before diving toward the bar. Luke Flint fired, too, and that shot punched a hole in the left side of Jess's red-and-tan shirt. It burned his skin, too. Jess grimaced, came up, cocking the revolver, but holding his fire.

Flint had lost his nerve—not to mention his brother—but not his instincts. He made for the bat-wing doors, carrying the carpetbag full of his winnings and plunder, including at least one bottle of whiskey, pulling the trigger as he ran.

Jess sat up as Flint's bullet smashed into the spittoon next to Jess, sending its foul contents up and out to splash on the brim and crown of Jess's hat and the shirt he had just put on.

Jess let loose with a vile curse and thumbed back the Colt's hammer. If he had counted right—and ciphering had never been his strongest subject back when he went to the subscription school—Luke Flint had only one bullet left in his revolver.

Unless it held more than six bullets. You could never tell about those foreign weapons.

And, naturally, it only took one bullet to send you to Boot Hill.

Luke Flint had a clear shot as he reached the doors. He just never got the chance to squeeze the trigger.

Jess's shot caught him square in the chest and sent the carpetbag falling by a bowler hat somebody had lost while leaving Gabe's Place in a hurry and sent Luke Flint flying through the batwing doors.

# CHAPTER TWENTY-SEVEN

*Tuesday, 4:55 a.m.*

"It's the damnedest thing, Sheriff," Morris Stokes was telling Jess. "I've been doing this job for seventeen years now here in Fort Worth. Thirty-five years altogether in the business. And this is the damnedest thing. In all my time here in Fort Worth, folks rarely die on Monday. Tuesdays were the slow day back in Nacogdoches, and they're a tad slow here in Fort Worth, but not compared to Mondays. Why I can count on one hand how much business I've had on a Monday in seventeen years here. They just don't die on Monday. Not in Fort Worth. Not from natural causes, accidents, *or* gunshots. The damnedest thing. They just don't croak here on Mondays, so I've often considered not even opening for business. But here . . . this day . . . I've got . . ." He had to count, and use two hands. "Eight cadavers. Eight! It's the damnedest thing, Sheriff. Eight men needing my embalming and burial services. On a Monday."

"It's Tuesday," Jess reminded the undertaker.

\* \* \*

He collected written statements from the hurdy-gurdy girl, the bartender, and the few men brave enough to wait outside Gabe's Place and see who came out alive. He half-expected county solicitor Mort Thompson or Mayor Harry Stout to wander over and stick their heads into this mess, but it was far too early—or late—for those two fiends to make their way this deep into Hell's Half Acre. He told Morris Stokes to send his bill to Kurt Koenig when the marshal got back from Huntsville, and once the bodies had been hauled out of the saloon, he blew out the lights, took the key that had been removed from the late Hank Blackwell's vest pocket, and locked the door. Then he used the butt of the late Ira Flint's Colt .45 as a hammer and nailed a crudely painted sign—the hurdy-gurdy girl had done it with some whitewash they found in the storeroom, though Jess had to tell her how to spell most of the words— over the front door and just below the sign that had read Gabe's Place for too many years.

### CLOSED TILL
### NEW OWNER
### CAN BEE FOUND

She had spelled *BE* with one too many E's, mis-understanding Jess's dictation, but Jess figured that the sign would do the job well enough. It was legible anyway.

He had the carpetbag full of money and miscellaneous items, which he would have to sort through and document before turning it over to the county officials, or Kurt Koenig if the marshal decided to come back to Fort Worth, and a sack full of weapons—a derringer, a Colt .45, a fancy pinfire revolver with one round in the chamber, the dead gambler's Colt Lightning, and a Colt rimfire .22 that had been found in Herb Blackwell's boot—that would likely be auctioned off.

It was quite the load, especially since Jess still had the Colt hammerless shotgun, and nobody volunteered to help. In fact, by the time Jess had finished everything, undertaker Stokes had already hauled the five dead men back to his office to be prepared for burial, and even the bartender and the hurdy-gurdy girl were gone.

Only a couple of banjos still played in a saloon, and most of the other joints Jess passed were sparsely populated, a drunk or two at the bar, a gambler in sleeve garters playing solitaire, and bored bartenders wiping down their mugs and shot glasses.

The church bells over at St. Stanislaus sounded six times when Jess pushed open the door to the jail's office.

Hoot Newton slept in Jess's chair, his spurred boots resting on Jess's desk. He dropped the sack of weapons on the floor, returned the shotgun to the gun case, and shoved the carpetbag into the cabinet below the gun case, thinking it would be safe there. His hat wound up on his desk, and he pulled off his shirt and replaced it with his Sunday-go-to-meeting shirt, a laundered French percale, ivory with pink hairline stripes. He was pinning on the fancy gold badge when Hoot Newton woke up.

Jess planned on waking him anyway as soon as he had the sleeves buttoned, not wanting to risk his jailer slipping into a coma.

The big cowboy's boots dragged off the desktop and landed with a thud on the floor. Hoot touched his bandaged head with a grimace, then saw Jess's hat.

"That hat's covered with tobaccy juice," Hoot told him.

"And other things," Jess said.

"About time for breakfast, ain't it?"

"That's where I'm going."

"Hotcakes would be nice. The ones with the pecans in 'em. With syrup. Maple syrup. From Vermont. And some bacon."

"Where do you want the bacon to hail from?" Jess asked.

Hoot grinned. "Hell, Jess. You ain't that dumb. From a pig, of course."

He had no spare hat. So he went out into the graying morning without one.

Workers were preparing the mule-drawn streetcars, and city employees were turning off the streetlamps as Jess walked to Main Street and headed up the street. The cafés had begun preparing for the first rush, and Jess could smell ham and eggs, but mostly coffee. A number of eateries would have been closer to pick up a meal for a jailer with a concussion and a prisoner with a bullet in his thigh and a dreadful fear of the dark, but Jess kept walking. The air cleared his head.

He stopped at Second Street and looked at the sky. It remained dark, of course, and most of the stars could no longer be seen, but he made out enough. He took in a deep breath and let it out. No rain. Whatever winter thunderstorm had been threatening last night had gone another way.

It remained cold, and Jess told himself that he should have pulled on the coat back at the jail. But he didn't feel cold. He just walked.

He entered the Trinity River Hotel through the lobby door. A few early risers were staring at the tarp that covered the blown-out plate glass window, china cups of coffee in their hands. They shut up when Jess entered.

After a quick look upstairs, he moved to the dining room and found his way to the counter. It remained too early for most occupants in the upstairs rooms. The only ones dining—and they were mostly drinking coffee or tea or wolfing down biscuits and gravy— were those who had to catch an early train east or west. None paid much attention as Jess leaned against the bar before lifting his tired, weary body onto a stool.

"What'll it be, Sheriff?" the counterman said when he finally decided he had read enough of the *Gazette* and made his way to the end of the counter. He did have the decency, however, to pour aromatic, freshly brewed coffee into a cup and place that in front of Jess.

"Two plates," Jess told him. "Bacon and hotcakes. To take to the jail."

"You want syrup?"

"Yeah."

"Vermont? It'll cost a little extra."

"I don't give a damn. The syrup can come from a pig as far as I care."

The man stared, considered Jess, and then retreated for the kitchen. Jess picked up the coffee, hoping good coffee might improve his mood. It didn't.

"Aren't you grouchy this morning," a pleasant voice came to his left, and Jess turned.

His mood improved. Caroline Dalton was standing next to him.

She wore a green and gray blazer-style suit, with a full-sweep skirt lined with taffeta and bound with velvet. Pinned into her well-groomed hair sat a hat of braids and chiffon ribbon, with a pleated satin edge, highlighted with a large rosette. Jess guessed that she had stayed up all night after he had left, just getting fixed up.

Caroline Dalton took his breath away, especially when she smiled.

"Tough night?"

He shrugged. "I've had better evenings."

She came closer to him, and he caught the scent of lilac and perfumed soaps. "My father can be a handful."

"It wasn't your father," he said.

"Oh."

Now came that awkward silence, Jess holding his cup, wondering what to say, fearing that his beard must look as if he were coming off a six-day drunk and without a hat to cover his mangled hair. He wondered if any of that slop from the spittoon at Gabe's Place had splashed on his cheeks, or hair, or neck, or pants. He wanted to chcck, but just couldn't take his eyes off the stunning woman standing before him.

She broke the silence.

"Would you care to have breakfast with me?" she asked.

# CHAPTER TWENTY-EIGHT

*Tuesday, 6:15 a.m.*

They had a selection of tables, so Jess led Caroline Dalton to the remote one near a corner window. The fellow who had taken Jess's order for Hoot Newton and the prisoner came out, frowned, and made his way to take their orders. Jess told him he'd just stick with coffee and for him to bring the plates to the jail whenever they were ready, and Caroline asked for some hot tea and a couple of biscuits.

"I reckon neither one of us has much of an appetite," Jess told her when the surly waiter left.

"I guess so."

The quietness was broken up only by the sound of another early morning diner stirring sugar or cream into a coffee cup.

Jess glanced out the window to find one of the newspaper waifs getting ready to start hawking to businessmen heading to work. At least what had happened at Gabe's Place would not be in the headlines until the afternoon newspapers came out. Reporters had likely heard about the shootings, though, and they'd be searching all over town to find Jess Casey.

"You make good copy, Jess," one inkslinger had told him a few months back.

They would be staked out in front of the jail, though, and he frowned, because Hoot Newton would likely tell them about the escape of Burt McNamara last night, and the afternoon papers might have that bit of news, too.

The waiter returned with Caroline's tea, topped off Jess's coffee, then left without speaking. Well, there wasn't going to be much of a tip on a couple of biscuits, coffee, and tea. He settled back behind the counter and picked up the newspaper.

"My father," Caroline said after a long while. She had not even sipped the steaming tea in front of her. Her eyes left the checkered tablecloth and found Jess. "He was at his best last night?"

Best? Jess nodded, although he didn't understand the statement. Best at what? Being a doddering old fool or a veritable curmudgeon, maybe.

"His memory," Caroline said. "It isn't just the cancer that's killing him. His mind is going. His memories. There are times when he can't remember what he ate for breakfast."

"I have that same problem," Jess told her, and he smiled, hoping she might return one. She did, but he could tell it was forced.

"He could remember a lot," she said. "Last night. That's rare these days. Sometimes, he's good, but other times . . ." Her voice trailed off.

Jess tasted the coffee. Something struck him, and

he asked, "When's the last time your father gave one of his lectures?"

The Texas newspapers used to report those items a lot, usually under headlines like THE BUTCHER'S LATEST LIES or MURDERING YANKEE SPEAKS AGAIN, reports sent by other newspapers or telegraphed by the Western Associated Press. Yet Jess couldn't remember seeing one of those items in any newspaper for . . . for how long?

"It's been five years . . . not quite five. The Fourth of July in Wheeling, West Virginia. He said then that this was to be his farewell address, but nobody really believed him. He'd said that at Columbus and Louisville and Cleveland and Indianapolis. That time he meant it, though. He came home. His memory got worse. Then the doctors said he had the carcinoma. And then he woke up one morning, memory clear, his body seemingly stronger than ever, and said he had to make one final speech."

She paused to sip her tea and allow a Mexican girl to place the two biscuits on the table. *"¿De salsa?"*

Caroline glanced at Jess. "She wants to know if you want gravy."

"Oh." She shook her head.

*"No gracias,"* Jess told the woman, who nodded and left.

Caroline looked up with a smile. "I do not understand how you people put that white soup on your biscuits. It's disgusting."

"But filling," Jess told her, and her smile widened.

She found a fork, cut off a piece of biscuit, and ate some. Jess had never seen a person eat a dry biscuit with a fork. She even dabbed her mouth with the napkin before she continued, after another sip of tea.

"That's when he told me he wanted to give his final speech in Texas." She shook her head. "I never knew he'd ever settled in Texas, but he showed me his diary and some of Mother's letters. All these years, giving talks and lectures and appearing at parades and carnivals and circus acts, he'd never gotten farther south than the border states. Only in St. Louis in Missouri, never western Missouri or south toward Springfield."

"Confederate strongholds," Jess said.

"Even today," Caroline added.

Jess had to nod his agreement.

"Kentucky . . . Maryland . . . that's about it. I told him it would be suicide, and he told me he was . . ." Her head dropped. Jess searched his pockets for a handkerchief but had nothing but the bandana, and he didn't think it appropriate to hand her that. It didn't matter. She found one and dabbed her eyes. ". . . that he . . . was dead anyway."

"So," Jess said, "he bought the circus wagon and . . ."

"Oh, no. We've had that for years. I told you that Mother played the calliope and taught me how to play it. We just had to fix it up some, grease the axles, freshen up the paint, and get rid of the mouse nests."

She ate some more biscuits. Jess drank some more coffee.

"Where is home?" Jess asked.

"Terre Haute," she said. "Western part of Indiana. It was far enough away from Baxter Pass."

"Long way to Texas," he said.

"We stopped. Sometimes he'd arrange for lectures, though often I'd have to fill in for him, when he'd just sit in his rocking chair and drool. They'd ask me what it was like to be the daughter of a butcher—and this is in Union states."

"You'd answer that?" Jess set his coffee cup down.

"I'd tell them that he was a good father to me." She smiled. "Then they'd ask me to play the calliope. That always lightens the mood."

He drank coffee and listened as she kept on talking, telling him of their journey to Texas. Terre Haute to Seymour to Cincinnati. Charleston to Frankfort to Louisville. Hogdenville to Memphis, General Dalton's first appearance in a Southern state. Little Rock to Texarkana to Dallas. And now Fort Worth.

"They wouldn't let us a room in Little Rock. We slept in a wagon yard in Texarkana, arriving at dark, leaving at dark. They threw tomatoes at us in Dallas. Mr. Custer was the only person who would agree to let us rent his theater."

"But you got Governor Ross's agreement. That took some doing."

She drew in a deep breath. "That letter, Jess," she said, "is a forgery. Major Clarke—I don't believe he ever served in any army, let alone the Union—spent two years in Michigan City." She gave Jess a knowing look.

Jess didn't know anything about Michigan City.

"That's where the Indiana State Prison is now," she said.

He nodded.

"And I take it that Lee Bodeen is not a Texas Ranger," Jess said.

She wet her lips. "He met us in Texarkana. Major Clarke hired him."

She finished the biscuits, let the waiter refill the cup with more tea—he didn't ask Jess if he wanted any more coffee—and then said, "You can run us out of town now, Jess. With a clear conscience."

His head shook. "You have a legitimate contract to perform this evening at the Opera House," he said. "I'm paid to uphold the law. You and your father are legal."

"And Bodeen?"

He finished his coffee. "I'll deal with Bodeen and the major later."

Maybe now. Jess leaned back in his chair. Just entering the dining room were Bodeen, Major Clarke, and the Butcher of Baxter Pass himself, Brevet Brigadier General Lincoln Everett Dalton, who was being pushed in a wheelchair by Clarke.

The Butcher was yelling in his ugliest voice, turning Caroline Dalton's eyes cold as she looked toward him, whispering. "This morning, he didn't remember Baxter Pass at all. He didn't even know . . . who . . . I was."

"What are we doing here? I don't want any damned breakfast. I already ate breakfast. Get me out of here!"

"You haven't had breakfast, General," Jedediah Clarke said, as if speaking to a toddler or a dog. "Since Dallas."

A few patrons tossed coins on their tables and

hurriedly left for work, or the depot, or anyplace far, far from the Trinity River Hotel.

Once Clarke had wheeled the Butcher to the table closest to Jess and Caroline, he faced the man at the counter with the newspaper, bellowing: "Three cups of coffee. Immediately, sir. Don't keep General Dalton waiting."

The man turned another page in the newspaper. He did not look up.

"Bacon and eggs," Bodeen said. "Fried. Three of them. Now."

That prompted the man to fold his newspaper and disappear into the kitchen. By the time he had returned, the restaurant was empty except for two tables, and Jess wanted to leave now. But the damned waiter hadn't brought out the plates for Hoot Newton and Pete Doolin.

"Damnation," General Dalton whined. "I think I've wet my britches."

He wasn't the same man Jess had seen the previous evening. His arms trembled, and his eyes appeared vacant, almost dead. He was dressed in a nightshirt, and Jess could tell that indeed, the old-timer had lost control of his bladder. If he had not been such a lout last night, and if he had not possibly murdered two hundred paroled Texans, Jess Casey might have felt sorry for him.

"You look plumb tuckered out, Sheriff," Lee Bodeen said. His chair scraped the floor, purposefully, making Jess's and Caroline's skin crawl. "Rough night?"

"I've had worse," Jess told him, and added, "*Ranger*." He even looked over at Clarke, who settled into a chair across from the Butcher. "Good morning, *Major.*"

He stressed their titles, hoping they would understand that he knew their little secrets. Clarke's reaction reaffirmed everything Caroline Dalton had told him. The gunman with the Ranger badge showed nothing on his face.

Dalton turned to face his daughter and Jess.

"Who the hell are you?"

He was looking at Caroline, but Jess came to her rescue. He could not bear to see her break down again, not here. Not in front of these men.

"Sheriff Jess Casey, General Dalton," he said. "Are you ready for your lecture tonight, sir?"

"What the blazes is he talking about?" He turned back to the men at his table. "Who the hell are you? What am I doing here?"

He was still firing out insults and questions and nonsensical statements when the waiter returned. He put two covered plates on the table in front of Jess and dropped a bill. He walked back to the kitchen, taking his newspaper with him, and Jess had to smile at the man's spunk. Clarke, Dalton, and Bodeen would be waiting a long time before they got served in this hotel.

They didn't notice. General Clarke probably never would. Jess turned his attention to the window. The streets and boardwalks were crowding up, and he excused himself and went to the window, drawing the shade.

"Cautious man," Bodeen told Clarke.

"I don't mind a cautious man," the major said. "I don't fancy getting killed in this Southern pesthole."

"You can always go back to Indiana," Bodeen told him.

"No," Clarke said. "I can't."

A man came out from the kitchen and walked directly toward the only patrons in the place. He wore black shoes, black pants, and a white tie with a black string tie around the collar. A fancy towel hid his hands. Bodeen gave him no more than a moment's glance. The general and the major did not even consider him, but Jess did.

He stood up, told Caroline that he had to be leaving, and walked away. Jess didn't bother picking up the plates the other waiter had left on the table. Nor did he leave any money for the check. He was moving toward the man, on instinct, and reached him just as the man's hands appeared as the towel fell to the floor.

He held a revolver.

# CHAPTER TWENTY-NINE

*Tuesday, 7:25 a.m.*

The 1875 Schofield .45 trembled in two small hands, and the man struggled to pull back the hammer to full cock. That was the trouble with those old thumb-busters. Someone had sawed this model's barrel down to maybe three inches.

Jess Casey didn't want to kill the man. In less than a full day, he had seen enough dead men, but he knew he had to react quickly and prevent the waiter from murdering General Dalton—and even faster to keep Lee Bodeen from carving another notch on his revolver. With his right hand gripping the butt of his holstered Colt, Jess brought his left hand down on the Schofield just as the frightened would-be assassin pulled the trigger.

The hammer smashed into Jess's hand, ripping into the flesh just below his pinky finger and tearing out a chunk a little less than the size of a dime. It hurt like hell, sent blood spurting, but it stopped the firing pin from striking the bullet, and at least it missed the bone in Jess's hand.

As the Schofield fell to the floor, dropped by the waiter in a moment of panic, Jess brought his own pistol out of the holster and slammed the barrel onto the man's black hair. Stunned, but still conscious, the man fell at Jess's feet, and Jess was turning, thumbing back the hammer on his .44-40, and lining the front sight up with Lee Bodeen's belly.

"Holster it," Jess ordered.

Bodeen's right-hand pistol had scarcely cleared leather. For a split second, his eyes burned with hatred, and Jess thought the gunman might even make a play—even though he had no chance—but then the man let the pistol slip back into that hog-greased holster, and he moved his hand to hook the thumb by the belt buckle. Lee Bodeen even grinned. "You're fast, Casey."

"I'm alive," Casey told him.

Something flashed again in the killer's eyes, and Bodeen sang out, "Look out!" He stepped to his right and palmed the revolver.

It could have been the oldest trick in the book, but Jess sensed danger himself. Besides, Major Clarke was spilling out of his chair, pulling his arms over his head as he dived for the floor, and Caroline Dalton screamed something and leaped, tackling her father and sending them both sliding across the dining room floor.

Whirling while dropping to a knee, Jess saw another figure in the doorway to the kitchen. So big, Jess couldn't even see that door, but he had a clear view of the shotgun the man held.

The double barrels belched flame and smoke, obscuring the man's face, and Jess felt a rush of buckshot sail over his head and heard panes of glass in the corner window shatter. The gunman had dropped the old percussion pistol and had grabbed some hogleg that had been tucked in his waistband.

Jess couldn't tell who fired first . . . the gunman, himself, or Lee Bodeen. He knew who fired the next three rounds, though, because Lee Bodeen was walking as he pulled the trigger, and the gunman was leaning against the wall beside the door, pain etched into his face as Bodeen's bullets struck him in the chest.

A second later, the big brute crashed behind the counter.

"Paul Bunyan?" Lee Bodeen joked. "Or Goliath?"

"Big Dan McNamara," Jess told him.

They stood at the corner of the counter, staring at the dead man whose right hand still clutched the old dragoon revolver he had purloined when he and his brothers had busted Burt out of jail. Jess didn't know where the shotgun came from.

"Biggest man I've ever seen. Took four of my slugs and one of yours to drop him. What's his story?"

Jess had holstered his gun after peering into the kitchen to find only the cooks and other workers kneeling on the floor with their hands clasped behind their heads. The rear door to the alley remained open. If the other brothers had been involved in this murder attempt, they had fled quickly. Jess began to remove his bandana and tie it across his bleeding left hand.

"His father was killed at Baxter Pass," Jess told Bodeen and Major Clarke, who had pulled himself off the floor and walked feebly to the counter. Jess saw Caroline helping her father into the wheelchair, which she had already righted. The first of the gunmen, the waiter, remained on the floor, though he had managed to pull himself into a seated position and was holding his head in both hands.

"This is Texas," Major Clarke said, his voice shaky and his face pale. "I suppose there are many more men in Texas whose fathers were killed at that prison camp."

"There are at least three more in town," Jess told him. His head tilted toward the late Big Dan McNamara. "His brothers."


Usually dour-faced undertaker Morris Stokes could not contain his glee that Tuesday was shaping up to be as crackerjack of a day as Monday had been, even though he had to pay for extra help to haul Big Dan McNamara to the horse-drawn hearse parked next to the Dalton circus wagon on Main Street.

The clerk at the desk had ordered two other desk clerks to nail up a tarp to cover the latest window blasted apart with a shotgun, and he had the audacity to ask Jess Casey to do something about all those onlookers standing outside on the boardwalk, pointing, gawking, and gossiping.

"It's a city matter," Jess told him. "Ask Kurt Koenig to take care of it. I'm county. Remember?"

Even as Doctor Amanda Wilson burned his hand with whatever medicine she had kept in a little rectangular bottle and then went to bandaging it, Jess did his job as a lawman, trying to piece together what—and how—everything had happened.

Bodeen and Major Clarke took General Dalton back upstairs to his room, the crazy old loon crying out that he had not gotten to eat his supper one moment, and the next saying something about what cowards these Pennsylvanians were for running him out of Danville on a rail. Caroline Dalton sat at the table across from Jess while Doc Wilson, sitting in a chair, finished working on the bloody left hand.

"That's going to leave a scar," Amanda Wilson told Jess.

"It won't be my first."

The waiter that Jess had coldcocked sat at the next table, still holding the head that Doc Wilson had examined and pronounced that he would live.

So, the way Jess's investigation had sorted everything out, three McNamara brothers had come into the kitchen through the back door after one of the workers had hauled out the morning's trash. They made everyone drop to their knees and put their hands behind their heads. That included the surly man who had been working the counter. Jess had thought that that fellow had just been showing the Dalton crew who was the boss in the Trinity River Hotel's dining room.

"They told us that if we made any sound at all, they'd shoot every last one of us," one of the dishwashers had said.

And knowing the McNamara brothers, Jess figured, that had not been a bluff.

Burt McNamara had sent out Emilio Garcia first; he had a wife and eight children, never missed Mass at St. Stanislaus, and had never owned a revolver or even fired one. That record, thanks to Jess Casey's sore, soon-to-be-scarred left hand, remained intact. McNamara had given Garcia the cut-down Schofield and told him to walk up to the old man in the wheelchair and put a bullet in the back of his head. If he did not do it, Burt McNamara had threatened, he would have no wife to love; and as soon as they had killed her, they would go to the Garcia home and kill Garcia's children and Garcia's mother-in-law, who lived with the family in a shack across the Trinity River near the Union Stockyards. Emilio Garcia's wife, Maria, washed dishes and was a chambermaid for the upstairs rooms. Jess made a note that he would not eat at the Trinity River Hotel anymore if they had chambermaids washing dishes.

Emilio Garcia said that once he had killed the old man in the wheelchair, he planned on killing himself—even though it was the worst sin a man could commit—if Sheriff Casey and the other men sitting with the old man had not ended Emilio Garcia's memory. He apologized profusely to Caroline Dalton.

"You had no choice, señor," she told him, and relief washed over Emilio Garcia's face as he thanked the kind dark-haired woman a good dozen times, while making the sign of the cross repeatedly.

Jess told Emilio Garcia to go home, to take his

wife home, to spend the rest of the day with his family and mother-in-law.

*"¿Y cuándo vas a llevarme a la horca?"* Emilio Garcia asked.

Amanda Wilson released Jess's bandaged left hand. Jess looked at the poor Mexican and shook his head. "You're free to go, Señor Garcia. You won't be hanged. You're not going to the gallows." He repeated that in the best Spanish he could muster and grimaced when the poor man sprang out of his chair, fell to his knees, and began kissing Jess's soon-to-be-scarred left hand.

Tears streaming down his face, Emilio Garcia got to his feet, and, making the sign of the cross while continuing to bless Jess, he hurried to the kitchen to fetch his wife and run home.

Amanda Wilson said, her voice flat, without any emotion. "I believe our solicitor, Mort Thompson, decides who goes free and who faces charges, Sheriff."

"That coyot' isn't here," Jess said. Which surprised him. Usually, the Tarrant County prosecutor and Mayor Harry Stout would be hovering over Jess like turkey buzzards. He looked at the crowded entryway to the restaurant, but saw only the assortment of men with morbid curiosity.

The gent who had been working at the counter—his name was William McCutcheon, according to the statement he had given Jess—got up to let the people waiting to eat breakfast know that the dining room would not be open today. Some of them likely had no appetite anyway for food and were just wanting to see where the latest killings had happened. When they didn't leave quickly enough, McCutcheon cursed them, and that cleared out the lobby.

McCutcheon came back, picked up the cup of coffee that he had poured for himself, and told Jess, "We're about out of windows on the ground floor, Sheriff. When are our guests leaving town?"

"First thing tomorrow," Caroline Dalton said, her voice stern.

"If y'all live that long." He left through the kitchen door.

"I did not mean to bring all this to you, Jess," Caroline Dalton. "I did not mean to bring this to your city."

Jess was about to tell her that he knew that, but Doc Wilson leaned over and said, "What the hell did you expect?"

What was that saying? *Hell hath no fury . . . ?*

Snapping her black satchel shut, Doc Wilson leaned closer toward Caroline Dalton. "Your father butchered two hundred men . . . and I don't know how many others he killed at Baxter Pass before the war was over."

Twelve hundred and seventy-four, thought Jess.

Caroline Dalton stood. "I thought," she said, "that nigh twenty-five years later, you might think that the war is over." She took a step toward the lobby, stopped, turned, and said, her voice still stern. "Shouldn't the war be over?"

And with that, Caroline Dalton was gone, leaving Jess in an empty dining room that still smelled of burnt gunpowder and drying blood, alone with Amanda Wilson.

A moment later, Jess was alone. Doc Wilson stood, mumbled something about what Jess could take if his hand got to hurting something awful, and then she walked straight into the empty lobby and out the front door. Jess figured he could watch her storm down the boardwalk, and bowl over anyone in her way, but the corner window was covered with a canvas tarp, and the front desk clerk had ordered that the shutters be closed on all other windows.

# CHAPTER THIRTY

*Tuesday, 11:25 a.m.*

"Damn, Jess," Hoot Newton said when the door to the jail opened. "That shore took ya long enough."

Jess handed the big cowboy both plates, telling him to give one to Pete Doolin unless Pete Doolin had escaped from jail, too.

"Nah," Hoot said. "He ain't gone nowheres." He stopped, thinking. "I don't think so nohow . . ."

Picking up the second plate, Jess told Hoot that he would deliver the food to the prisoner himself. By the time Jess was settling into the chair behind his desk, Hoot Newton was dropping the plate in the wreck pan. Turning, the cowhand stopped, stared, and finally pointed.

"What happened to yer hand?"

"Cut it."

"You shore ain't talkative this morn, Jess," Hoot said.

No. Jess had talked himself out that morning,

after he had finished asking all those questions about the McNamara brothers and Emilio Garcia.

Once he had stepped out of the Trinity River Hotel and onto the boardwalk, it had taken Jess practically an hour to walk from the hotel back to the jail. Every newspaperman in town had wanted to hear the story, so Jess had told them. These boys would be kind to Emilio Garcia, especially after Jess had lied that the waiter had fired the pistol shot that missed General Dalton, in a brave attempt to fool the cowards hiding in the kitchen, and that Big Dan McNamara's shotgun blast had been meant for Emilio Garcia. That's what wounded Jess's hand; he had lied. One of the buckshot had plucked at his hand.

And that, Jess had figured, might also keep Mort Thompson from ruining some other poor man's life.

Jess had learned a few things himself from the newspapermen, though. Mort Thompson wasn't in town. He had taken last night's train to Dallas, although no one knew why. Mayor Stout had gone with the solicitor.

"Maybe Dallas'll keep the both of 'em!" one of the editors had joked. That had gotten a round of applause from a few of the other scribblers.

Not having Stout and Thompson around could make Jess's day a bit easier. They would stay out of his hair, and Jess would have his hands full just trying to keep Lincoln Everett Dalton alive until 5:30 p.m. Besides, Jess knew why those two elected officials had left town. Whatever happened today, they would be able say they, having been in Dallas on important matters (like cards or cribs or charging Dallas restaurant prices to the taxpayers), were not responsible. And without City Marshal Kurt Koenig around, any and all blame would be pasted on Jess Casey's back like an oversized bull's-eye target.

"Why don't you run those Yanks out of town?" one reporter had asked Jess.

"They have a legal contract to perform," he had answered. "And a legal right to be wherever they please. They have broken no laws that I am aware of."

He had realized that mistake and figured it would cost him when he ran for sheriff. If he ran for sheriff. Cowboying looked pretty good right about now.

"On the contrary, Sheriff Casey," the oldest of the reporters had said, "I do believe the murder of two hundred Texas soldiers is against the laws of Texas and the laws of God."

"You'd be right," Jess had told him, "except that twenty-five years ago he was not charged with any crime and has not been charged with murder or anything—as far as I know—over the past quarter of a century." Then he had let the newspapermen finish writing down that quote, though he wondered how much of it would be accurate in the next editions.

Finally, hearing no more questions shoveled in his face, Jess Casey had finished: "The war's over."

"The hell you say," someone had said. A few reporters had laughed, but Jess and most of the journalists had known that the man who had spoken had not been joking.

*Well*, Jess now thought, *this will all be over come tomorrow.*

Every bone in his body ached, his muscles refused to unclench, and his eyes burned from the lack of sleep. On top of all that, his chewed-up left hand began throbbing, and he couldn't remember what Doc Wilson had told him to do about the pain.

That's when Jess saw the yellow telegraph paper on the desktop.

"That come fer you," Hoot told him.

Jess picked it up, saw that it came from Dallas Constable Paul Parkin and read no further. He looked at the coffeepot on the stove, decided against drinking that, and, after a weary sigh, asked Hoot Newton, "How's the head?"

"Hurts." The cowhand sank into the chair and touched the bandage Doc Wilson had put on him. "You wouldn't happen to have no whiskey on you, eh, Jess?"

Jess was about to answer when the door opened and a cowhand, sweeping his hat off his head, stepped into the office and closed the door behind him.

"Uh . . . Sheriff . . ." he drawled.

"Howdy, Eustace!" Hoot called out.

The cowhand shot a surprised look at Newton, nodded a greeting in return, and looked back at Jess.

Jess remembered this man. He had been playing poker last night at Gabe's Place when Luke Flint had killed the late owner of the saloon and the man who had accused Flint of cheating.

"Eustace," Jess said. "What can I do for you?"

Jess figured the cowboy was legitimate. After all, Hoot Newton knew him and had not immediately challenged him to a fight. Besides, what kind of trouble could a man named Eustace cause?

"Well, Sheriff, it's this way, you see. All my money was on that poker table last night. I was a-wonderin' if . . . well . . . I ain't et in a while, and I gots me a powerful thirst, and . . . well . . . ain't it possible for me to get some of that cash back? After all, that Flint, the one you shot deader'n a dog, he was a-cheatin'."

There hadn't been any proof that Flint had been cheating, though Jess knew the sharper had been. And there was this little fact that Eustace, from all accounts—including Eustace's own—had folded his hand. So without substantiated proof that Flint had been dealing off the bottom of the deck, the poor, broke cowhand really had no claim to the money.

And then there were those technicalities Mayor Harry Stout and Solicitor Mort Thompson were so fond of pointing out.

"Eustace," Jess said with a sigh, "I can't turn over any money to you without an order from a judge. And then there would be other claims to money in the pot. It wasn't just your table that Flint stuffed in his grip."

Eustace's face turned sour.

Jess cursed himself for being a softhearted fool and pulled out his billfold. He handed the cowboy three greenbacks and a Morgan silver coin.

"I'm good fer it," Eustace said, stuffing the money into a mule-ear pocket on his pants.

"I know that." Jess knew no such thing. Even Hoot Newton seemed skeptical.

The hat returned to the cowboy's head, and his left hand found the doorknob. The door opened, Eustace started outside, but stopped, turned, his face all apologetic again.

"You wouldn't happen to have no whiskey on you, would you?" Eustace asked.

"Coffee's all we have, Eustace," Jess told him, and, frowning, Eustace stepped onto the boardwalk, closed the door, and headed for his horse to ride to the nearest saloon.

"No whiskey?" Hoot Newton said.

Jess shook his head.

"But my head hurts."

"What about those pain pills Doc Wilson gave you?"

"Ate 'em for breakfast."

"All of them?"

"They was tiny. Ain't like they was beefsteaks or brisket from that joint you go to oftentimes."

"Sorry, Hoot. And that was the last of my money I gave to Eustace. I'll be on tick till payday."

"Don't your hand hurt, Jess?"

"It does."

"Well, whiskey'll make it feel a mite better. 'Specially if it's rye. Like Old Overholt."

"I'll keep that in mind."

From the jail, Pete Doolin was yelling about

something to drink, so Hoot filled a cup and took it through the heavy door, leaving Jess alone.

He thought of the McNamara brothers. One of them had taken a shot at him in the Fort Worth Opera House. He was sure of that. He remembered Hoot telling him about what one of the brothers had said before leaving the jail with Burt. Something that did not add up.

Tom McNamara had said, "Tell the law we'll be goin' home."

And Neils had added: "As soon as we pay a Yankee-lovin' cur dog opery house owner a visit and deliver him a reminder 'bout folks he shouldn't be bookin'."

One of those boys had taken a shot at Jess in the darkened hallway of the opera house, likely thinking that Jess was Gary Custer.

"But," Jess said, testing his theory aloud. "If they had run Custer through with that sword, why would they come back?"

"You talkin' to yerself?" Hoot Newton asked, closing the door to the cells and heading to the wreck pan to deposit Pete Doolin's plate.

"Wash those two plates, Hoot, and take them back to the Trinity River Hotel," he said.

"You say something, Jess?"

"No. I'm talking to myself."

"Whiskey'll fix that."

It might at that. Jess remembered the satchel he had placed in the cabinet beneath the gun case. He slid over to the case, opened the door, and pulled the bag out, which he then set on the desk. Damn, but it was heavy. He had to wonder how he had managed to lug it back from way down in Hell's Half Acre with everything else he had been hauling.

He pulled out the bottle he had picked up and set it on the desk.

"It's bourbon," he told Hoot. "Not rye. Not Old Overholt."

"Don't matter none to me." Hoot found two glasses, relatively clean, and sat across the desk as Jess filled one for Hoot and poured about a finger in his own.

He coughed as the liquor burned like coal oil on the way down and ignited his stomach. Hoot Newton sucked his down as if it were water. With a groan, Jess turned the bottle around and read the label. It did say Pure Kentucky Bourbon, but Jess knew it was forty-rod, likely seasoned with snakeheads and tobacco juice, that had been refilled into an empty bourbon bottle.

"That all?" Newton smacked his lips.

"I need you sober today, Hoot," Jess told him, and corked the bottle.

"That's a hell of a thing for you to tell me, Jess."

But he didn't argue. He even washed the two plates and said he would take them to the hotel. Jess wondered if Hoot would return, before his thoughts turned to the McNamara brothers and Gary Custer.

Not that the brothers had been the ones to have killed the theater manager. Jess figured there were probably twenty thousand or more folks in town who would have done the job. But how many would use a sword—er, rapier—to kill a man? Gun. Knife.

Two-by-four. Sledgehammer. Fists. Those were more in line for murderers in Fort Worth.

He glanced at the telegram lying facedown on the desk again and reluctantly picked it up and read. The more he read, the closer he leaned, and the longer he held his breath.

# CHAPTER THIRTY-ONE

*Tuesday, Noon*

DID SOME CHECKING ON YOUR BOY
FLINT STOP HE WAS IN DALLAS TWO
DAYS STOP PLAYED POKER AT THE
BANKERS SALOON STOP LOST BIG
TO GARY CUSTER STOP CUSTER
IS A FORT WORTH BOY RIGHT STOP
CUSTER TOOK TRAIN BACK TO YOUR
DULL TOWN STOP FLINT TOOK STAGE
STOP PARKIN CONSTABLE DALLAS

"Well, I'll be a suck-egged mule." Jess leaned back in his chair, still holding the telegram, and checking the time that it had arrived this morning. Not only had the Dallas constable done some actual work, Paul Parkin had even helped out someone in Fort Worth.

"Maybe the war is over," Jess said aloud. "Maybe both wars can be over."

The Fort Worth–Dallas feud. And the Civil War/War Between the States/War of the Rebellion/War for the Southern Confederacy/War to Preserve the Union and/or Free the Slaves/War of Northern Aggression.

A thought struck him, and he again opened the grip setting atop the desk. At first, he rifled through the cash, coins, and other items with his hands, but then gave up and simply dumped the bag's contents onto the desktop. He shoved aside the watches and greenbacks and looked through the silver dollars, golden eagles, and half-eagles, and then he whistled and picked up what he had hoped to find.

A hand-carved bone fob. You could not mistake the Federal eagle icon, and Jess wondered if the *National Police Gazette* might write about him and his investigative prowess. He even found a diamond stickpin.

Not that he could ever prove it officially, not unless he found an eyewitness who saw Luke Flint, or maybe his brother, sneaking into the Fort Worth Opera House, or maybe one of the poker players might remember Luke Flint betting the fob, stickpin, or the watch he had taken off Gary Custer's body. He glanced at the pocket watches, wondering if perhaps someone might identify Gary Custer's out of the three he had collected.

Luke Flint had been an idiot. Betting plunder he had taken off the man he, or his brother, had murdered—in the same town where Gary Custer had lived.

Not that it really mattered, but it made sense. Everything fit. The McNamara boys had not run

Gary Custer through with the rapier. It had been Luke or, possibly, Ira Flint.

He deposited the fob into an envelope, which he stuck in his top desk drawer. Next, he swept the contents back into the satchel, quickly, before someone came into the office and jumped to the conclusion that he was stealing from what he had confiscated at Gabe's Place. He did not, however, return the bottle of rotgut to the satchel, but slipped it back into the cabinet under the gun case.

He drank coffee, mostly to remove the awful taste of the whiskey that had burned his mouth and throat and done no telling what kind of damage to his innards. In a moment of charity, or maybe something completely the opposite, he brought the rotgut into the cells and let a grateful Pete Doolin take the bottle.

"When you're done," he told his prisoner, "toss it through the window out back. And don't let Hoot Newton have any."

"That'd never happen, Sheriff," Doolin said.

As Jess headed back to the office, the prisoner called out happily, "Appreciate it."

*Not after you drink that,* Jess thought before closing the door.

When Hoot Newton returned, Jess pulled on his coat, grabbed his hat and a Winchester repeater, and told his new deputy that he would likely spend the rest of the day at the Trinity River Hotel.

"When will you come back?" Hoot asked.

Jess pushed three more cartridges into the Winchester, thinking, *The question should be "Will I come back?"* "After the show this evening," he answered.

"What show?" Hoot asked.

"Doesn't matter."

His hand was on the doorknob when Hoot whined, "Yeah, but what am me and Pete s'posed to do fer our dinner? And supper?"

Jess looked at the big lug. "You just ate . . ." Yet he leaned the Winchester against the wall and returned to the grip in the cabinet, pulled out one of the gold pieces, thinking of it as a loan, if he remembered to pay it back, and went back to the rifle.

"I'll send over some dinner right now and have supper delivered to you and the prisoner, too."

With a beaming look, Hoot Newton nodded and settled into Jess's chair.

Closing the door and pulling up the collar to fight the sinking temperature, Jess moved down the road, headed for the Trinity River Hotel.

He stopped at a Chinese restaurant and bought cheap dinners for Hoot and the prisoner, although Jess figured he splurged by adding a pitcher of hot tea for the two boys, and also tipped the owner of the place for agreeing to send two specials of something that sounded like fried rice and some noodle dish with beef to the jail around suppertime. He did not splurge on tea for supper, though.

When he reached Main Street, he jumped aboard the mule-drawn trolley and settled onto a seat with a drummer and a lady in a green dress. Jess settled into the seat right behind the driver.

"Cold, ain't it," said the driver, an old man bundled up in a Mackinaw and woolen blanket.

Jess agreed.

"Gettin' colder, too," the driver said.

This time, Jess only nodded. He had taken the streetcar because his feet ached. Jess didn't know if he would ever get used to all the walking a sheriff had to do in Fort Worth. He was a cowboy. In his day, you would ride across the street from the saloon to the next saloon, rather than walk. Yet in a town with more than twenty thousand people, Jess found it getting harder and harder to find room at a hitching rail to tether his horse.

He studied the rooftops, the brick and stone buildings, and the wooden façades. Good places to put a man with a Winchester. Jess would have to consider every rooftop when General Dalton decided to make his way to the opera house for his final public appearance.

Jess was trying to figure out the most likely place an assassin would hide when he heard the rifle shot.

The old driver yelled out a curse while pulling hard on the lines to stop the mule. The woman in the green dress screamed—no, that was the drummer, who leaped over the back railing and bolted toward the courthouse.

"Get down!" Jess had wasted his breath. Both the woman and the driver had ducked as Jess stepped out of the trolley, levering a .44-40 shell into the Winchester, as he moved cautiously beside the mule.

Another shot boomed, and Jess heard the smashing of glass. He spotted shards of glass falling like rain from the third floor of the Trinity River Hotel. Across the street, standing on the boardwalk in front of the Cattleman's Bank, a kid—he could not be out of his teens—butted the rifle on the pine planks and struggled to cock his Winchester. A bottle of redeye, uncorked and only a quarter full, sat on the edge of the water trough in front of the kid.

The boy was dressed in worn-out brogans, duck trousers, a muslin shirt, and a floppy hat. He had curly blond hair. Probably fresh from the cotton fields. Utterly harmless.

Except for the Winchester that he brought to his shoulder again, aimed, and fired. Another window smashed on the third floor of the hotel.

Down along both sides of the street, people huddled behind wooden columns, barrels, troughs, corners of buildings, or in the doorways of businesses. Jess glanced at the hotel, the tarps over the windows flapping in the wind. A curtain moved from the second floor on the opposite end from where the kid was shooting.

That would be General Dalton's room. Jess figured the man who had moved the curtain would be Lee Bodeen.

Sighing, Jess stepped away from the mule and walked down the center of the street. He had to work fast. Before Bodeen decided to take action.

"Ya low-down Yankee dawg!" the kid shouted, slurring his words. "C'mon an' show yer yeller face. Afore I sends ya to yer maker!"

Again, the boy struggled to work the lever. This time he needed to fortify himself with another pull from the bottle. After slaking his thirst, he jacked the lever—and saw Jess Casey standing in the street.

"What ya wants?" the kid asked.

"You're shooting at the wrong room," Jess said,

and tilted his head toward the hotel. "The Butcher of Baxter Pass isn't in that room."

The kid seemed to have trouble understanding the words. He swayed, and it took the column near the trough to keep him upright.

"He's not even staying on that floor," Jess said.

Wetting his lips, the boy shot a quick glance at the third-floor window he had pockmarked with rifle shots. His eyes struggled to focus on Jess.

"Why don't you put the rifle away, son," Jess said. "Before you hurt yourself. Or some paying customer in the hotel."

Jess wondered if the hotel had any customers after all that had happened over the past two days. He expected everyone had checked out for safer places—except for the Butcher, Major Clarke, Lee Bodeen, and Caroline Dalton.

The wind picked up. It practically blew the kid into the water trough, but he managed to keep his feet. He nodded at the circus wagon still parked out front.

"He's got that cannon."

"Gatling gun," Jess corrected.

"If he wasn't no low-down blue-belly dawg, he'd come out an' . . . an' . . . I'd gives him a chance. His cannon . . . ag'in my ri-rifle."

"But he's a low-down Yankee dog," Jess said. He chanced a step toward the boy, who didn't seem to notice, so he took a few more steps. He kept walking, slowly, cautiously, never taking his eyes off the kid and never letting his smile fade.

The rifle came up. Only now it aimed at Jess's stomach, only twenty feet away.

Jess stopped.

"Ya stop right thar, mistah." He was sweating. Even from twenty feet away, Jess could smell the sour stink of whiskey sweat—despite the cold.

"I have stopped." Jess widened his grin. "My name's Casey. Jess Casey."

He waited. The kid didn't introduce himself.

"Now," Jess said, "I told you my name." Cowboy etiquette didn't allow you to ask a person's name, or where he hailed from. You told him your name and expected him to do the same, but if he didn't, well, you didn't push matters.

"He's a low-down Yankee dawg," the boy slurred. "And I's a mind to kills him."

"But he's not in the room you've been shooting at," Jess said, and watched the words register. By now, at least, if anyone were staying in that room, he or she would have been able to crawl to the hallway.

If, Jess understood, he or she weren't already dead.

"Son . . ." Jess began, but then he knew. He read the boy's eyes.

Turning and diving to his left, Jess felt the warming blast as the bullet tore through the air. Even before he hit the ground, he saw Lee Bodeen stepping from the main entrance of the hotel, big Centennial rifle in his hands. Jess's rifle was cocked, and he squeezed the trigger. That's all he could do. The Winchester's barrel Jess held had been pointed, more or less, in the general direction of the hotel. He had no chance of hitting Lee Bodeen—didn't even want to—but the shot might jolt the gunman with the Texas Ranger badge.

It did. Lee spun, half-thinking another farm boy with a rifle might be shooting.

By then, Jess was on the ground, rolling over the dirt and mud-covered paved street, letting go of the Winchester and coming up to his knees with the Colt revolver in his right hand.

He came up to find himself staring down the barrel of the boy's own big rifle.

# CHAPTER THIRTY-TWO

*Tuesday, 12:40 p.m.*

Jess had no choice. He pulled the trigger.

The Colt bucked in his hand, and the boy screamed, dropping the rifle and grabbing his thigh as he fell into the water trough just as another bullet splintered the column behind the boy. The Winchester bounced off the street, and Jess sprang to his feet, leveling the .44-40 toward the Trinity River Hotel.

"It's over, Bodeen!" he shouted.

Bodeen had a rifle. Holding a revolver, Jess knew he lacked the advantage at this distance, and if Bodeen decided to shoot, they would likely be burying Jess Casey tomorrow morning. But Caroline Dalton stepped out of the hotel behind Bodeen, and she sported one of her own pistols that was conveniently aimed at Lee Bodeen's back.

The gunman felt her presence, and her pistol, and butted the rifle on the boardwalk in front of the hotel. He grinned.

"Like I said, Sheriff," Bodeen called out. "You're

fast." He turned, tipped his hat at Caroline Dalton, and stepped back inside the hotel, but not before he paused, turned, and yelled back. "But, Casey . . . you're also soft."

The farm kid Casey had shot emerged from the freezing water, shivering, pale, and cussing Jess Casey. That brought a warm smile to Casey's face as he walked to the trough, picked up the boy's rifle, and, after holstering his Colt, extended his hand to pull the boy out of the horse trough.

"Do I send you the bill?" Amanda Wilson asked when she closed the door to the cells and dropped her satchel on Jess's desk.

"Give it to the mayor." Jess filled two cups with steaming black coffee. He handed one to Doc Wilson, and sat on the side of the desk. "How is he?"

"He should live," she said. "Unless he catches pneumonia."

Jess had put a tourniquet over the boy's leg and made the trolley driver haul his prisoner back to the jail. The jail, Jess figured, might be a safer place for the farm kid. Now, the local citizens might want to give that boy a medal, but Lee Bodeen and maybe even Jedediah Clarke might be inclined to some form of lethal punishment. So might the owner of the Trinity River Hotel, who was going to be paying a lot of money to replace various windows in his establishment.

Doc Wilson had jumped aboard the trolley as the mule headed down the street and was already at work on the latest wounded prisoner before the wagon had turned at the courthouse.

"He could use a couple of blankets," Doc Wilson said, and sipped some coffee.

"Hoot," Jess said.

Hoot Newton stood in the corner, finishing his plate of food the Chinese kid had brought a few minutes earlier. He licked his fingers and picked up the cup of tea, frowning at the taste. "Uh-huh," he said.

"Bring the prisoner a couple of blankets. And let him have the tea. It'll do him some good."

"Sure, Jess. I'd rather have coffee anyhow."

"You'd rather have rye," Jess said, but the big cowboy didn't hear him. Hoot, moving spry with a full belly, had picked up a couple of blankets and was already heading toward the jail cells with his hands full.

"How many more men must be killed by the Butcher?" Amanda Wilson said without trying to conceal her animosity.

Jess set his cup on the desk. "Well, Dalton hasn't killed anyone in Fort Worth since he arrived." She turned, ready to bark back, although Jess had kept his tone pleasant enough, but Jess jerked his thumb toward the open door to the cells. "That boy in there's lucky he didn't kill anyone himself. You know how Mort Thompson is. He'd have that kid lined up for a necktie party. And I couldn't do anything to stop that had the kid shot anyone."

She started to say something, but Hoot Newton was back, empty-handed. Amanda Wilson bit her tongue and drank more coffee.

"Did he tell you his name?" Jess asked.

She shook her head.

"Have you seen that boy before?" he asked Hoot.

"What boy?"

Jess motioned toward the cells.

"Pete Doolin?" the big lug asked.

"No," Jess said, rolling his eyes. "The kid."

"Oh. No, Jess. Ain't never laid eyes on him till you brung him in."

The door opened, and the newspaper boys entered. Amanda Wilson finished her coffee, grabbed her black bag, and left while the journalists hovered over Jess like horseflies. This time, though, Jess wasn't sorry to see them or answer their questions. He even let them go into the jail, though not inside the cells, and interview both prisoners. He hoped the kid might mention his name, or at least where he hailed from, but that didn't happen. Still, the boys would write up their articles, and maybe the prisoner's ma and pa might read it and come to fetch their son.

With luck, the parents could lay a claim on the kid and get that boy out of here before Mort Thompson returned from Dallas and filed a charge.

A clerk brought the mail that had arrived with the stagecoach, which Jess put aside to sort through later, but then the clerk handed him a note written on Trinity River Hotel stationery. The handwriting was beautifully feminine, and he knew who had written it. When the clerk started for the door, Jess stopped him.

"Any passengers on the stages today?" Jess asked.

The clerk turned, sniffled, and looked at Jess as if he had lost his mind. Jess grinned and could not blame the clerk. After all, it was a stagecoach, generally stagecoaches carried passengers, and in a town the size of Fort Worth, usually a few of those passengers got off.

"Any strangers?" Jess stressed.

"I reckon so. A few."

"Any one of them carrying a weapon?"

"Not that I noticed." The clerk scratched his balding head, thinking, picturing the passengers, and understanding Jess's reason for asking. "Couple of drummers. . . . And a preacher man. Had a white collar anyhow, and a big, thick Bible in his lap, but he was older than Methuselah. Them's all that come on the westbound." He opened the door, but stopped in the doorway and faced Jess again. "But, come to think on it, the northbound had a passenger, too."

For a moment, Jess tensed, thinking that the northbound could have been coming from Stephenville. He tried to remember if the McNamara boys had any other brothers . . . or friends.

"But it was just some ol' cripple," the clerk said, and Jess let out a breath of relief.

The door closed behind the clerk, and Jess considered the newcomers: drummers, a preacher, and a cripple. Well, maybe those visitors wouldn't be a threat to the peace of Fort Worth. After unfolding the note addressed to him, Jess read:

*Sheriff Casey—*
    *Received shortly after noon today a note, printed in big block letters, that read:*

*THE BUTCHER WILL NOT MAKE IT
TO THE OPERA HOUSE ALIVE NOR
WILL ANYONE WHO GOES THERE
WITH HIM LEAVE FORT WORTH
NOW. OR DIE.*

*BROTHERS OF THE CONFEDERACY*

Letting out a breath, Jess dropped the note on the desk. Brothers of the Confederacy? Those would likely be the brothers McNamara.


He finished his coffee, sorted through the mail, glanced at the clock, and stood. Hoot Newton was asleep on the little couch in the corner, and Jess let him sleep. He pulled on his coat, took the Winchester from the case, and stepped outside, quickly pulling up his collar. The wind had turned bitter, biting, furious, and gray clouds loomed ominously overhead. By the time he had turned onto Main Street, the sleet had begun, stinging him and pelting the hat he had pulled low onto his head. The blustery, frigid weather had cleared most of the streets, and when he reached the Trinity River Hotel, Major Clarke and one of the hotel busboys were busy securing a tarp over the Gatling gun atop the circus wagon.

Jess didn't offer to help. He stepped inside and moved to the potbelly stove in the center of the lobby.

"It's warmer in here most times, Sheriff," a snotty

hotel clerk said from behind the front desk. "Or was . . . back when we had windows."

With the rifle tucked up underneath his armpit, Jess merely gave the clerk an evil eye and blew on his hands. The sleet drummed against the hotel's tin roof, and the clerk turned his attention to a hangnail. By then, the busboy and Major Clarke had finished their chore and were walking back inside.

The busboy headed into the vacant restaurant. Major Jedediah Clarke stopped in front of Jess.

"Miserable out there," Clarke said as he held out his hands toward the stove.

Jess didn't feel like commenting on the weather. "How do you plan on getting General Dalton to the opera house?"

Clarke sniffed and rubbed his cold face. "Same as always. He climbs atop the wagon, Caroline plays that steam organ, and we ride down the Main Street to cheers and hurrahs. Turn at the courthouse, then down the street, turn onto Calhoun, and roll right up to the opera house. A grand parade!" Sarcasm accented the voice.

"Let me rephrase that, Clarke," Jess said. He decided to shun calling this fraud *Major*. "How do you plan on getting General Dalton to the opera house . . . alive?"

The pelting sleet softened for a minute, then picked up with the wind, which flapped the tarp over the busted front window.

"You heard about our death threat, eh?"

Jess nodded.

"You realize, of course, that General Dalton has gotten many death threats over the past twenty-five years. This is not unusual. Copperheads and Southern sympathizers often frequented his lectures in northern cities such as Terre Haute, Danville, Indianapolis, Columbus, Pittsburgh . . ."

"You're not in Terre Haute," Jess reminded him. "Danville. Indianapolis. Columbus. Pittsburgh. You're in Fort Worth, Texas, formerly of the Confederacy."

"I think we can handle matters, Sheriff."

That's when one side of the tarp covering what had been a nice, expensive plate glass window collapsed in a heap, covering rocking chairs and a settee. Ice poured in, and Jess stepped over the supine body of Major Jedediah Clarke, who had screamed and dropped to the floor at the sudden noise.

"I see how you handle things, Major," Jess said. He left his rifle on a chair and moved toward the window with the busboy, who had rushed out from the restaurant to help. The clerk did not move from the counter. Major Clarke did manage to find his knees.

"You got a hammer?" Jess had to shout to the busboy. The wind roared, and the sleet came down like rain in a spring thunderstorm. The street was already covered with two inches of ice, and Fort Worth was gray and white, and bitterly cold.

"Yes-suh!" The busboy hurried back to the restaurant.

Jess grabbed one corner of the fallen tarp and shouted out, "And some nails."

Wind and sleet pricked his ears and neck. He backed his way toward the wall, pulling the heavy, frozen canvas tarp with him. His boots crunched the ice that already covered the rug near the window.

Lowering his head, Jess turned and glanced outside. The circus wagon looked frozen, the one bit of color in a veritable tundra. No one was outside, for only a fool would venture out in this weather. He braced himself against the wall and looked at the clock.

Maybe nobody would show up for Lincoln Dalton's final lecture. Maybe the Butcher would even cancel the event. No, he knew those were forlorn hopes and that the McNamara boys would be waiting to kill the general and anyone else, even if the weather worsened.

Which, from the looks of things, seemed impossible.

# CHAPTER THIRTY-THREE

*Tuesday, 3:20 p.m.*

"What are you doing in my house?" Brevet Brigadier General Lincoln Everett Dalton called out from the bed where he had stretched out over the quilts and blankets.

Ignoring the old man, Jess Casey pointed toward the window, even though the curtains were closed tightly, not allowing even the slightest afternoon light into the suite.

"In this weather," Jess said, "the McNamara boys could be anywhere. On any rooftop. One shot is all they need. And in this weather, it will be tough to spot a rifle barrel before the trigger's pulled."

Lee Bodeen spit into a cuspidor. "Be hard to hit a target in this weather, too."

Jess nodded. He had considered that.

"Where's my supper?" the Butcher called out. "Private! I asked for ham and eggs and black coffee. Bring me my supper or you, boy, will join those Rebs in the stockade."

"Hush, Father." Caroline Dalton walked from the corner of the bed to the window. She started to pull on the curtain, but her hand dropped, and she looked at Jess. "So how do we get Father to the opera house?"

"You don't have to do this," Jess said. "Call it off. Go home to Decatur. Let him finish his last days in peace."

Although Jess wondered how much peace the Butcher would find in Wise County, Texas. The old fool should have stayed in Terre Haute, Indiana.

"That, sir, is out of the question." General Dalton sat upright in bed, eyes no longer rheumy but full of fierce pride. He swung his feeble legs over the bed-side and tried to stand, but that's where his strength failed him. Yet even though the old man could not stand, he raised his arm and pointed a long finger at Jess Casey.

"You are secessionist trash, boy. A traitor to the Stars and Stripes. I'd have you shot, only that is not good enough for the likes of you. I am Major Dalton, and I will speak tonight. Everyone will hear what I have to say about our glorious nation and about Baxter Pass. Do you understand me, boy?"

Every eye had trained on the old man. Major Clarke's mouth hung agape. Even Caroline seemed surprised by her father.

"Boy." The old man lowered his arm, but not his burning eyes. "When I ask a question, I expect an answer, and that answer should come immediately. Now . . ." The eyes closed, and he sank back in bed, calling up toward the tin ceiling, "Where is my supper?"

"We can't cancel," Caroline said. She lowered her head, drew up a deep breath, and slowly exhaled. "It's Father's wish."

"He might be like that, Miss Caroline." Well, Major Jedediah Clarke had some ounce of decency in his veins. "Just mumble about idiotic things, forget where he is, forget who we are, why he's here."

"Forget who he is," Lee Bodeen said with a snort. "Damned idiot."

"He won't," Caroline said. "I've seen Father like this before. He'll sharpen his tongue . . ."

"When?" Jess asked. "Five years ago? When was the last time he spoke in front of more than ten or twelve people?"

"It's his wish, Jess," she said as she moved back toward her father. "I have to grant him that. It might be his last request."

Silence filled the room, except for the sleet and wind outside, and the Butcher of Baxter Pass's snores from the bed.

"So . . ." Major Clarke began. "How do we get him to the opera house?"

"Take him in that chariot out yonder," Bodeen said. "See what kind of guts anyone has in this fleabag of a town. Parade him right down the street and dare anyone to test." He held out his right hand with an evil grin. "Test the hand of Lee Bodeen."

The wind moaned. Sleet slapped the roof and sides of the hotel. General Dalton mumbled something incoherently.

"I have an idea," Jess Casey said.

* * *

Getting the old man down the stairs wasn't as hard as Jess thought it could have been—and probably should have been. Caroline Dalton had gone to the desk clerk, and, without too much effort, lured him into the restaurant on the pretense of needing a glass of wine. Who wouldn't follow a stunning woman into a restaurant?

With the lobby vacant, Jess, Major Clarke, and Lee Bodeen hurried down the stairs, the Butcher being carried by Clarke and Bodeen. Oh, Lincoln Dalton sang out his protests and sang out *Tenting Tonight*, but the wind moaning through all the broken windows and the pounding of the sleet outside drowned out his lyrics. Sprinting ahead of the two Dalton employees, Jess raced to the storeroom, opened the door, and held his breath as Clarke and Bodeen carried the singing old man inside. Quickly, he closed the door before anyone came to investigate.

Breathing a sigh of relief, Jess lighted a candle and led the way to the hotel's rear entrance. He pointed to a crate, and Bodeen and Clarke deposited their load and stepped back.

"Now what?" Bodeen asked.

"You go back upstairs," he said. "I'll be there directly. What time is it?"

Clarke didn't answer, but he pulled out his watch and showed it to Jess.

"Not much time," Clarke said before returning the watch.

"Go rescue Miss Dalton," Jess said. "Then you wait for us upstairs."

"You think you can pull this off?" Bodeen asked.

"I can try," Jess said, and watched as the two men walked back toward the lobby.

"Where's my breakfast?" Dalton said.

"Won't be long now, Major," Jess said, and leaned against the door.

"Major? I'm a store clerk."

Ignoring the Butcher, Jess could hear the sleet and the wind and even feel the bite of the winter storm. The door opened into a rear alley, and Jess recognized the potential problems. Servants, cooks, busboys all entered the hotel through the storeroom, and if one happened to come to work now, Jess's plan could be shot.

"I killed twelve hundred and seventy-four Confederates, boy," the Butcher said, his memory working again, and then he doubled over into a massive coughing spell.

Jess came to him. The old man wheezed, groaned, moaned, and then tears poured down his stubbled cheeks.

"This ain't . . ." the old man gasped. "This ain't . . . a fitting . . ." He coughed again, and, even with only the small candle for light, he detected the flecks of blood. Finding a handkerchief in his pocket, he handed it to the general, who wiped his mouth as soon as the spell had lessened.

"Thank you, Sheriff," the old man said, cognizant of his surroundings.

"You're . . . welcome," Jess said. A moment later, he heard the clopping of a mule's hoofs outside.

He stood, one hand gripping the butt of his Colt

and the other the door's latch. Wetting his lips, he waited, heard a voice, and cautiously pulled the door open. The fierce wind greeted him, but the sleet seemed to be lessening.

Wearing a heavy cloak, Caroline Dalton came down from the surrey someone had left in front of the Cattleman's Bank.

"Anybody see you?" Jess asked, as he grabbed her hand and pulled her inside.

"I don't think so."

"All right."

Caroline helped her father to his feet and pulled the quilt over his head and shoulders. "Father," she said softly, "we're going now. I'll help you. I'll be with you."

"I am responsible for the deaths of twelve hundred and seventy-four men," the Butcher said. "And I do not give a tinker's damn."

Jess opened the door and hurried to the buggy. The draft horse looked miserable, and if Jess ever found out who had left a horse like this hitched to a wagon in front of the bank, he'd arrest the lousy fiend. He looked up and down the alley, but saw only the whiteness of the ground and the grayness of the skies. Then he was back, taking the general by his other arm, guiding him to the surrey.

The old man pulled away and slipped on the ice. Caroline let out a shout as her feet shot out from underneath her, and she landed hard. Jess found himself facedown on the cold, frozen earth, and slipped again when he tried to push himself up.

"I'm not going anywhere with you!" General Dalton shouted.

On his third try, Jess managed to get himself to his feet and pulled the Butcher up. Caroline came up, next, and tried to cover her father with the quilt, but the old man tossed it off.

Cursing and praying, Caroline fetched the ice-covered quilt and tossed it over her father's head. He put up a fight, but Jess wrapped his arms around the man's chest, dragged him to the surrey, then pulled him into the back of the wagon behind him. The surrey's roof stopped the hail from stinging Jess's body, but the wind numbed him.

Caroline jumped into the driver's seat, released the brake, and flipped the lines.

"Straight down this alley?"

"Yeah," Jess said as he wiped the ice off his face.

The mule seemed relieved to be moving again, warmer if he kept going. Jess didn't feel any relief. He peered over the side of the surrey, careful not to hit his head or arms against the rear walls of the buildings. It was a tight fit. The sky was darkening, though more than an hour remained before sundown. When they reached the intersection, Jess gave Caroline directions, and he looked both ways, then at the rooftops.

No one was out. Who would be?

Ten minutes later, they reached the Fort Worth Opera House. Jess leaped from the buggy before they even reached the building. Somehow, he managed not to slip on the ice, and he came to the front door and opened it.

He was back by the surrey as Caroline set the

brake, and he began pulling the old man out, tossing him over his shoulder like a pair of saddlebags, and stepping under the awning and into the opera house.

The room was warm. It felt like heaven.

Caroline shut the door.

"We made it," she said, but her smile did not lessen any tension.

"This far," Jess said, as he lowered the old Butcher onto the floor and let Caroline take off the quilt.

"Where are we?" Dalton demanded. "Are you Mosby? Have you kidnapped me, you gray-coated traitor?"

"This way," Jess said, "General."


The way this lecture was supposed to go, Caroline had explained back in the hotel, was that the wagon would pull up to the front of the theater, where throngs of people would be waiting. As Caroline played the final notes on the steam organ, Major Clarke and Lee Bodeen would escort General Dalton into the theater.

"Who takes the tickets?" Jess had asked. "Seats everyone?"

That, Caroline had explained, had been left up to Gary Custer. Since Mr. Custer was now awaiting his own burial, and no one had volunteered or said they had been hired, Caroline figured she would do the seating, Major Clarke would take the tickets, and Lee Bodeen would stay with her father until the curtain was raised.

Jess wasn't sure how many people the opera house

would seat, but doubted if it would be less than three hundred. Maybe even four hundred.

"I'm not sure two people can handle that kind of a crowd," Jess had said.

"This isn't about money, Jess," Caroline had told him. "It's for my Father. For his legacy. His place in history."

Now, Jess led the old Butcher into the theater. He kept his pistol out, though he doubted if the McNamara boys would be here, ready for an ambush.

They came onto the stage, went behind the curtain, and disappeared into the nether reaches of the theater. Jess checked the side door, but found that it had been fixed and remained locked. He saw the light on in the late Mr. Custer's office and heard the squeaking hinges as the door opened.

Jess waited, hoping, praying.

He lowered the pistol when Amanda Wilson stepped out of the room.

# CHAPTER THIRTY-FOUR

*Tuesday, 4:10 p.m.*

"Are you sure you can trust her?" Caroline Dalton asked as they took the surrey back to the hotel.

Jess debated with himself how he should answer before choosing to be honest. "No. She lost a cousin at Baxter Pass."

Caroline knew that. Amanda Wilson even told her before they had left. "I guess she could have killed him when we first arrived," Caroline said.

"I reckon so," Jess said. He kept hoping that oath those doctors had to take might rein in any homicidal tendencies stirring up in the redheaded doctor's insides. "I could have asked Hoot Newton," Jess said, "but . . ."

"No," Caroline said. "She'll do. Doctor Wilson will have to do."

When they reached the hotel, Jess tugged on the lines and helped Amanda down. "I'll be upstairs in a few minutes," he said. "I'm taking this to the livery, getting your team, and I'll hitch those animals to your wagon."

"No need." Amanda pointed, and Jess saw the stable hands leading the team. "Major Clarke has done his job."

Jess looked at the rooftops. The sleet had stopped. The streets were stark white.

He hoped they would not be running red in the next hour.

In the second-story hotel suite, Jess held up General Dalton's pants, shook his head, and began doubting his plan. Sure, it would be dark and cloudy, and all that ice on the ground might play in his favor. Snickering, Lee Bodeen tossed the Butcher's white wig onto the bed behind Jess.

"I'll laugh over your corpse, Casey," the gun-fighter said, and Jess understood that the killer was dead serious.

"I'll laugh at myself," Jess said, and sat on the bed, pulled off his boots, and began to unfasten his britches.

By the time Jess had finished dressing, Caroline Dalton knocked on the door. Bodeen answered, let her in, and saw Major Clarke bounding down the hallway. He closed the door after Clarke came in.

"Folks are coming outside now, Sheriff," Casey said. "Waiting along the boardwalks."

"We don't get much snow or sleet in this country," Jess said. "It's like a free stereoscopic card."

"I don't think that's their reasoning," Clarke said. "I think they want to see the show."

"Well," Jess pulled an ill-fitting kepi over the wig. He felt ridiculous. He looked ridiculous. "They just might get to see a show. A whopper of a show."

Bodeen shook his head and spit into the cuspidor. "So. They'll shoot you. Then I shoot them."

"Preferably, you shoot them before they shoot me, or even get a shot at me," Jess said.

"Uh-huh."

"You expect them to be on the rooftops?" Caroline said.

Jess shrugged. "With Burt, yeah, I'd expect that. But Tom's the older brother. Remember, he wasn't in the kitchen when Burt sent that old Mexican out to try to kill the general. That's not Tom's style. He never struck me as a squat assassin. More of a stand-up kind of man. Unlike some gunmen I've known." He made sure that Lee Bodeen knew who he meant by the last statement.

"It's time," Major Clarke said.

Jess felt his innards turning into quicksand. "I sure wish that Gatling gun of yours fired real bullets," he said wistfully.

"I'll blow the damn Yankee's head clean off," Burt McNamara said. "He'll never know what kilt him, the low-down dog."

Tom McNamara shoved the last cartridge into the newly cleaned revolver, shut the loading gate, and holstered his pistol, pushed himself off the cracker barrel, and strode across the alley to his younger brother. Neils, sensing what was about to occur, moved away from Burt.

The youngest brother started up from the hay bale, but prison had not slowed down Tom, nor softened him. He snatched the whiskey bottle Burt had stolen from one of Hell's Half Acre's worst saloons and backhanded Burt to the ice-covered alley.

"Your brother Dan never knew who killed him, either." Vapor shot out of Tom McNamara's mouth and nose, like smoke from a dragon. "That was your convoluted plan, boy. One brother dead. And our pa dead. I want everyone in Fort Worth to know who killed the Butcher of Baxter Pass. And I especially want Dalton to know who it was that sent him to hell."

The slap in the frigid weather stung Tom's hand as much as it did his kid brother's face.

"They got a Gatling gun atop that wagon, Tom!" Burt yelled out, his right hand against his red-marked face.

"It don't work," Neils said casually. "Just for show."

"Even if it did work, I ain't killing that Butcher without a call." Tom had to control his voice, his temper. "We're men. We're Texans. We give him the chance he didn't give our Pa . . . or two hundred others who fought with Gen'ral Hood."

"So . . ." Neils pursed his lips. "How do you plan it?"

"They'll come straight down the street. Toward the courthouse." Neils grinned, and Tom knew why. He was thinking that if Tom had planned that bank robbery, the boys likely would have gotten clear away with it. They never would have seen the inside of the prison at Huntsville.

"That fella guardin' the Butcher," Burt said. "He's s'posed to be right handy with those revolvers."

"Which is one reason Dan's dead."

Burt lowered his head, and Tom regretted his words. He loved his brother. Even when he hated him. It wasn't Burt's fault. Pa had gotten killed, murdered at the end of the War Between the States, and that had left Tom as the man of the house. It was Tom's fault Burt—and Neils, and even himself—had spent time behind bars. It was all Tom's fault.

But he could right all of that this evening. He could avenge the death of Bass McNamara. He could go down in history as a legend of Texas. He'd bring glory to the McNamara name. To Neils. To Burt.

They'd be the men who killed the Butcher of Baxter Pass.

Tom stepped back and picked up the bottle that he had knocked from his kid brother's hand. He took a swig—it was awful—and tossed it to Neils, who caught it with a grin.

Then Tom extended his hand and helped Burt to his feet. He brushed off the ice and took the bottle from Neils, which he passed to Burt.

"Finish it, Burt," Tom said. "Can you shoot with that busted hand of yours?"

Burt looked at his right hand, then grinned. "That's why God give me two hands. And why you taught me how to use both of 'em."

"Let's go," Tom said. "Go make things right with Pa. Go make history."

As Burt McNamara, now grinning, finished the last two fingers of rotgut, a loud wailing commenced. Dropping the now-empty bottle onto the ice at his feet, Burt wiped his mouth with the back of his coat sleeve, and asked, "What the hell is that infernal racket?"

Neils was checking his revolver. "It's that steam piano," he said, and dropped the Colt into the leather. "The general's beginning his journey in that crazy-looking wagon."

"It'll be his last journey," Tom McNamara said.

Mounting their horses, they rode out of the alley and onto Throckmorton Street, pulling up the collars of their coats to fight off the temperatures, already freezing but not plummeting with the coming of dark. After they reached the Eclipse Saloon, they turned east onto Weatherford Street and approached the courthouse grounds. When people on the boardwalks saw the three riders, they stopped to whisper among themselves. A few of the wiser men, sensing what would soon happen, went inside businesses and closed the doors behind them.

Tom McNamara pointed with his gloved hand at the hay wagon still parked across from the courthouse. He looked at the clock in the tower, led his brothers to the wagon, where he swung out of the saddle, and pulled the rifle from the scabbard. He led his horse around the wagon, on the courthouse side and wrapped the reins around the rear wheel. That would offer his horse more protection from the bullets that would soon be flying down Main Street. Tom waited for his brothers, who also tied their mounts to the wagon, loose enough that the horses could paw away the ice-covered ground to munch on the dead grass below.

He leaned the Winchester against the sleet-coated wagon and held out his right hand. First, he shook Neils's hand, then Burt's.

"Ready?" he asked.

The calliope wailed down the street.

Neils gave a slight nod. Burt's voice, higher than usual, cracked as he said something that Tom couldn't quite make out, but Burt was already moving, stepping over the wagon tongue and moving toward Main Street. Tom and Neils quickly caught up.

As they passed the *Standard* building, the editor, with a pencil tucked above his ear, hurried back into the newspaper office, yelling, "Jimmy, rip up that front page! Big bold headline. All caps. DEATH ON MAIN STREET!"

They stopped in the middle first, waiting in the brick-lined street, covered with dust and dirt, coated with two inches of ice. The wind blew, but could not drown out the calliope's belching noise that sounded a little like "When Johnny Comes Marching Home."

The men, women, and children standing on the boardwalks between First and Second streets quickly vanished. Those past Third Street found safer spots to be. The wagon was coming past the El Paso Hotel at the corner of Main and Third.

Tom ratcheted the lever of the Winchester and took a few steps ahead of his two brothers. "Spread out a little, boys," he said, and stared at the freakish wagon coming toward them. Neils moved to Tom's right. Burt shuffled off a few feet to the left.

The calliope grated on Tom's nerves. He tried to

remember his father playing the washtub as his uncle clawed a banjo and a cousin kept time on a jaw harp while his mother sang in her angelic soprano voice. Yet that Butcher's daughter pounding those keys on the steam-powered organ drowned out those memories.

That damn Yankee fool who called himself a major sat in the driver's box, working the lines to the big horses pulling the heavy, loud, and obnoxiously painted wagon. The tarp had been pulled off the Gatling gun, and the white-haired General Dalton sat in his rocking chair, one hand on the gun, the other hand holding the kepi atop his head. The clothes seemed tight on the old man, who looked uncomfortable.

Standing next to the Butcher of Baxter Pass on the colorful wagon was the murdering gunman, Lee Bodeen, a rifle in his hands. The wind, blowing harshly from the north, pinned up the brim of his hat against the crown, but if that killer felt cold, he did not show it.

Tom could not see the woman playing the steam piano. He could just hear that dreadful noise, though, almost like a dirge instead of some jaunty Yankee tune.

The wagon passed the intersection and the major turned his head to call out something to either the general or Bodeen, but the wind prevented Tom from hearing what was said. Both General Dalton and Bodeen answered, for Tom could see the white vapor escaping their mouths when they spoke to the wagon's driver.

Both sides of the block had been deserted, except

for one brave individual who secured the heavy shutters to protect the windows of the apothecary. Then that man, too, was gone, disappearing inside his store and slamming the door behind him. He was close enough for Tom to hear the bolt latch.

The major tugged on the lines, slowing the wild-looking wagon into a crawl.

Tom wet his chapped lips and frowned.

"Something ain't right," he told Neils.

"What?" Burt's voice remained unnaturally high.

"It's Dalton," Neils said. "Something peculiar about the Butcher. Something just don't set well about him."

Tom's head nodded. "Yeah." He focused on the old man in the rocking chair, and when the major pulled the wagon to a stop several yards from where Tom stood with his brothers, the woman stopped playing the calliope.

Now, Tom could hear the steam pump belching in the insides of the wagon. He could hear the wind and feel the icy breath of death.

General Lincoln Everett Dalton, the Butcher of Baxter Pass, the man who had murdered Tom's father and two hundred other paroled Confederate soldiers, pushed himself out of the rocking chair.

# CHAPTER THIRTY-FIVE

*Tuesday, 5:20 p.m.*

At that moment, Tom McNamara knew that he had been played for a fool.

One second later, Jess Casey ripped the Federal kepi and the dying old general's long, flowing white wig off his head. The wind carried both sailing over the street and onto the boardwalk next to City Hall. Jess felt relief. If he died now, at least he wouldn't look like a complete idiot, although he still wore General Dalton's ill-fitting pants and moth-eaten army blouse.

"Tom!" Jess called out. "It's over. Give it up."

His left hand rested on the brass end of the Gatling gun. His right held the crank's grip. The weapon was eight feet long, or thereabouts, and the barrels stretched thirty-one inches. Jess could sense the power at his command, and he did not like it one bit. A weapon like this was the devil's handiwork. It could destroy this entire street, maybe even all of Fort Worth, Texas.

"Caroline!" Jess kept talking. "Get out of here. Now."

He heard her as she stepped out of the wagon, heard her feet crunching the ice, and caught a glimpse of her out of the corner of his eye as she crossed the slippery, frozen street—the wind blowing her raven-dark hair—and slid around the corner of the two-story City Hall.

Clouds had swallowed the sun, which would be setting in fifteen or twenty minutes. The wind lashed hard. Major Clarke set the brake.

"Where the hell is the Butcher?" Burt McNamara called out, right hand wrapped up, left hand on the butt of a revolver.

Jess didn't answer. He appealed to Tom, the wisest of the brothers. "You got no chance, Tom. Don't make me use this." He patted the brass with his left hand, and his fingers tightened around the Gatling gun's crank.

"That thing's just a prop, Casey," Tom said, but his face showed doubt. "Everybody in town knows that already."

Jess let himself grin, even though as cold as it had turned, and still turning, the motion made his face hurt.

"Tom," Jess said softly, "you know better than trust a damn Yankee. Major?"

"Brake's set. These Percherons are trained."

Tilting the heavy weapon down just a notch, Jess pulled the crank and felt the lethal weapon come alive. He worked the handle slowly but surely, smelling the bitter tangy scent of powder as .45-70 slugs ripped into the icy street about ten yards in front of the McNamara boys. The ten-barrel weapon was said to be able to fire twenty rounds a second, but Jess knew these weapons were prone to jam, and he didn't want things to get out of hand. He turned the crank slowly, just fast enough to send a steady round of lead into Main Street. The draft horses jerked a bit, but Major Clarke had been right. They were trained for the sound of the Gatling gun. Some animals would have bolted, but the Percherons did not.

The sudden explosion of gunshots caused some folks hiding in the nearby buildings to scream, and when the smoke cleared, Jess saw Neils lying on his back, trying to scramble to his feet, and Burt on his knees, both hands clasped over his ears, his face as white as the ground in front of him. Only Tom remained standing, still clutching the Winchester with two gloved hands, staring hard at Jess, anger etched into his face, but Tom wasn't fool enough to bring that rifle into a firing position.

Jess drew in a breath and slowly let it out.

"I don't want to kill you boys," Jess said. "Leave your guns on the ice. Get your horses. Ride home. The war's over. It's been over for a long, long time."

Neils had pulled himself to his feet and kept his hand far from the holstered revolver. Burt remained on his knees, though he had lowered his hands from his aching ears.

"What about him?" Tom gestured toward his youngest brother.

Yeah, Jess knew about him. Mort Thompson wanted to try the boy, send him back to Huntsville, and lock him up for another five or ten years. And

Burt had broken out of jail—thanks to Neils and Tom—and left Hoot Newton with an aching head and plaster over his busted nose. Thompson would be furious, but Jess was getting used to that.

"I don't think the Tarrant County prosecutor will come looking for y'all down Stephenville way."

"You sure?"

"I give you my word." Even if it meant whipping the Tarrant County solicitor with his pistol barrel.

"The Butcher murdered our pa!" Burt McNamara managed to stand but made no play for his pistol with his one good hand. His voice sounded like a girl's, Jess thought as he considered the youngster but kept his attention on Tom.

"Dalton's a sick old man. He'll be dead soon. Let God be his judge and his punisher."

The wind blew. The skies darkened.

"I don't want this to end badly, boys, and it will," Jess said, "unless you drop those guns. Now."

His heart pounded, and his throat went dry, even when Tom McNamara let the big rifle slip from his hands and fall to the ice by his boots.

Following Tom's lead, Neils began to unbuckle the shell belt around his waist, and when Burt made no move to disarm himself, Tom McNamara crossed the icy street, leaving his gun belt on the ground, not far from where the Gatling gun had plowed the ice.

"It's over, Burt," Tom was saying, and Jess was letting out a sigh of relief, watching Caroline Dalton step around the corner, her face revealing the relief that was washing away her fear.

Jess stepped away from the Gatling gun but kept his right hand on the butt of the holstered .44-40.

This wouldn't be over until Burt McNamara had dropped his guns. The kid didn't move until his big brother put both hands on his shoulders and turned him around to face Tom. Tom said something, but he was whispering, and Jess could only hear the wind and see the icy vapor as Tom spoke softly.

Relaxing, Jess shot Caroline another look. She smiled at him, but her expression immediately changed, and Jess sensed what was happening, turning toward the Gatling, lifting his left hand just in time to take the full force of the big Centennial Lee Bodeen was swinging.

Bodeen screamed something that Jess couldn't quite understand. Foreign? Crazy words? Unintelligible? The wind drowned out most of what Bodeen had yelled.

Likely, if Jess had not reacted when he did, the fraudulent Texas Ranger would have stove in Jess's head with the .45-75. Instead, the big weapon broke Jess's left forearm and sent him toppling over the side of the wagon.

"You yellow sons-of-bitches!" Bodeen shouted, dropping the Winchester and moving toward the Gatling gun. Jess understood that, "I'll kill all of you cowards!"

Landing on his back, the air whooshed out of Jess's lungs, and he lay stunned, trying to get his breath working again. He could barely see the top of the wagon and make out Major Clarke standing in the box, turning, crying out, "Lee, what in the name of—"

And that was all, because the Gatling gun barked again, and Major Jedediah Clarke's body exploded in streaks of crimson as his body flailed about like a fish tossed onto the riverbanks, and then the dead man was flying onto the backs of the team of draft horses the Gatling's deadly bullets had also cut into pieces.

Jess realized that if he didn't move—and quickly—he'd be blown apart himself.

He rolled underneath the wagon, just managing to see Lee Bodeen's insane face, and the pistols he held in both hands, as the killer abandoned the Gatling gun—it would have been impossible for Bodeen to hit Jess at that angle with the automatic weapon—and fired twice. Ice stung Jess's ears as the bullets tore into Main Street.

Those lungs sucked in freezing air, and Jess turned and saw Caroline Dalton screaming something from the boardwalk. He tried to tell her to get back but couldn't make his voice work. It didn't matter, because the daughter of the Butcher understood that if she didn't move, she'd be dead, too. She dived back behind the City Hall as the Gatling spoke again, tearing apart the wooden planks along the corner of the structure, littering the boardwalk and parts of the street corner with splinters, just as Caroline Dalton reached safety.

Jess rolled onto his belly, managed to turn around, seeing the bloody bodies of Major Jedediah Clarke and the horses in front of him. He could also see the McNamara boys, still in the middle of the icy street, and Jess grimaced.

There was absolutely nothing he could do in time to save any of them.

Neils had reacted the quickest, probably because the gun belt he had dropped remained right at his feet. He dropped, jerked the revolver from the holster, and was bringing it up. Above Jess came the roar of a gunshot, and blood spurted from Neils McNamara's left shoulder. The ex-convict grimaced, but kept his grip on the revolver as he jerked the trigger.

The bullet smashed through a window. That's how much the shoulder wound have spoiled his aim, but it also told Jess that, atop the wagon, Lee Bodeen was shooting one of his revolvers—not the Gatling. Neils turned again, thumbed back the Colt's hammer. The second round from Bodeen caught the brother in his belly, doubling him over as again he jerked the trigger. That bullet plowed a furrow in the ice, and Neils was kneeling on the street, turning the frozen ground crimson, but not completely down.

Until Lee Bodeen put a bullet through the brother's head.

Through the front spokes of the wagon wheel, Jess saw Tom McNamara shoving Burt down First Street. Tom had managed to jerk the Colt out of his kid brother's holster and was turning to fire.

"Tom!" Burt screamed.

"Get out of here, kid!" his big brother boomed.

The kid darted, slipping and sliding on the ice, down First, toward Calhoun. Tom was thumbing back the hammer of the Colt, and Jess Casey was moving.

Back. Toward the rear of the wagon. He came up, and started climbing, getting foot and hand holds in the ornate carvings, using the calliope when he could. His left arm dangled uselessly at his side, burning in agonizing pain from the busted bone.

Jess couldn't see Tom McNamara, but he heard the Gatling gun on the wagon's rooftop. It sickened him.

His ears rang as the gun erupted in rapid fire. Jess caught a glimpse of Burt McNamara as he ran, bullets now digging past him. The kid lost his hat, hunched over, ran—and through some sort of miracle—cleared the mercantile on the corner.

The Gatling's slugs ripped through the building's plate glass window, reduced the pickle barrel to kindling, and destroyed the bench on the boardwalk. Jess remembered Major Clarke saying that General Dalton's Gatling was an 1881 model and fed two rows of cartridges housed in a hopper. Already, Jess saw smoking brass casings rolling off the side of the wagon's top and onto the ice.

The deafening roar of the gun stopped, and over the echoes reverberating across Fort Worth, Jess heard the demonic cackling of Lee Bodeen.

That man was insane. No doubt about it.

Jess knew he couldn't climb any higher up the wagon. His left arm wouldn't let him, but that didn't matter. He had a clear view of Lee Bodeen as the gunman replaced the hoppers of the Gatling gun with new ones containing fresh loads.

He brought the gun up, but he knew he was too late. Bodeen must have seen him, or heard him—maybe felt his presence. The gunman dropped to his knee as Jess squeezed the trigger.

Jess knew his shot had missed, and he knew he

was a dead man. Because he lost his hold, his feet slipping out and away from the wagon, and he was falling backward, onto the hard ice and hard street. And Lee Bodeen was coming after him.

To finish the job.

# CHAPTER THIRTY-SIX

*Tuesday, 5:25 p.m.*

His head exploded with pain from the impact with the hard street, but that didn't feel anywhere near as intense as the screaming sensation that shot through his broken arm.

Jess saw Lee Bodeen standing on the edge of the circus wagon, guns in each hand. The man was grinning as his fingers tightened on both triggers while Jess tried to bring his own revolver up.

A bullet roared, and Lee Bodeen sang out in surprise, lost his balance, and slipped backward, banging against the Gatling gun. Jess looked to his right, finding Caroline Dalton standing beside the chewed-up corner of the City Hall, clutching a smoking revolver with both hands.

"You wench!" Bodeen screamed from atop the wagon.

"Get back!" Jess yelled, and pulled the trigger. He couldn't see Bodeen. He just hoped the bullet may give the crazed gunman second thoughts.

Caroline fired again, her pistol shot echoed by one of Bodeen's guns. The Butcher's daughter dropped to her knee, unharmed, and aimed the big revolver, squeezing the trigger. By then, Jess had gotten his legs to work. He moved back, onto the boardwalk, until he had a clear shot at Lee Bodeen.

As Caroline pulled the trigger yet again, Bodeen turned, saw Jess, and snapped a shot that busted out a windowpane to Jess's right. He snapped a shot, saw the spark, and heard the ricochet as the bullet whined off the Gatling gun. Bodeen leaped backward, off the wagon's rooftop, and Jess dropped to his knee, trying to get a clear shot at the killer.

No good. Bodeen landed, slipped, and came to his feet on a run. Jess moved down the boardwalk toward First Street. Bodeen rushed a shot over his shoulder as he ran in the same direction as Burt McNamara had gone. Caroline fired, her shot well off the mark. Jess came down the boardwalk. Maybe he could have hit Bodeen before he rounded the corner and got out of view, but that would have been nothing short of a scratch shot. He slipped on a patch of ice on the boardwalk, and while he didn't lose his feet, his shot dug into the ice, well to the left of Bodeen.

After that, it didn't matter. Bodeen was out of view.

Jess ran after him, just glancing at the bullet-riddled body of Tom McNamara, who lay in a freezing lake of blood on Main Street.

"Stay here!" Jess yelled at Caroline, who charged down the east side of Main Street toward First.

She didn't listen. Jess didn't argue. They reached

the corner at the same time. They charged down First, with Jess shucking out the empty cartridges of his Colt, replacing them with fresh loads he had shoved into the pocket of the Butcher's blouse. Caroline fired once more, but Bodeen had turned the corner ahead.

Jess swore. Bodeen had turned southward on Calhoun.

He stopped at the cooper's place, and held out his left arm to keep Caroline Dalton from running onto Calhoun Street—and possibly into a bullet from one of Bodeen's pistols.

"What?" She caught her breath.

"He's heading toward the opera house," Jess said, and cautiously peered around the corner.

"I don't . . . understand."

Jess did. At least, he thought he understood, because now he remembered exactly what Lee Bodeen had shouted before knocking him off the wagon, before he killed Major Clarke and two of the McNamara brothers with that Gatling gun.

"Bodeen yelled, *'Sic semper tyrannis'* just before he started this ball," Jess told her.

That Latin phrase was becoming popular in Fort Worth. One of the McNamara boys had shouted the same thing before taking a shot at Jess, mistaking him for Gary Custer, in the opera house earlier.

"All right." Caroline looked over Jess's shoulder. The street appeared clear. "Like John Wilkes Booth at Ford's Theatre."

"Bodeen's Southern. He wants to kill your father, too."

Her head shook. "If he wanted to do that, he had plenty of chances before."

Which did trouble Jess a bit, but he thought he had that problem solved, too. "Yeah, but he's a gunfighter. He wants style. Wants to be remembered." Jess stepped onto the boardwalk and walked cautiously down Calhoun, making sure to keep his body in front of Caroline Dalton's.

He shook his head, as the images of the dead bodies on Main Street flashed through his mind. Lee Bodeen would be remembered all right.

"He's mad," Caroline said, understanding. "Completely mad."

"As a hatter," Jess said.

"Father!" She started, but Jess blocked her path.

"Bodeen knows he has to take care of us first."

He studied both corners on Third and Calhoun and kept the Colt cocked.

"What about the other one?" Caroline asked. "The McNamara boy?"

Jess shook his head. "I don't know."

Panic filled her voice. "I have to get to Father," she said.

"I know." He stopped. The opera house lay three blocks away. No throngs crowded the theater. In fact, no one dared show his or her face in Fort Worth.

Darkness began covering the streets like a shroud.

He reached a water trough. "Get down," he said, and when Caroline Dalton didn't follow his orders quickly enough, he snapped at her, "Now, damn it."

This time, she obeyed.

"I don't know where he is. Or where Burt is." He cringed at the pain shooting up and down his left arm. "But I'm going to see if I can't draw Bodeen's fire. With luck, he'll go after me. Then you take off fast as you can and find your father."

He didn't like that, but he couldn't see any other options. Besides, Amanda Wilson was waiting with the Butcher of Baxter Pass, and Lee Bodeen would kill her along with General Dalton.

Jess wet his lips and stepped off the boardwalk. Ice crunched beneath his boots. He drew in a deep breath, let it out, and broke into a sprint, hoping he wouldn't slip and break his neck on the ice, moving cattycorner across the street.

He saw the flash of Bodeen's revolver. Felt the bullet whistle behind him and snapped a shot in the general direction. Bodeen had taken cover at the wagon yard on the eastern side of Calhoun. Jess practically flew the last few yards and slammed his back against the wall of an abandoned old shanty just as Bodeen's next bullet splintered the old rotten wood.

Jess looked at the water trough across the street, praying that Caroline Dalton would have the good sense to stay put.

He thumbed back the hammer on the Colt and yelled, "Bodeen! You couldn't hit the back side of a barn if it were two inches from your pistol barrel."

The next bullet tore through the shanty, showering the top of Jess's hat with splinters and almost tearing Jess's head off. Dropping to his knees, he came around the corner of the dilapidated building, pulled the trigger, and ducked back. "Come on, you Southern trash!"

Stumbling backward, he heard the roar of Bodeen's pistol, followed by the crazed man's curse. Bodeen would be coming now, and Jess had to lead the gunman away from Caroline Dalton, away from the Fort Worth Opera House, away from Calhoun Street and the Butcher of Baxter Pass. He raced down the boardwalk, reached Jones Street, and dived past the rain barrel at the corner of the Masonic Lodge.

Barely. A bullet from one of Bodeen's pistols tore off the heel of his left boot.

There were no boardwalks on Jones. Jess landed on the frozen ground, came up on his hands and knees, and crawled until he could scramble to his feet. Running with one heel shot off, on ice for that matter, was awkward, but he saw the livery on the eastern side of the street and raced for it, hearing Bodeen's boots pounding the street behind him.

Jess made it. A bullet whined through the open doorway. A horse whinnied and began kicking its stall. Jess landed in the hay, felt dust sting his eyes, and came to his feet.

"Who's the damned coward?" Bodeen yelled from outside. "Who's the traitor to the South? That's you, Casey! And I'm gonna put you under before I kill that old Butcher."

Jess moved down the darkened livery, quickly, hoping to lure Bodeen in. He found an empty stall, leaped into it, and peered through the wooden slats. It was fairly dark now, and night was falling quickly. No one had the guts to start lighting the streetlamps, and it wouldn't matter on Jones Street, anyway. There were no streetlamps here.

Yet a few buildings had lanterns still burning inside, and Jess could make out the grayness of the open door, the silhouette of the bales of hay stacked near the beginning of the stalls.

He tried to control his breathing. Tried to forget the pain shooting through his busted arm.

"You're gutless, Casey!" Bodeen barked from outside, the sound coming from Jess's right, unless the wind played tricks on him. "You run. You run like the Yankees did at Manassas. Well, I'm gonna track you down, you blue-belly-loving coward. I'm gonna kill you."

"Come on, Bodeen!" Jess called out.

He had done his job. By now, Caroline Dalton had to be at the opera house. Yet he frowned again, remembering Burt McNamara. That boy could be anywhere. He could have run out of town at a high lope. Could have gone to check on his dead brothers. Or he could have decided to kill the Butcher of Baxter Pass, too.

"Let's finish this, Bodeen!" he yelled. He couldn't wait here any longer. He had to make sure the Butcher . . . and Caroline . . . and Doc Wilson were all right.

"Come on out!" Bodeen laughed. His voice seemed a bit farther away now. "I'll hold my fire till you're ready."

Like hell, Jess thought, but he guessed what Bodeen was doing, and an idea quickly popped into Jess's head. He came out of the stall, shoving the Colt—still cocked—into his holster, and slipping off the coat. He had to bite down on his lips to keep from crying out as he pulled his busted arm through the left sleeve and kept moving to those shadowy hay bales. He placed the coat on the top bale, let it hang down, and made sure the right sleeve dropped clear of the hay. He found a hat, likely the liveryman's, and put it atop the hay just over his coat.

Backing up, Jess studied the dummy he had created. It probably would not work.

Then again, in this darkness, it just might. A horse snorted. At least the other animal had quit kicking the stall. Jess kept backing up to the stall where he had first taken shelter. He looked at the hay bales holding his hat and coat.

Next he turned. The open door to the livery drew air from the opening to the corral that faced the Grove Street side, to the east. He saw nothing but blackness out there, although he could hear the hoofs of horses as they wandered about in the dark, and another noise struck him. One of the animals had started drinking water. Again, he turned and looked at the hay bales. Maybe it looked like a man standing there. Maybe.

Could it work? Would it work? Was there any chance?

He would find out soon enough. Jess slipped back inside the stall and drew the Colt from the holster.

Time became stubborn, unmoving. The wind howled. A mule in a nearby stall began to urinate. The nerves in Jess's broken arm screamed out in agony.

Yet he waited. He had to be patient.

Bodeen hadn't yelled anything for a while now, and Jess figured he was making his way around the livery, into the corral. The killer had planned on sneaking in the back way. At least, that's what Jess hoped Bodeen had thought up. Listening as the wind roared through the livery from the open door and out into the corral, Jess felt his heart hammering against his chest.

A new sound struck instantly, and Jess could not help but shiver. The sleet had started again, ice coming down with fierce intensity, pelting the rooftop, bounding off the street, startling the horses in the corral.

Jess heard the animals moving inside. He made out a big draft animal as it moved down the aisle toward the hay bales.

No. . . . That could ruin everything. The animal went past, but Jess couldn't see if it had knocked his coat or hat off the hay. Another horse turned and stopped, snorting. Horses had much better eyesight than humans in the dark, and Jess knew this quarter horse wondered what in blazes a man was doing in its stall. The animal pawed the hay-covered floor, but snorted again, and went on inside, walking past Jess for the bucket of water in the corner.

It started slurping. Another horse—no, that one was too small, had to be a donkey—walked in and stopped to eat some hay just across from Jess.

He bit his lips. The sleet drummed all around him, and the temperatures plummeted even more. The Colt he was holding felt like an anvil. He kept thinking, praying.

*Come on, Bodeen. Hurry up, damn it.*

The pistol's report sounded like a cannon, and the muzzle flash practically blinded him.

# CHAPTER THIRTY-SEVEN

*Tuesday, 5:40 p.m.*

Right in front of the open stall, Lee Bodeen had fired at the dummy Jess had rigged up. Jess hadn't heard the gunman's footsteps. In fact, he had not even seen the killer until the gunshot.

Bodeen pulled the trigger again and laughed.

The horse in the stall overturned the bucket, snorted, kicked, and Jess had to dive out of its way to keep from getting trampled. Bodeen whirled, but saw only the panicking eyes of the horse as it charged out of the stall, turned right, and raced back into the corral and numbing sleet.

Jess bounced off the stall, heard other horses screaming. The donkey took off running toward the open door. Jess fell to the ground. His arm felt as if someone had chopped it off with an ax.

"Bodeen!" Jess called out. He couldn't make out Bodeen. Didn't even know where the man was.

"What the—!"

Bodeen's Remington barked again. Jess felt the

tug of the collar on his shirt, and he squeezed the trigger. The Colt bucked, and Jess was diving to his right, thumbing back the hammer, aiming up, below the muzzle flash.

Another bullet blasted past Jess.

He rolled to his left, cocked, and fired. Cocked. Fired. Came to his knees. Cocked. Fired. The flashes gave him enough light. He saw Bodeen staggering backward. Jess aimed carefully this time.

Cocked.

Fired.

There was another pistol shot, but it was low on the ground, muffled, and the muzzle flash ignited the hay on the livery's ground floor.

He could barely hear anything now. Not the sleet. Just the roaring in his ears. He blinked. Then held his eyes shut for the longest time, waiting for the orange flashes to diminish.

Jess was standing now. He smelled gun smoke. And the smoke from the burning hay. The fire was small but could quickly send the livery stable up like an effigy.

Walking out of the stall, Jess holstered his Colt.

Lee Bodeen lay facedown in the muck. His last shot had been spasmodic and had touched off the fire, which gave enough light for Jess Casey to see that Lee Bodeen was dead.

After stomping out the fire, Jess hurried toward the livery's front entrance. At least one of Bodeen's bullets had knocked his coat to the ground, and Jess didn't want to bend over to pick it up—and he certainly remembered the pain taking off that coat had caused him—but that hat remained on top of the hay.

He snatched it as he ran outside and into the sleet. It fit, barely, but kept his head warm, barely.

His arm throbbed. Sleet beat him without mercy. He stumbled once but kept his feet. He kept running, as fast as he could, ignoring the bitter cold, the brutal pain in his arm.

He made his way to the Fort Worth Opera House.

A block away from the building, he heard the muffled sound of a pistol shot from inside.


He hurried, smashed through the double doors, with his Colt drawn. Jess made his way down the aisle, onto the stage, and toward the curtains. The theater had been lit, but no one sat in any of the seats. Jess even looked at the balcony. His boots echoed as he hurried down the aisle and kept his .44-40 trained on the man standing beside the curtain.

The stranger in front of him wore a sack suit, with the left sleeve pinned up at the elbow, and a crutch under the armpit. Jess saw the man's left leg was wooden, and he remembered the mail clerk telling him about the cripple who had gotten off the north-bound stage.

He was a thin man, old, with a neatly groomed mustache and goatee, dark hair but streaked with silver. Spectacles pinched his nose. He held no gun in his right hand, which pointed toward the curtain.

"The shot came from behind the curtain," the man spoke. It was a Texas drawl but with an intelligence.

"Stay there," Jess told him, and climbed the side steps to the stage. Taking a breath, he stepped through the curtain to find Burt McNamara holding

Caroline Dalton's revolver, the barrel pressing into General Lincoln Everett Dalton's temple. The Butcher of Baxter Pass sat in a rocking chair, center stage, not seeming to notice that if the sobbing boy with the pistol in his one good hand pulled the trigger, Lincoln Dalton would be dead.

Amanda Wilson sat on the floor, stage left, holding her head, from which blood trickled down. Otherwise, she seemed unharmed, and her eyes locked on Jess's for a moment before turning back to Burt McNamara. Caroline Dalton stood behind the general, her face pale, her eyes pleading, and her lips trembling with fear.

"Please . . ." she begged.

Jess stepped onto the stage.

"Burt." Jess's voice seemed to echo across the theater. "Put the gun down, son."

"H-h-he . . . he k-k-kilt Tom. He k-kilt . . . Neils."

"No. Bodeen killed your brothers. And I've killed Bodeen."

Behind him, Jess heard the wooden leg and crutch treading the boards as the stranger came closer. Jess didn't like that. He couldn't see the man on the other side of the curtain, didn't know him, and questioned what a stranger would be doing in the opera house. But stopping Burt McNamara from murdering the old man remained Jess's top priority.

"H-he . . . he . . . or-ordered it." The gun shook in Burt's hand.

Caroline wet her lips.

Jess figured what had happened. Burt had barged in, taken the pistol from Caroline Dalton's hand, with the gun discharging in the scuffle. Doc Wilson had tried to help, and Burt had buffaloed her slightly with the barrel.

"No. Bodeen was crazy. You're not, Burt."

"He kilt my pa, too."

"That was war." Jess felt the curtain move behind him, heard the crutch and peg leg, and felt the stranger's presence behind him. He wouldn't take his eyes off Burt, though, except for quick glances at Amanda and Caroline. They seemed confused by the newcomer's presence but not scared.

"I-it wa-wa-wasn't . . . w-war. It w-was . . . murder."

"Twenty-five years ago," Jess said. "The war's over, Burt. Three of your brothers are dead. You need to go on living."

The boy's head shook savagely.

"I don't want this to end badly, Burt. Put the gun down. He's a dying old man. He's not worth it."

"He . . . k-kilt . . ."

"The war's over, Burt. It has been over for a long time."

The head shook again. Jess feared that the way the kid kept shaking, he might accidentally jerk the trigger.

"It'll never be over," Burt said.

"Maybe." Jess knew enough Texans to believe what Burt had just said. "But you can start the peace right now. Just lower than pistol, son."

The head shook again. "He . . . k-kilt . . . Pa."

"No." The voice came from the cripple standing behind Jess. "No, son. General Dalton killed no one. At least, not on the night of the thirtieth of May in the year of our Lord eighteen and sixty-five."

It was a voice meant for the theater, though more for *Hamlet* or *King Lear* than what was being played on this stage this night.

Burt glanced at the man behind Jess, but did not lower his pistol. "Who are you?"

"Professor Mitchell Vogt," the man said. "I teach at AddRan Male & Female College down at Thorp Spring. And I served with Hood's First Texas. I was wounded and captured at Sharpsburg. The rest of the war I spent at Baxter Pass. Who was your father?"

He started to answer, but then General Dalton blurted out, "I killed twelve hundred and seventy-four traitors."

"No, you did not, sir," Vogt said, addressing the Butcher now and not Burt McNamara. "Disease killed most of them. Wounds. Our own men. And a few died trying to escape, which was their duty, as it was yours to stop them."

"I cut two hundred boys down with a Gatling gun." Even Dalton sounded like a veteran thespian and not the blithering idiot whose mind wandered and whose body had been eaten up with the carcinoma.

The clopping of the crutch and peg leg sounded, and Jess stood still as Professor Mitchell Vogt crossed the stage and stopped just a few feet in front of the old man and the kid with the pistol.

"No, sir. You saved my life." Vogt's head turned from Dalton to Burt.

"Your father's name, son?"

"B-B-Bass. Bass Mc-Namara."

Vogt's head shook sadly. "It has been too many

years. I'm sorry. I don't remember him, but there were many, many brave Texans under Hood's command. I was a mere private."

"Pa was . . . a . . . sergeant."

"And a brave man."

"He was gunned down . . ."

"No. It didn't happen that way."

"But . . ."

"Yes. The stories. The lies. Hell, I was partly responsible for that myself. I wrote an article, sent it to Dallas—that's where I'd lived before I rode south to join the cause. The *Dallas Mercury* published my lies."

Jess found himself lowering his pistol.

"W-what . . . happened?" That came from General Dalton himself. "I do not remember . . . anymore."

Vogt's head bowed.

"We boarded the steamboat, the *Fancy Belpre*. A ship built for cargo and maybe sixty passengers and crew, loaded down with more than three hundred or thereabouts. Alas, the *Belpre* was also carrying weapons and ammunition. Bound for a war that was already over. When the boilers exploded that awful night, the ship went up like a tinderbox, and the flames set off all that ammunition. Bullets ripped through the bodies of so many men—even women passengers and children—tore them to pieces. Dalton, though." Vogt bowed at the seated old man. "He raced from the hotel. He pulled a few survivors out of the Ohio River. One of those men he saved . . . was me."

"I . . . was . . . a . . . hero?" the Butcher of Baxter Pass asked.

"Yes, Father," Caroline said softly. "As I always knew . . . in my heart."

"Indeed, General," the stranger said.

Burt McNamara had lowered the revolver, and Jess holstered his own, crossed the stage, and took the pistol from the boy's left hand.

"But . . . why?" Amanda Wilson asked. "Why did you lie? Why did you write that . . . article?"

Vogt shrugged. "I was young. I was bitter. I hated General Dalton. For letting me live and not drown. It's . . . it's . . . hard to . . . explain." His head bowed, but only for a moment. "But do not . . . do not forgive me. I do not deserve such mercy."

He held out his hand. Which the Butcher of Baxter Pass accepted.

# CHAPTER THIRTY-EIGHT

*Wednesday, 7:50 a.m.*

"I can't believe," Jess told Hoot Newton in the jail, "that you slept through that Gatling gun last night."

"I was tired, Jess," Hoot said between slurps of coffee and chewing bacon and scrambled eggs. "I'm still tired."

"You're tired!" Jess laughed, although that hurt his broken arm. "I haven't slept since Sunday night!"

He had spent all Tuesday night and most of this morning straightening everything out. Having Doc Wilson set his broken arm and put it in a cast and sling. Cleaning up the streets. Getting the bodies of dead men to a very happy undertaker. Telling every newspaper reporter—including those that came from Dallas via special trains—what had happened. Setting the record straight about the Butcher of Baxter Pass after twenty-five years.

At dawn, Caroline Dalton had loaded her senile father into the circus wagon—with a new team, although mules and not Percheron draft animals, donated by Stewart's Wagon Yard—and paraded him down Main Street toward his home up north in Wise County. Men and women, boys and girls cheered the new hero . . . the man who had tried to save so many lives of Texas Confederates at the awful prison camp in Baxter Pass, Ohio.

Jess didn't know how much longer the old man had, but he'd live the rest of his days as a hero. Jess wondered if he would ever see Caroline Dalton again. Certainly, he hoped so.

Burt McNamara had gone south before the big parade and without any fanfare. He had been given a buckboard, loaded with three coffins, and ridden in the frosty morning toward Stephenville.

After the Daltons had left, Jess had walked into the jail, opened the cells, and kicked the teenage kid who still hadn't told anyone his name and Pete Doolin out. Run both of them out of town and did not ask for any fines to be paid. Mort Thompson and Harry Stout wouldn't like that one bit. But they weren't here. Actually, Jess hoped they stayed in Dallas. And become Constable Paul Parkin's problem. Maybe Fort Worth Marshal Kurt Koenig would also stay gone. This town could be a right peaceable place if you got rid of certain undesirables.

The door opened as Jess finished his coffee. Professor Mitchell Vogt hobbled inside. Leaning on his crutch, his right hand disappeared into his sack suit's pocket.

"Sheriff," Vogt said, his voice still booming. "I have something for you."

"Would you like some cof—" The sentence died in his throat as Vogt withdrew a Colt Thunderer double-action revolver and dropped it on Jess's desk.

Jess didn't have any words. He looked across the room, but Hoot Newton had finished his breakfast and was lying on the cot in the corner. A few seconds later, and Hoot started snoring.

"I don't understand," Jess said.

"It's simple, Sheriff." Vogt straightened. "That's the weapon I bought in Granbury after receiving your telegram and before catching the stage. I came here to kill the Butcher of Baxter Pass."

Jess's arm ached, but his head hurt more.

"But . . ."

"Last night?" Vogt grinned. "I love the theater, sir. Love to perform. I lied."

"You mean . . ."

"Dalton was the devil incarnate, and he opened fire from the Union Hotel's balcony on that night with a Gatling gun. He murdered everyone who died aboard the *Fancy Belpre* He had been driven mad. The article I wrote for the *Mercury* might have been biased, but it was the truth, sir."

Jess slumped in his chair.

"Oh, the Butcher did try to get food for the prisoners. I think that's what drove him insane. No one helped. It was war. But when Dalton destroyed the steamboat, he was mad. Mad. He shouted that no one had any right to survive the hell they had endured. It was nothing short of murder, but the murder of a man driven insane by the horrors at Baxter Pass. The Yankees knew what Dalton had done. But Lincoln was dead, the war was over, Booth was dead, and there were conspirators to be hanged. They ignored what Dalton had done. Made him a general. Conveniently swept the matter under that proverbial rug."

Hoot Newton rolled over, said something in his sleep, and resumed snoring.

"How did you live?" Jess asked.

"That's the crux of things, Sheriff. It was Dalton. He refused to let me take the steamboat. Said I was too sick. But he knew. He knew my fellow Texans knew that I had been a traitor, informing the guards of tunnels being dug, of escapes being planned. I did what I needed to do to survive, Sheriff. Had the steamboat made it down the Ohio, I would have been murdered. But in the general's hotel room, I heard the Gatling gun. I wanted to die. I wanted Dalton to die for letting me live."

Jess's head shook. "So why didn't you kill him last night?"

"You stopped me, Sheriff. I guess I should thank you for that. When you told that boy that the war was over, that he could start the peace . . ." Vogt opened the door and stepped outside. "I knew then that twenty-five years was long enough to hate. Hate Dalton. And hate myself. I knew I should get back to living. Thank you, Sheriff. If you ever decide to come down to Thorp Spring, please, don't. I'd like to forget everything and just teach young men and women to be better than I was, or could ever be."

The door closed. Like that, Mitchell Vogt was gone, leaving Jess alone in the office with a dumbstruck look on his face and a snoring Hoot Newton.

Exhausted, Jess stared at the clock, stood, and walked to the cells. After closing the heavy door behind him to drown out Hoot Newton's snores, Jess stepped inside the first cell. He sat on the cot, and then lay down carefully with his busted arm in the sling, and closed his eyes. Immediately, he fell asleep.

# Connect with Us